THE FOOLISH VIRGIN

THOMAS DIXON

1st WORLD
LIBRARY
Literary Society

The Foolish Virgin

Thomas Dixon

© 1st World Library – Literary Society, 2006
PO Box 2211
Fairfield, IA 52556
www.1stworldlibrary.org
First Edition

LCCN: 2006905735

Softcover ISBN: 1-4218-2164-8
Hardcover ISBN: 1-4218-2064-1
eBook ISBN: 1-4218-2264-4

Purchase *"The Foolish Virgin"*
as a traditional bound book at:
www.1stWorldLibrary.org/purchase.asp?ISBN=1-4218-2164-8

1st World Library Literary Society is a nonprofit
organization dedicated to promoting literacy by:

- Creating a free internet library accessible from any
  computer worldwide.
- Hosting writing competitions and offering book
  publishing scholarships.

The Foolish Virgin
contributed by Tim, Ed & Rodney
in support of
1st World Library Literary Society

TO
GERTRUDE ATHERTON
WITH GRATITUDE AND ADMIRATION

CONTENTS

LEADING CHARACTERS OF THE STORY

MARY ADAMS, An Old-Fashioned Girl.

JIM ANTHONY, A Modern Youth.

JANE ANDERSON, An Artist.

ELLA, A Scrubwoman.

NANCE OWENS, Jim Anthony's Mother.

A DOCTOR, Whose Call was Divine.

THE BABY, A Mascot.

CHAPTER I

A FRIENDLY WARNING

Mary Adams, you're a fool!"

The single dimple in a smooth red cheek smiled in answer.

"You're repeating yourself, Jane -"

"You won't give him one hour's time for just three sittings?"

"Not a second for one sitting -"

"Hopeless!"

Mary smiled provokingly, her white teeth gleaming in bstinate good humor.

"He's the most distinguished artist in America -"

"I've heard so."

"It would be a liberal education for a girl of your training to know such a man -"

"I'll omit that course of instruction."

The younger woman was silent a moment, and a flush of anger slowly mounted her temples. The blue eyes were fixed reproachfully on her friend.

"You really thought that I would pose?"

"I hoped so."

"Alone with a man in his studio for hours?"

Jane Anderson lifted her dark brows.

"Why, no, I hardly expected that! I'm sure he would take his easel and palette out into the square in front of the Plaza Hotel and let you sit on the base of the Sherman monument. The crowds would cheer and inspire him - bah! Can't you have a little common- sense? There are a few brutes among artists, as there are in all professions - even among the superintendents of your schools. Gordon's a great creative genius. If you'd try to flirt with him, he'd stop his work and send you home. You'd be as safe in his studio as in your mother's nursery. I've known him for ten years. He's the gentlest, truest man I've ever met. He's doing a canvas on which he has set his whole heart."

"He can get professional models."

"For his usual work, yes - but this is the head of the Madonna. He saw you walking with me in the Park last week and has been to my studio a half-dozen times begging me to take you to see him. Please, Mary dear, do this for my sake. I owe Gordon a debt I can never pay. He gave me the cue to the work that set me on my feet. He was big and generous and helpful when I needed a friend. He asked nothing in return but the privilege of helping me again if I ever needed it. You can do me an enormous favor - please."

Mary Adams rose with a gesture of impatience, walked to her window and gazed on the torrent of humanity pouring through Twenty-third Street from the beehives of industry that have changed this quarter of New York so rapidly in the last five years. She turned suddenly and confronted her friend.

"How could you think that I would stoop to such a thing?"

"Stoop!"

"Yes," she snapped, "- pose for an artist! I'd as soon think of rushing stark naked through Twenty-third Street at noon!"

The older woman looked at her flushed face, suppressed a sharp answer, broke into a fit of laughter and threw her arms around Mary's neck.

"Honey, you're such a hopeless little fool, you're delicious! You know that I love you - don't you?"

The pretty lips quivered.

"Yes."

"Could I possibly ask you to do a thing that would harm a single brown hair of your head?"

The firm hand of the older girl touched a rebellious lock with tenderness.

"Of course not, from your point of view, Jane dear," the stubborn lips persisted. "But you see it's not my point of view. You're older than I -"

Jane smiled.

"Hoity toity, Miss! I'm just twenty-eight and you're twenty-four. Age is not measured by calendars these days."

"I didn't mean that," the girl apologized. "But you're an artist. You're established and distinguished. You belong to a different world."

Jane Anderson laid her hand softly on her friend's.

"That's just it, dear. I do belong to a different world - a big new world of whose existence you are not quite conscious. You are living in the old, old world in which women have groped for thousands of years. I don't mind confessing that I undertook this job of getting you to pose for Gordon for a double purpose. I wished to do something to repay the debt I owe him - but I wished far more to be of help to you. You're living in the Dark Ages, and it's a dangerous thing for a pretty girl to live in the Dark Ages and date her letters from New York to-day -"

"I don't understand you in the least."

"And I'm afraid you never will."

She paused suddenly and changed her tone.

"Tell me now, are you happy in your work?"

"I'm earning sixty dollars a month - my position is secure -"

"But are you happy in it?"

"I don't expect to teach school all my life," was the vague answer.

"Exactly. You loathe the sight of a school-room. You do the task they set you because your father's a clergyman and can't support his big family. You're waiting and longing for the day of your deliverance - isn't it so?"

"Perhaps."

"And that day of deliverance?"

"Will come when I meet my Fate!"

"You'll meet him, too!"

"I will -"

Jane Anderson shook her fine head.

"And may the Lord have mercy on your poor little soul when you do!"

"And why, pray?"

"Because you're the most helpless and defenseless of all the things He created."

Mary smiled.

"I've managed to take pretty good care of myself so far."

"And you will - until the thunderbolt falls."

"The thunderbolt?"

"Until you meet your Fate."

"I'll have someone to look after me then."

"We'll hope so anyhow," was the quick retort.

"But can't you see, Jane dear, that we look at life from such utterly different angles. You glory in your work. It's your inspiration - the breath you breathe. I don't believe in women working for money. I don't believe God ever meant us to work when He made us women. He made us women for something more wonderful. I don't see anything good or glorious in the fact that half the torrent of humanity you see down there pouring through the street from those factories and offices is made up of women. They are wage-earners - so much the worse. They are forcing the scale of wages for men lower and lower. They are paying for it in weakened bodies and sickly, hopeless children. We should not shout for joy; we should cry. God never meant for woman to be a wage-earner!"

A sob caught her voice and she paused.

The artist watched her emotion with keen interest.

"Neither do I believe that God means to force woman at last to do the tasks of man. But she's doing them, dear - and it must be so until a brighter day dawns for humanity. The new world that opens before us will never abolish marriage, but it has opened our eyes to know what it means. You refuse to open yours. You refuse to see this new world about you. I've begged you to join one of my clubs. You refuse. I beg you to meet and know such men of genius as Gordon -"

"As an artist's model!"

"It's the only way on earth you can meet him. You stick to your narrow, hide-bound conventional life and dream of the Knight who will suddenly appear some day out of the mists and clouds. You dream of the Fate God has prepared for you in His mysterious Providence. It's funny how that idea persists even today in novels. As a matter of fact we know that the old-fashioned girl met her Fate because her shrewd mother planned the meeting - planned it with cunning and stratagem. You're alone in a great modern city, with all the conditions of the life of the old regime reversed or blotted out. Your mother is not here. And if she were, her schemes to bring about the mysterious meeting of the Fates would be impossible. You outgrew the limits of your village life. Your highly trained mind landed you in New York. You've fought your way to a competent living in five years and kept yourself clean and unspotted from the world. Granted. But how many men have you met who are your equals in culture and character?"

Jane paused and held Mary's gaze with steady persistence.

"How many - honest?"

"None as yet," she confessed.

"But you live in the one fond, imperishable hope! It's the only thing that keeps you alive and going - this idea of your Fate. It's an obsession - this mysterious Knight somewhere in the future riding to meet you -"

"I'll find him, never fear," the girl laughed.

"Of course you will. You'll make him out of whole cloth if it's necessary. Our ideals are really the same when you come to analyze my wider outlook."

The artist paused and laughed softly.

"The same?" the girl asked incredulously.

"Certainly. Mine is based on intelligence, however - yours on blind instinct perverted and twisted by the idiotic fiction you read morning, noon and night."

"I don't see it," Mary answered emphatically. "Your ideal is fame, achievement, the applause of the world - mine just a home and a baby -"

Jane laughed softly.

"And that's all you know about me?"

"Isn't it true?"

"You've been in this room five years, haven't you?" the older girl asked musingly.

"Yes -"

"And though you've kept your lamp trimmed and burning, you haven't yet seen a man whom you could recognize as your equal."

"I'm only twenty-four."

"In these five years I've met a hundred men my equal."

"And smashed the conventions of Society whenever you saw fit."

"Without breaking a single law of reason or common-sense. In the meantime I've met two men who have really made love to me. I thought I loved one of them - until I met the other. The second proved himself to be an unprincipled scoundrel. If I had held your views of life and hated my work, I would have married this man and lived to awake in a prison whose only door was Death. But I loved my work. Life meant more than one man who was not worth an hour's tears. I turned to my studio and he slipped back into the gutter where he belonged. I'll meet MY Fate some day, too, dear. I'm waiting and watching - but with clear eyes and unafraid. I'll know mine when he comes, I shall not be blinded by passion or the fear of drudgery. Can't you see this bigger world of realities?"

The dimple flashed again in the smooth red cheek.

"It's not for me, Jane. I'm just a modest little home body. I'll bide my time -"

"And eat your foolish heart out here between the narrow walls of this cell you've built for yourself. I should think you'd die living here alone."

The girl flushed.

"I'm not lonely -"

"Don't fib! I know better. Your birds and kitten occupy daily about thirty minutes of the time that's your own. What do you do with the rest of it?"

"Sit by my window, watch the crowds stream through the streets below, read and dream and think -"

"Yes - read love stories and dream about your Knight."

"Well?"

"It's morbid and unhealthy. You've hedged yourself about with the old conventions and imagine you're safe - and you are - until you meet HIM!"

"I'll know how to behave - never fear."

"You mean you'll know how instantly to blindfold, halter and lead him to the Little Church Around the Corner?"

Mary moved uneasily.

"And what else should I do with him?"

"Compare him with other men. Weigh him in the balances of a remorseless common-sense. Study him under a microscope and keep your reason clear. The girl who rushes into marriage in a great city under the conditions in which you and I live is a fool. More girls are ruined in New York by marriage than by any other process. The thunderbolt out of the blue hasn't struck you yet, but when it does -"

"I'll tell you, Jane."

"Will you, honestly?"

The question was asked with wistful tenderness.

"I promise. And you mustn't think I don't appreciate this visit and the chance you've given again to enter the 'big world' you're always telling me about. I just can't do it, dear. It's not my world."

"All right, my little foolish virgin, have it your own way. When you're lonely, run up to my studio to see me. I won't ask you to pose or meet any of the dangerous men of my circle. We'll lock the doors and have a snug time all by ourselves."

"I'll remember."

The clock in the Metropolitan Tower chimed the hour of five, and Jane Anderson rose with a quick, business-like movement.

"Don't hurry," Mary protested. "I know I've been stubborn, but I've been so happy in your coming. I do get lonely - frightfully lonely, sometimes - don't think I'm ungrateful -"

"You're dangerously beautiful, child," the artist said, with enthusiasm. "And remember that I love you - no matter how silly you are - good-by."

"You won't stay for a cup of tea? I meant to ask you an hour ago."

"No, I've an engagement with a dreadful man whom I've no idea of ever marrying. I'm going to dinner with him - just to study the animal at dose range."

With a jolly laugh and quick, firm step she was gone.

Mary snatched the kitten from his snug bed between the pillows of the window-seat and pressed his fuzzy head under her chin.

"She tempted us terribly, Kitty darling, but we didn't let her find out - did we? You know deep down in your cat's soul that I was just dying to meet the distinguished Gordon - but such high honors are not for home bodies like you and me -"

She dropped on the seat and closed her eyes for a long time. The kitten watched her wonderingly sure of a sudden outbreak with each passing moment. Two soft paws at last touched her cheeks and two bright eyes sought in vain for hers. The little nose pressed closer and kissed the drooping eyelids until they opened. He curled himself on her bosom and began to sing a gentle lullaby. For a long while she lay and listened to the music of love with which her pet sought to soothe the ache within.

The clock in the tower chimed six.

She lifted her body and placed her head on a pillow beside the window. The human torrent below was now at its flood. Two streams of humanity flowed eastward along each broad sidewalk. Hundreds were pouring in endless procession across Madison Square. The cars in Broadway north and South were jammed. Every day she watched this crowd hurrying, hurrying away into the twilight - and among all its hundreds of thousands not an eye was ever lifted to hers - not one man or woman among them cared whether she lived or died.

It was horrible, this loneliness of the desert in an ocean of humanity! For the past year it had become an increasing horror to look into the silent faces of this crowd of men and women and never feel the touch of a friendly hand or hear the sound of a human voice in greeting.

And yet this endless procession held for her a supreme fascination. Somewhere among its myriads of tramping feet, walked the one man created for her. She no more doubted this than she doubted God Himself. It was His law. He had ordained it so. She had grown so used to the throngs below her window and so loved the little park with its splashing fountain that she had refused to follow her landlady uptown when the brownstone boarding-house facing the Square had been turned into a studio building.

Instead of moving she had wheedled the landlord into allowing her to cut off a small space from her room for a private bath and kitchenette, built a box couch across the window large enough for a three-quarter mattress and covered it with velour. For five dollars a week she had thus secured a little home in which was combined a sitting-room, bed-room, bath and kitchenette.

It had its drawbacks, of course. The Professor downstairs who taught music sometimes gave a special lesson at night, and the Italian sculptor who worked on the top floor used a hammer at the most impossible hours. But on the whole she liked it better than the tiresome routine of boarding. She was not afraid at night. The stamp-and-coin man who occupied the first floor, lived with his wife and baby in the rear. The janitress had a room on the floor above hers. Two elderly women workers of ability in the mechanical arts occupied the rear of her floor, and a dear little fat woman of fifty who drew designs for the New England weavers of cotton goods lived in the room adjoining hers.

She had never spoken to any of these people, but Ella, the janitress, who cleaned up her place every morning, had told her their history. Ella was a sociable soul, her face an eternal study and an inscrutable mystery. She spoke both German and English and yet never a word of her own life's history passed her lips. She had loved Mary from the moment she cocked her queer drawn face to one side and looked at her with the one good eye she possessed. She was always doing little things for her comfort - and never asked tips for it. If Mary offered to pay she smiled quietly and spoke in the softest drawl: "Oh, that's nothing, child - Ach, Gott im Himmel - nein!"

This one-eyed, homely woman who cleaned up her room for three dollars a month, and Jane Anderson, were the only friends she had among the six million people whose lives centered on Manhattan Island.

Man had yet to darken her door. The little room had been carefully fitted, however, to receive her Knight when the great event of his coming should be at hand.

The box couch was built of hard wood paneling and was covered with pillows of soft leather and silk. The bed-clothes were carefully stored in the locker beneath the mattress cushion. No one would ever suspect its use as a bed. The bathroom was fitted with a bureau and no signs of a sleeping apartment disfigured the effect of her one library, parlor, and reception-room. A desk and bookcase stood at either end of the box couch. The bookcase was filled with fiction - love stories exclusively.

A large birdcage swung from a staple in the window and two canaries peered cautiously from their perches at the kitten in her lap. She had trained him to ignore this cage.

The crowds below were thinning down. A light snow was falling. The girl lifted her pet and kissed his cold nose.

"We must get our own dinner tonight, Mr. Thomascat - it's snowing outside. And did you hear what she said, Kitty dear - 'More girls are ruined by marriage in New York than by any other process!' A good joke, Kitty! - You and I know better than that if we do live in our own tiny world! We'll risk it some day, anyhow, won't we?"

The kitten purred his assent and Mary bustled over the little gas stove humming an old love song her mother had taught her in a far-off village in Kentucky.

CHAPTER II

TEMPTATION

Her kitchenette was a model of order and cleanliness. The carpenter who built its neat cupboard and fitted the drawers beneath the tiny gas range, had outdone himself in its construction. He had given the wood-work four coats of immaculate white paint without extra charge. Mary had insisted on paying for it, but he waved the proffered money aside with a gesture that spoke louder than words:

"Pooh! That's nothing to what I'd like to do for you."

She was not surprised when he called the following Saturday and stood at her door awkwardly fumbling his hat, trying to ask her to spend the afternoon and evening at Coney Island with him. There was no mistaking the manner in which he made this request.

She had refused him as gently as possible - a big, awkward, good-natured, ignorant boy he was, with the eyes of a St. Bernard dog. He apologized for his presumption and never repeated the offense.

Somehow her conquests had all been in this class.

The tall, blushing German youth from the butcher's around the corner had been slipping extra cuts into her bundle and making awkward advances until she caught him red-handed

Thomas Dixon

with a pound of lamb chops which he failed to explain. She read him a lecture on honesty that discouraged him. It was not so much what she said, as the way she said it, that wounded his sensitive nature.

The ice man she had not yet entirely subdued. Tony Bonelli had the advantage of pretending not to understand her orders of dismissal. He merely smiled in his sad Italian way and continued to pack her ice-box so full the lid would never close.

She was reminded at every turn tonight of these futile conquests of the impossible. They all smelled of the back stairs and the kitchen. Her people had been slaveholders in the old regime of southern Kentucky. A kindly tolerant contempt for the pretensions of a servant class was bred in the bone of her being.

And yet their tribute to her beauty had its compensations. It was the promise of triumph when he for whom she waited should step from the throng and lift his hat. Just how he was going to do this without a breach of the proprieties of life, she couldn't see. It would come. It must come. It was Fate.

In twenty minutes her coffee-pot was boiling, the lamb chops broiled to perfection and she was seated before the dainty, snow-white table, the kitten softly begging at her feet. Half an hour later, every dish and pot and pan was back in its place in perfect order. She prided herself on her mastery of the details of cooking and the most economical administration of every dollar devoted to housekeeping. She studied cooking in the best schools the city afforded. She meant to show her Knight a thing or two in this line when the time came. His wife would not be an ignorant slattern, the victim of incompetent servants. No servant could fool her. She would know the business of the house down to its minutest detail.

Not that she loved dish-washing and pot-polishing and scrubbing. It was simply a part of the Game of Life she must play in the ideal home she would build. There was no drudgery in it for this reason. She was a soldier on the drill grounds preparing for the battle on the successful issue of which hung her happiness and the happiness of the one of whom she dreamed. She might miss some of the dangerous fun which Jane Anderson could enjoy without a scratch, but she would make sure of the fundamental things which Jane would never stop to consider.

She threw herself on the couch in her favorite position against the pillows, drew the kitten into her arms and hugged him violently.

"It's all right, Mr. Thomascat; we'll show them," she purred softly. "We'll see who wins at last, the eagle who soars or the little wren in the hedge close beside the garden wall - we'll see, Kitty - we'll see!"

The room was still, the noise of the street-cars below muffled with the first soft blanket of snow. The street lamps flickered in the wind with a pale subdued light that scarcely brought out the furnishings of her nest. She was in the habit of dreaming in this window for hours with only the light from the lamps on the street.

The Square, deserted by its tramp lovers, lay white and still and cold. The old battle with the Blue Devils was on again within. The fight with Jane had been easy. She had always found it easy to face temptation in the concrete. The moment Satan appeared in human shape she was up in arms and ready for the fray. It was this silent hour she dreaded when the defenses of the soul were down.

There was no use to lie to herself. She was utterly lonely and heartsick.

She had guarded the portals of life with religious care - with a care altogether unnecessary as events had proved. There had been no crush of rude men to assault her. Only an awkward carpenter, a butcher's boy and the ice man! It was incredible.

Of all the men whose restless feet pressed the pavements of New York, not one, save these three, had apparently cared whether she lived or died.

The men whom she met in her duties in the schoolroom she had found utterly devoid of imagination and beneath contempt. They had each been obviously on guard against the machinations of the female of the species. They had, each of them, shown plainly their fear and hatred of women teachers. The feeling was mutual. God knows she had no desire to encroach on their domain any longer than absolutely necessary.

Perhaps she was making a mistake. The thought was strangling. Only the girl who waived conventions in the rushing tide of the modern city's life seemed to live at all. The others merely existed. Jane Anderson lived! There could be no mistake about that. She had mastered the ugly mob. Its cruel loneliness was to her a thing unknown. But Jane was an exception - the one woman in a thousand who could defy conventions and yet keep her soul and body clean.

The offer she had made had proved a terrible temptation. The artist who had asked with such eagerness to use her head for his portrait of the Madonna on the canvas he was executing for the new cathedral, had long appealed to her vivid imagination. Two prints of his famous work hung on her walls. She had always wished to know him. He had married a Southern girl.

That was just the point - he WAS married!

No girl could afford to be shut up alone in a studio with a fascinating married man for three hours - or half an hour. What if she should fall in love with him at first sight! Such things had happened. They could happen again. Only tragedy could be the end of such an event. It was too dangerous to consider for a moment.

She would have consented had it been possible for Jane to

chaperon her. That would have been obviously ridiculous. No artist with any self-respect would tolerate such a reflection on his honesty. No girl could afford to confess her fears in this brazen fashion.

The necessity for her refusal had depressed her beyond any experience she had passed through in the dreary desert of the past five years.

She lifted the sleeping kitten and whispered passionately:

"Am I a silly fool, Kitty? Am I?"

The tears came at last. She lay back on the pillows and let them pour down her cheeks without protest or effort at self-control. Every nerve of her strong, healthy body ached for the love and companionship of men which she had denied herself with an iron will. At nineteen it had been easy. The sheer animal joy in life had been enough. With the growth of each year the ache within had become more and more insistent. With each ripening season of body and mind, the hunger of love had grown more and more maddening. How long could she keep up this battle with every instinct of her being?

She rose at last, determined to go to Jane, confess that she had been a fool, and step out into the new world, New York's world, and begin to live.

She seized her hat and furs and put them on with feverish haste.

"God knows it's time I began - I'll be an old maid in another year and dry up - ugh!"

She looked in the quaint oval mirror that hung beside her door and lifted her head with a touch of pride.

She had reached the street and started for the Broadway car before she suddenly remembered that Jane was "dining with a dangerous man."

She couldn't turn back to that little room tonight without new courage. Her decision was instantaneous. She couldn't surrender to the flesh and the devil by yielding to Jane.

She would go to prayer-meeting!

Religion had always been a very real thing in her life. Her father was a Methodist presiding elder. She would have gone to the meeting tonight in the first place but for the snow. Dr. Craddock, the new sensational pastor of the Temple, was giving a series of Wednesday-night talks that had aroused wide interest and drawn immense crowds.

His theme tonight was one that promised all sorts of sensations - "The Woman of the Future." The only trouble with the Doctor was that the substance of his discourses sometimes failed to make good the startling suggestions of his titles. No matter - she would go. She felt a sense of righteous pride infighting her way to the church through the first storm of the winter.

In spite of the snow the church was crowded. The subject announced had evidently touched a vital spot in modern life. More people were thinking about "The Woman of the Future" than she had suspected. The crowd sat with eager, upturned faces.

The first half-hour's prayer and song service had just begun. Mary joined in the singing of the stirring evangelistic hymns with enthusiasm. Something in their battle-cry melody caught her spirit instantly tonight and her whole being responded. In ten minutes she was a good shouting Methodist and supremely happy without knowing why. She never paused to ask. Her nature was profoundly religious and she had been born and bred in the atmosphere of revivals. Her father was an aggressive evangelist both in his character and methods of work, and she was his own daughter - a child of emotion.

The individuals in the eager crowd which packed the popular church meant nothing to her personally. They had passed before her unseeing eyes Sunday after Sunday the past five years as mere shadows of an unknown world which swallowed them up the moment they reached the street. She had never seen the inside of one of their homes. Not one of them had drawn close enough to her to venture an invitation.

Two of the stewards she knew personally - one a bricklayer, the other a baker on Eighth Avenue. The preacher she had met in a purely formal way as the bishop of the flock. She liked Dr. Craddock. He was known in the ministry as a live wire. He was a man of vigorous physique - just turning fifty, magnetic, eloquent and popular with the masses.

Mary was curious tonight as to what the preacher would say on "The Woman of the Future." The Methodist Church had been a pioneer in the modern Feminist movement, having long ago admitted women to the full ordination of the ministry. Craddock, however, had been known for his conservatism in the woman movement. He abhorred the idea of woman's suffrage as a dangerous revolution and the fact that he consented to treat the topic at all was a reluctant confession of its menacing importance.

With keen interest, the girl saw him rise at last. A breathless hush fell on the crowd. He walked deliberately to the edge of the platform and gazed into the faces of the people.

"I have often been asked," he slowly began, "where I get my sermons." He paused and laughed. "I'll be perfectly honest with you. Sometimes I get them from the Bible - sometimes from the book of life. The genesis of this talk tonight is very definite. I found it in the liquid depths of a little girl's eyes. She asked a simple question that set me thinking - not only about the subject of her query but on the vaster issues that grew out of it. She looked up into my face the other night after my call for volunteers for the new mission we are beginning in the slums of the East Side, and asked me if the girls were not going to be given the chance to do something worth while in this church's work.

"I couldn't honestly answer her off-hand and in my groping I forgot the child and her question. I saw a vision - a vision of that broader, nobler future toward which human civilization is now swiftly moving.

"I say deliberately that it is swiftly moving, because the progress of the world during the last fifty years has been greater than in any five hundred years of the past.

"The older I grow the stronger becomes my conviction that the problems of the age in which we now live cannot be solved by masculine brain and brawn alone. The problems of the city and the nation and the great fundamental social questions that involve the foundations of modern life will find no solution until the heart and brain of woman are poured into the crucible of our test.

"They talk about a woman's sphere
As though it had a limit:
There's not a place in earth or heaven,
There's not a task to mankind given,
There's not a blessing or a woe,
There's not a whisper yes or no,
There's not a life, or death, or birth
That has a feather's weight of worth
Without a woman in it!

"The difference between a man and a woman is one that makes them the complementary parts of a perfect unit. God made man in His own image - male and female. The person of God therefore combines these two elements unseparated. The mind of God is both male and female. In man we have the strength which lifts and tugs and fights the elements. This is the aspect turned primarily toward matter. In woman we have the finer qualities of the Spirit turned toward the source of all spirit in God. The idea of a masculine deity is a false assumption of the Dark Ages. God is both male and female.

"I used to wonder why Jesus Christ was a man, until I realized that the Incarnation expressed the depth of human need. God stooped lower in assuming the form of man. The form of the divine revelation through Jesus Christ was determined solely by this depth of human need -"

For half an hour in impetuous eloquence, in telling incidents wet with tears and winged with hope, he held his listeners in a spell. It was not until the burst of applause which greeted his closing sentence had died away that Mary Adams realized that another landmark had toppled before the onrushing flood of modern Feminism. The conservatism of Doctor Craddock had yielded at last to the inevitable. He, too, had joined the ranks of the prophets who preach of a Woman's Day of Emancipation.

And yet it never occurred to her that this fact had the slightest bearing on her personal outlook on life. On the contrary she felt in the spiritual elation of the triumphant eloquence of her favorite preacher a renewal of her simple religious faith. At the bottom of that religion lay the foundation of life itself - her conception of marriage as the supreme and only expression of woman's power in the world.

She walked back to her home on the Square, in a glow of ecstatic emotion.

Surely God had miraculously saved her this night from the wiles of the Devil! No matter what this eloquent discourse had meant to others, it had renewed her faith in the old-fashioned woman and the old-fashioned ways of the old-fashioned home. Her vision was once more clear. She was glad Jane Anderson had come to put her to the test. She had been tried in the fires of hell and came forth unscorched.

She stood beside her window dreaming again of the home she would build when her Knight should stand before her revealed in beauty no words could describe. The moon was shining now in solemn glory on the white-shrouded Square. Temptation had only strengthened the fiber of her soul. She knelt in the moonlight beside her couch and prayed that God should ever keep her faith serene. She rose with a sense of peace and joy. God would hear and answer the cry of her heart. The City might be the Desert - it was still God's world and not a sparrow that twittered in those bare trees or chattered on her window-ledge in the morning could fall to the ground without His knowledge. God had put this deathless passion in her heart; He could not deny it expression. She could bide His time. If the day of her deliverance were near, it was good. If God should choose to try her faith in loneliness and tears, it was His way to make the revelation of glory the more dazzling when it came.

She drew the covering about her warm young body with the firm faith that her hour was close at hand, and fell asleep to dream of her Knight.

CHAPTER III

FATE

Mary waked next morning with the delicious sense of impending happiness. A wonderful dream had come to thrill her half-conscious moments, repeating itself in increasing vividness and beauty with each awakening. The vision had been interrupted by the unusual noise of the snow machines on the car tracks, and yet she had fallen asleep after each break and picked up the rapturous scene at the exact moment of its interruption.

She was married and madly in love with her husband. His face she could never see quite clearly. His business kept him away from home on long trips. But his baby was always there - a laughing, wonderful boy whose chubby hands persisted in pulling her hair down into her face each time she bent over his cradle to kiss him.

Ella was chattering in German to someone on the stairs. She wondered again for the hundredth time how this poor, slovenly, one-eyed, ill-kempt creature, scrub-woman and jani-tress, could speak two languages with such ease. Her English, except in excitement, seemed equally fluent with her German. How did such a woman fall so low? She was industrious and untiring in her work. She never touched liquor or drugs. She was kind and thoughtful and watched over her tenants with a motherly care for which no landlord could pay in dollars and cents. She was on her knees on the stairs now, scrubbing down the steps to be crowded again with muddy feet from the street below.

Mary lay for half an hour snuggling under the warm blankets, weaving a romance about Ella's life. A great love for some heroic man who died and left her in poverty could alone explain the mystery that hung about her. She never spoke of her life or people. Mary had ventured once to ask her. A wan smile flitted across the haggard face for a moment, and she answered in low tones that closed the subject.

"I haven't any people, dear," she said slowly. "They are dead long ago."

The girl wondered if it were really true. In her joy this morning she felt her heart go out to the pathetic, drooping figure on the stairs. She wished that every living creature might share the secret joy that filled her soul.

She drew the kitten from his nest beside her pillow and rubbed her cheek against his little cold nose. He always waked her with a kiss on her eyelids and then coiled himself back for a tiny cat-nap until she could make up her mind to rise.

She sprang from the couch with sudden energy and stretched her dainty figure with a prodigious yawn.

"Gracious, Kitty, we must hurry!" she cried, thrusting her bare feet into a pair of embroidered slippers and throwing her blue flannel kimono on over her night-dress.

The coffee-pot was boiling busily when she had bathed and dressed. Each detail of her domestic schedule was given an extra care this morning. The stove was carefully polished, each pot and pan placed in its rack with a precision that spoke an unusual joy within the heart of the housewife.

And through it all she hummed a lullaby that haunted her from the memories of a happy childhood.

Breakfast over, the kitten fed, the birds given their bath, their sand and seed, she couldn't stop until the whole place had been thoroughly cleaned and dusted. Exactly why she had done this on Thursday morning it was impossible to say. Some hidden force within had impelled her.

Then back into the dream world her mind flew on joyous wings. It was a sign from God in answer to prayer. Why not? The Bible was full of such revelations in ancient times. God was not dead because the world was modern and we had steam and electricity. The routine of school was no longer dull. Around each commonplace child hung a halo of romance. They were love-children today. She wove a dream of tenderness, of chivalry, and heroic deeds about them all. She searched each face for some line of beauty caught in the vision of her own baby who had looked into her heart from the mists of eternity.

Three days passed in a sort of trance. Never had she felt surer of life and the full fruition of every hope and faith. Just how this marvelous blossoming would come, she could not guess. Her chances of meeting her Fate were no better than at any moment of the past years of drab disillusionment, and yet, for some reason, her foolish heart kept singing.

Why?

There could be but one answer. The event was impending. Such things could be felt - not reasoned out.

She applied herself to her teaching with a new energy and thoroughness. She must do this work well and carry into the real life that must soon begin the consciousness of every duty faithfully performed.

A boy asked her a question about a little flower which grew in a warm crevice of the stone wall on which the iron fence of the school yard rested. She blushed at her failure to enlighten him and promised to tell him on Monday.

Botany was not one of her tasks but she felt the tribute to her personality in his question, and she would take pains to make her answer full and interesting.

Saturday afternoon she hurried to the Public Library, on Fifth Avenue and Forty-second Street, to look up every reference to this flower.

The boulevard of the Metropolis was thronged with eager thousands. Handsome men and beautifully dressed women passed each other in endless procession on its crowded pavements. The cabs and automobiles, two abreast on either side, moved at a snail's pace, so dense were the throngs at each crossing. Her fancy was busy weaving about each throbbing tonneau and limousine a story of love. Not a wheel was turning in all that long line of shining vehicles that didn't carry a woman or was hurrying to do a woman's bidding.

Her hero was coming, too, somewhere in the crowd with his gloved hand on one of those wheels. She could feel his breath on her cheek as he handed her into the seat by his side and then the sudden leap of the car into space and away on the wings of lightning into the future!

She ascended the broad steps of the majestic building with quick, springing strength. She loved this glorious library, with its lofty, arched ceilings. The sense of eternity that brooded over it and filled the stately rooms rested and inspired her.

Besides, she forgot her poverty in this temple of all time. Within its walls she belonged to the great aristocracy of brains and culture of which this palace was the supreme expression. And it was hers. Andrew Carnegie had given the millions to build it and the city of New York granted the site on land that was worth many millions more. But it was all built for her convenience, her comfort and inspiration. Every volume of its vast and priceless collection was hers - hers to hold in her hands, read and ponder and enjoy. Every officer and manager in its inclosure was her servant - to come at her beck and call and do her bidding. The little room on Twenty-third Street was the symbol of the future. This magnificent building was the realization of the present.

She smiled pleasantly to the polite assistant who received her order slip, and took her seat on the waiting line until her books were delivered.

This magnificent room with its lofty ceilings of golden panels and drifting clouds had always brought to her a peculiar sense of restful power. The consciousness of its ownership had from the first been most intimate. No man can own what he cannot appreciate. He may possess it by legal documents, but he cannot own it unless he has eyes to see, ears to hear, and a heart to feel its charm. This appreciation Mary Adams possessed by inheritance from her student father who devoured books with an insatiate hunger. Nowhere in all New York's labyrinth did she feel as perfectly at home as in this reading-room. The quiet which reigned without apparent sign or warning seemed to belong to the atmosphere of the place. It was unthinkable that any man or woman should be rude or thoughtless enough to break it by a loud word.

This room was hers day or night, winter or summer, always heated and lighted, and a hundred swift, silent servants at hand to do her bidding. Around the room on serried shelves, dressed in leather aprons, stood twenty-five thousand more servants of the centuries of the past ready to answer any question her heart or brain might ask of the world's life since the dawn of Time.

In the stack-room below, on sixty-three miles of shelves, stood a million others ready to come at her slightest nod. She loved to dream here of the future, in the moments she must wait for these messengers she had summoned. In this magic room the past ceased to be. These myriads of volumes made the past a myth. It was all the living, throbbing present - with only the golden future to be explored.

Her number flashed in red letters on the electric blackboard.

She rose and carried her books to the seat number assigned her near the center of the southern division of the room on the extreme left beside the bookcases containing the dictionaries of all languages.

Her seat was on the aisle which skirted the shelves. She found the full description of the flower in which she was interested, made her notes and closed the volume with a lazy movement of her slender, graceful hand.

She lifted her eyes and they rested on a remarkable-looking young man about her own age who stood gazing in an embarrassed, helpless sort of way at the row of ponderous volumes marked "The Century Dictionary."

He was evidently a newcomer. By his embarrassment she could easily tell that it was the first time he had ever ventured into this room.

He looked at the books, apparently puzzled by their number. He raised his hand and ran his fingers nervously through the short, thick, red hair which covered his well-shaped head.

The girl's attention was first fixed by the strange contrast between his massive jaw and short neck which spoke the physical strength of an ox, and the slender gracefully tapering fingers of his small hand. The wrist was small, the fingers almost feminine in their lines.

He caught her look of curious interest and to her horror, smiled and walked straight to her seat.

There was no mistaking his determination to speak. It was useless to drop her eyes or turn aside. He would certainly follow.

She blushed and gazed at him in a timid, helpless fashion while he bent over her seat and whispered awkwardly:

"You look kind and obliging, miss - could you help me a little?"

His tone was so genuine in its appeal, so distressed and hesitating, it was impossible to resent his question.

"If I can - yes," was the prompt answer.

"You won't mind?" he asked, fumbling his hat.

"No - what is it?"

Mary had recovered her composure as his distress had increased and looked steadily into his steel blue eyes inquiringly.

"You see," he went on, in low hurried tones, "I'm all worked up about the mountains of North Carolina - thinkin' o' goin' down there to Asheville in a car, an' I want to look the bloomin' place up and kind o' get my bearin's before I start. A lawyer friend o' mine told me to come here and I'd find all the maps in the Century Dictionary. The man at the desk out there told me to come in this room and look in the shelves on the left and take it right out. Gee, the place is so big, I get all rattled. I found the Century Dictionary on that shelf -"

He paused and smiled helplessly.

"I thought a dictionary was one book - there's a dozen of 'em marked alike. I'm afraid to pull 'em all down an' I don't know where to begin - COULD you help me - please?"

"Certainly, with pleasure," she answered, quickly rising and leading the way back to the shelf at which he had been gazing.

"You want the atlas volume," she explained, drawing the book from the shelf and returning to the seat.

He followed promptly and bent over her shoulder while she

pointed out the map of North Carolina, the position of Asheville and the probable route he must follow to get there.

"Thanks!" he exclaimed gratefully.

"Not at all," she replied simply. "I'm only too glad to be of service to you."

Her answer emboldened him to ask another question.

"You don't happen to know anything about that country down there, do you?"

"Why, yes. I know a great deal about it -"

"Sure enough?"

"I've been through Asheville many times and spent a summer there once."

"Did you?"

His tones implied that he plainly regarded her as a prodigy of knowledge. His whole attitude suggested at once the mind of an alert, interested boy asking his teacher for information on a subject near to his heart. It was impossible to resist his appeal.

"Why, yes," Mary went on in low, rapid tones. "My people live in the Kentucky mountains."

He bent low and gently touched her arm.

"Say, we can't talk in here - I'm afraid. Would it be asking too much of you to come out in the park, sit down on a bench and tell me about it? I'll never know how to thank you, if you will?"

It was absurd, of course, such a request, and yet his interest was so keen, his deference to her superior knowledge so humble and appealing, to refuse seemed ungracious. She hesitated and rose abruptly.

"Just a moment - I'll return my books and then we'll go. You can replace this volume on the shelf where we got it."

"Thank yoo, miss," he responded gratefully. "You're awfully kind."

"Don't mention it," she laughed.

In a moment she was walking by his side down the smooth marble stairs and out through the grand entrance into Fifth Avenue. The strange part about it was, she was not in the least excited over a very unconventional situation. She had allowed a handsomely groomed, young, red-haired adventurer to pick her up without the formality of an introduction, in the Public Library. She hadn't the remotest idea of his name - nor had he of hers - yet there was something about him that seemed oddly familiar. They must have known one another somewhere in childhood and forgotten each other's faces.

The sun was shining in clear, steady brilliancy in a cloudless sky. The snow had quickly melted and it was unusually warm for early December. They turned into the throng of Fifth Avenue and at the corner of Forty-second Street he paused and hesitated and looked at her timidly:

"Say," he began haltingly, "there's an awful crowd of bums on those seats in the Square behind the building - you know Central Park, don't you?"

Mary smiled.

"Quite well - I've spent many happy hours in its quiet walks."

"You know that place the other side of the Mall - that ragged hill covered with rocks and trees and mountain laurel?"

"I've been there often."

"Would you mind going there where it's quiet - I've such a lot o' things I want to ask you - you won't mind the walk, will you?"

"Certainly not - we'll go there," Mary responded in even, business-like tones.

"Because, if you don't want to walk I'll call a cab, if you'll let me -"

"Not at all," was the quick answer. "I love to walk."

It was impossible for the girl to repress a smile at her ridiculous situation! If any human being had told her yesterday that she, Mary Adams, an old-fashioned girl with old-fashioned ideas of the proprieties of life, would have allowed herself to be picked up by an utter stranger in this unceremonious way, she would have resented the assertion as a personal insult - yet the preposterous and impossible thing had happened and she was growing each moment more and more deeply interested in the study of the remarkable youth by her side.

He was not handsome in the conventional sense. His features were too strong for that. An enemy might have called them coarse. Their first impression was of enormous strength and exhaustless vitality. He walked with a quick, military precision and planted his small feet on the pavement with a soft, sure tread that suggested the strength of a young tiger.

The one feature that puzzled her was the size of his hands and feet. They were remarkably small and remarkable for their slender, graceful lines.

His eyes were another interesting feature. The lids drooped with a careless Oriental languor, as though he would shut out the glare of the full daylight, and yet the pupils flashed with a cold steel-blue fire. One look into his eyes and there could be no doubt that the man behind them was an interesting personality.

She wondered what his business could be. Not a lawyer or doctor or teacher certainly. His timidity in handling books was clear proof on that point. He was well groomed. His clothes were made by a first-class tailor.

Her heart thumped with a sudden fear. Perhaps he was some sort of criminal. His questions may have been a trick to lure her away. . . .

They had just crossed the broad plaza at Fifty-ninth Street and entered the walkway that leads to the Mall.

She stopped suddenly.

"It's too far to the hill beyond the Mall," she began hesitatingly. "We'll find a seat in one of the little rustic houses along the Fifty-ninth Street side -"

"Sure, if you say so," he agreed.

He accepted the suggestion so simply, she regretted her suspicions, instantly changed her mind and said, smiling:

"No, we'll go on where we started. The long walk will do me good."

"All right," he laughed; "whatever you say's the law. I'm the little boy that does just what his teacher says."

She blushed and shot him a surprised look.

"Who told you that I was a teacher?" she asked, with a smile.

"Lord, nobody! I had no idea of such a thing. It never popped into my head that you do anything at all. You know, I was awful scared when I spoke to you?"

"Were you?" she laughed.

"Surest thing you know! I'd 'a' never screwed up my courage to do it if you hadn't 'a' looked so kind and gentle and sweet. I just knew you couldn't turn me down -"

There was no mistaking the genuineness of the apology for his presumption. She smiled a gracious answer, and threw the last ugly suspicion to the winds.

He broke into a laugh and lifted his hand in the sudden gesture of a traffic policeman commanding a halt.

"What is it?" she asked.

"You know I was so excited I clean forgot to introduce myself! What do you think o' that? You'll excuse me, won't you? My name's Jim Anthony. I'm sorry I can't give you any references to my folks. I haven't any - I'm a lost sheep in New York - no father or mother. That's why I'm so excited about this trip I'm plannin' down South. I hear I've got some people down there."

He stopped suddenly as if absorbed in the thought. Her heart went out to him in sympathy for this confession of his orphaned life.

"I'm Mary Adams," she smiled in answer. "I'm a teacher in the public schools."

"Gee - that accounts for it! I thought you looked like you knew everything in those books. And you've been to Asheville, too?"

"Yes."

"Suppose it's not as big a burg as New York?"

"Hardly - it's just a hustling mountain town of about twenty-five thousand people."

"Lot o' swells from around New York live down there, they tell me."

"Yes, the Vanderbilts have a beautiful castle just outside."

"Some mountains near Asheville?"

"Hundreds of square miles."

"Mountains in every direction?"

"As far as the eye can reach, one blue range piled above another until they're lost in the dim skies on the horizon."

"Gee, it may be pretty hard to find your folks if they just live in the mountains near Asheville?"

"Unless your directions are more explicit - I should think so."

"You know, I thought the mountains near Asheville was a bunch o' hills off one side like the Palisades, that you couldn't miss if you tried. I've never been outside of New York - since I can remember. I'd love to see real mountains."

The last sentence was spoken in a wistful pathos that touched Mary with its irresistible appeal. Her mother instincts responded to it in quick sympathy.

"You've missed a lot," she answered gravely.

"I'll bet I have. It's a rotten old town, this New York -"

He paused, and a queer light flashed from his steel eyes.

"Until you get your hand on its throat," he added, bringing his square jaws together.

Mary lifted her face with keen interest.

"And you've got it by the throat?"

"That's just what - little girl!" he cried, with a ring of pride. "You see, I'm an inventor and I won a little pile on my first trick. I've got a machine-shop in a room eight-by-ten over on the East Side."

"A machine-shop all your own?"

"Yep."

"I'd like to see it some day."

He shook his head emphatically.

"It's too dirty. I couldn't let a pretty girl like you in such a place." He paused and resumed the tone of his narrative where she interrupted him. "You see, I've just put a new crimp in a carburetor for the automobile folks. They're tickled to death over it and I've got automobiles to burn. Will you go to ride with me tomorrow?"

The teacher broke into a joyous laugh.

"Why do you laugh?" he asked awkwardly.

"Well, in the language of New York, that would be going some, wouldn't it?"

"And why not, I'd like to know?" he cried with scorn. "Who's to tell us we can't? You've no kids to bother you tomorrow. I'm my own boss. You've seen Asheville, but you've never seen New York until you sit down beside me in a big six-cylinder racing car I'm handlin' next week. Let me show it to you. I'll swing her around to your door at eight o'clock. In twenty-five minutes we'll clear the Bronx and shoot into New Rochelle. There'll be no cops out to bother us, and not a wheel in sight. It'll do you good. Let me take you! I owe you that much for bein' so nice to me today. Will you go with me?"

Mary hesitated.

"I'll think it over and let you know."

"Got a telephone?"

"No."

"Then you'll have to tell me before I go - won't you?"

"I suppose so," she answered demurely.

They passed the big fountain beyond the Mall and skirted the lake to the bridge, crossed, walked along the water's edge to the laurel-covered crags and found a seat alone in the summer house that hides among the trees on its highest point.

The roar of the city was dim and far away. The only sounds to break the stillness were the laughter of lovers along the walks below and the distant cry of steamers in the harbor and rivers.

"You'd almost think you're in the mountains up here, now wouldn't you?" he asked, after a moment's silence.

"Yes. I call this park my country estate. It costs me nothing to keep it in perfect order. The city pays for it all. But I own it. Every tree and shrub and flower and blade of grass, every statue and bird and animal in it is mine. I couldn't get more joy out of them if I had them inclosed behind an iron fence, and the deed to the land in my pocket - not half as much, for I'd be lonely and miserable without someone to see and enjoy it all with me."

"Gee, that's so, ain't it? I never looked at it like that before."

He gazed at her a long time in silent admiration, and then spoke briskly.

"Now tell me about this North Carolina and all those miles

and square miles of mountains."

"You've a piece of paper and pencil?"

He lifted his hand school-boy fashion:

"Johnny on the spot, teacher!"

A blank-book and pencil he threw in her lap and leaned close.

"Tear the leaves out, if you like."

"No, I'll just draw the maps on the pages and leave them for you to study."

With deft touch she outlined in rough on the first page, the states of New Jersey, Pennsylvania, Delaware, Virginia and North Carolina, tracing his possible route by Trenton, Philadelphia, Wilmington, Dover, Norfolk and Raleigh, or by Washington, Richmond, and Danville to Greensboro.

"Either route you see," she said softly, "leads to Salisbury, where you strike the foothills of the mountains. It's about two hundred miles from there to Asheville and 'The Land of the Sky.'"

For two hours she answered his eager, boyish questions about the country and its people, his eyes wide with admiration at her knowledge.

The sun was sinking in a sea of scarlet and purple clouds behind the tall buildings beside the Park before she realized that they had been talking for more than two hours.

She sprang to her feet, blushing and confused.

"Mercy, I had no idea it was so late."

"Why - is it late?" he asked incredulously.

"We must hurry -"

She brushed the stray ringlets of hair from her forehead, laughed and hurried down the pathway.

They crossed the Park and took the Madison Avenue line to Twenty-third Street. They were silent in the car. The roar of the traffic was deafening after the quiet of the summer house among the trees.

"I can see you home?" he inquired appealingly.

"We get off at Twenty-third Street."

They stood on the steps at her door beside the Square and there was a moment's awkward silence.

He lifted his hat with a little chivalrous bow.

"Tomorrow morning at eight o'clock in my car?"

She smiled and hesitated.

"You'll have a bully time!"

"It's Sunday," she stammered.

"Sure, that's why I asked you."

"I don't like to miss my church."

"You go to church every Sunday?" he asked in amazement.

"Yes."

"Well, just this once then. It'll do you good. And I'll drive as careful as a farmer."

"All right," she said in low tones, and extended her hand:

"Good night -"

"Good night, teacher!" he responded with a boyish wave of his slender hand and quickly disappeared in the crowd.

She rushed up the stairs, her cheeks aflame, her heart beating a tattoo of foolish joy.

She snatched the kitten from sleep and whispered in his tiny ear:

"Oh, Kitty dear, I've had such an adventure! I've spent the happiest, silliest afternoon of my life! I'm going to have a more wonderful day tomorrow. I just feel it. In a big racing automobile if you please, Mr. Thomascat! Sorry I can't take you but the dust would blind you, Kitty dear. I'm sorry to tell you that you'll have to stay at home all day alone and keep house. It's too bad. But I'll fix your milk and bread before I go and you must promise me on your sacred Persian cat's honor not to look at my birds!"

She hugged him violently and he purred his soft answer in song.

"Oh, Kitty, I'm so happy - so foolishly happy!"

CHAPTER IV

DOUBTS AND FEARS

Mary attempted no analysis of her emotions. It was all too sudden, too stunning. She was content to feel and enjoy the first overwhelming experience of life. Hour after hour she lay among the pillows of her couch in the dim light of the street lamps and lazily watched the passing Saturday evening crowds. The world was beautiful.

She undressed at last and went to bed, only to toss wide-eyed for hours.

A hundred times she reenacted the scene in the Library and recalled her first impression of Jim's personality. What could such an utterly unforeseen and extraordinary meeting mean except that it was her Fate? Certainly he could not have planned it. Certainly she had not foreseen such an event. It had never occurred to her in the wildest flights of fancy that she could meet and speak to a man under such conditions, to say nothing of the walk in the Park and the hours she spent in the little summer house.

And the strangest part of it all was that she could see nothing wrong in it from beginning to end. It had happened in the simplest and most natural way imaginable. By the standards of conventional propriety her act was the maddest folly; and yet she was still happy over it.

There was one disquieting trait about him that made her a little uneasy. He used the catch-words of the street gamins of New York without any consciousness of incongruity. She thought at first that he did this as the Southern boy of culture and refinement unconsciously drops into the tones and dialect of the negro, by daily association. His constant use of the expressive and characteristic "Gee" was startling, to say the least. And yet it came from his lips in such a boyish way she felt sure that it was due to his embarrassment in the unusual position in which he had found himself with her.

His helplessness with the dictionary was proof, of course, that he was no scholar. And yet a boy might have a fair education in the schools of today and be unfamiliar with this ponderous and dignified encyclopedia of words. It was impossible to believe that he was illiterate. His clothes, his carriage, even his manners made such an idea preposterous.

Besides, no inventor could be really illiterate. He may have been forced to work and only attended night schools. But if he were a mechanic, capable of making a successful improvement on one of the most delicate and important parts of an automobile, he must have studied the principles involved in his inventions.

His choice of a profession appealed to her imagination, too. It showed independence and initiative. It opened boundless possibilities. He might be an obscure and poorly educated boy today. In five years he could be a millionaire and the head of some huge business whose interests circled the world.

The tired brain wore itself out at last in eager speculations, and she fell into a fitful stupor. The roar of the street-cars waked her at daylight, and further sleep was out of the question. She rose, dressed quickly and got her breakfast in a quiver of nervous excitement over the adventure of the coming automobile.

As the hour of eight drew nearer, her doubts of the propriety of going became more acute.

"What on earth has come over me in the past twenty-four hours?" she asked of herself. "I've known this man but a day. I don't KNOW him at all, and yet I'm going to put my life in his hands in that racing machine. Have I gone crazy?"

She was not in the least afraid of him. His face and voice and personality all seemed familiar. Her brain and common-sense told her that such a trip with an utter stranger was dangerous and foolish beyond words. In his automobile, unaccompanied by a human soul and unacquainted with the roads over which they would travel, she would be absolutely in his power.

She set her teeth firmly at last, her mind made up.

"It's too mad a risk. I was crazy to promise. I won't go!"

She had scarcely spoken her resolution when the soft call of the auto-horn echoed below. She stood irresolute for a moment, and the call was repeated in plaintive, appealing notes.

She tried to hold fast to her resolutions, but the impulse to open the window and look out was resistless. She turned the old-fashioned brass knob, swung her windows wide on their hinges and leaned out.

His keen eyes were watching. He lifted his cap and waved. She answered with the flutter of her handkerchief - and all resolutions were off.

"Of course, I'll go," she cried, with a laugh. "It's a glorious day - I may never have such a chance again."

Thomas Dixon

CHAPTER V

WINGS OF STEEL

She threw on her furs and hurried downstairs. Her surrender was too sudden to realize that she was being driven by a power that obscured reason and crushed her will.

Reason made one more vain cry as she paused at the door below to draw on her gloves.

"You have refused every invitation to see or know the unconventional world into which thousands of women in New York, clear-eyed and unafraid, enter daily. You'd sooner die than pose an hour in Gordon's studio, and on a Sabbath morning you cut your church and go on a day's wild ride with a man you have known but fifteen hours!"

And the voice inside quickly answered:

"But that's different! Gordon's a married man. My chevalier is not! I have the right to go, and he has the right."

It was settled anyhow before this little controversy arose at the street door, but the ready answer she gave eased her conscience and cleared the way for a happy, exciting trip.

He leaped from the big, ugly racer to help her in, stopped and looked at her light clothing.

"That's your heaviest coat?"

"Yes. It isn't cold."

"I've one for you."

He drew an enormous fur coat from the car and held it up for her arms.

"You think I'll need that?" she asked.

His white teeth gleamed in a friendly smile.

"Take it from me, Kiddo, you certainly will!"

She winced just a little at the common expression, but he said it with such a quick, boyish enthusiasm, she wondered whether he were quoting the expression from the Bowery boy's vocabulary or using it in a facetious personal way.

"I knew you'd need it. So I brought it for you," he added genially.

"Thanks," she murmured, lifting her arms and drawing the coat about her trim figure.

He helped her into the car and drew from his pocket a light pair of goggles.

"Now these, and you're all hunky-dory!"

"Will I need these, too?" she asked incredulously.

"Will you!" he cried. "You wouldn't ask that question if you knew the horse we've got hitched to this benzine buggy today. He's got wings - believe me! It's all I can do to hold him on the ground sometimes."

"You'll drive carefully?" she faltered.

He lifted his hand.

"With you settin' beside me, my first name's `Caution.'"

She fumbled the goggles in a vain effort to lift her arms over her head to fasten them on. He sprang into the seat by her side and promptly seized them.

"Let me fix 'em."

His slender, skillful fingers adjusted the band and brushed a stray ringlet of hair back under the furs. The thrill of his touch swept her with a sudden dizzy sense of excitement. She blushed and drew her head down into the collar of the shaggy coat.

He touched the wheel, and the gray monster leaped from the curb and shot down the street. The single impulse carried them to the crossing. He had shut off the power as the machine gracefully swung into Fourth Avenue. The turn made, another leap and the car swept up the Avenue and swung through Twenty-sixth Street into Fifth Avenue. Again the power was off as he made the turn into Fifth Avenue at a snail's pace.

"Can't let her out yet," he whispered apologetically. "Had to make these turns. There's no room for her inside of town."

Mary had no time to answer. He touched the wheel, and the car shot up the deserted Avenue. She gasped for breath and braced her feet, her whole being tingling with the first exhilarating consciousness that she too was possessed of the devil of speed madness. It was glorious! For the first time in her life, space and distance lost their meaning. She was free as the birds in the heavens. She was flying on the wings of this gray, steel monster through space. The palaces on the Avenue whirled by in dim ghost-like flashes. They flew through Central Park into Seventy-second Street and out into the Drive. The waters of the river, broad and cool, flashing in the morning sun, rested her eyes a moment and then faded in a twinkling. They had leaped the chasm beyond Grant's Tomb, plunged into Broadway and before she could get her bearings, swept up the hill at One Hundred and Fifty-fifth Street, slipped gracefully across the iron bridge and in a jiffy were lost in a gray cloud of dust on the Boston Turnpike.

When the first intoxicating joy of speed had spent itself, she found herself shuddering at the daring turns he made, missing a curb by a hair's breadth - grazing a trolley by half an inch. Her fears were soon forgotten.

The hand on the wheel was made of steel, too.

The throbbing demon encased within the hood obeyed his slightest whim. She glanced at the square, massive jaw with furtive admiration.

Without turning his head he laughed.

"You like it, teacher?"

"I'm in Heaven!"

"You won't worry about church then, will you?"

"Not today."

They stopped at a road-house, and he put in more gasoline, lifted the casing from the engine, touched each vital part, examined his tires, and made sure that his machine was at its best.

She watched him with a growing sense of his strength of character, his poise and executive ability. He was an awkward, stammering boy in the Library yesterday. Today with this machine in his hand he was the master of Time and Space.

She yielded herself completely to the delicious sense of his protection. The extraordinary care he was giving the machine was a plain avowal of his deep regard for her comfort and happiness. She had been in one or two moderately moving cars driven by careful chauffeurs through Central Park. She had always felt on those trips with Jane Anderson like a poor relation from the country imposing on a rich friend.

This trip was all her own. The car and its master were there solely for her happiness. Her slightest whim was law for both. It was sweet, this sense of power. She began to lift her body with a touch of pride.

She laughed now at fears. What nonsense! No Knight of the Age of Chivalry could treat her with more deference. He had tried already to get her to stop for a bite of lunch.

"Don't you want a thing to eat?" he persisted.

"Not a thing. I've just had my breakfast. It's only nine o' clock -"

"I know, but we've come thirty miles and the air makes you hungry. We ought to eat about six good meals a day."

She shook her head.

"No - not yet. I'm too happy with these new wings. I want to fly some more - come on -"

He lifted his hand in his favorite gesture of obedience.

"'Nuff said - we'll streak it back now by another road, hump it through town and jump over the Brooklyn Bridge. I'll show you Coney Island and then I know you'll want a hot dog anyhow."

He crossed the country and darted into Broadway. Before she could realize it, the last tree and field were lost behind in a cloud of dust, and they were again in the crowded streets of the city. The deep growl of his horn rang its warnings for each crossing and Mary watched the timid women scramble to the sidewalks five and six blocks ahead.

It was delicious. She had always been the one to scramble before. Her heart went out in a wave of tenderness to the man by her side, strong, daring, masterful, her chevalier, her protector and admirer.

Yes, her admirer! There was no doubt on that point. The moment he relaxed the tension of his hand on the wheel, his deep, mysterious eyes beneath the drooping lids were fixed on hers in open, shameless admiration. Their cold fire burned into her heart and thrilled to her finger-tips.

In spite of his deference and his obedience to her whim, she felt the iron grip of his personality on her imagination. Whatever his education, his origin or his environment, he was a power to be reckoned with.

No other type of man had ever appealed to her. Her conception of a real man had always been one who did his own thinking and commanded rather than asked the respect of others.

She had thrown the spell of her beauty over this headstrong, masterful man. He was wax in her hands. A delicious sense of power filled her. She had never known what happiness meant before. She floated through space. The spinning lines of towering buildings on Broadway passed as mists in a dream.

As the velvet feet of the car touched the great bridge she lazily opened her eyes for a moment and gazed through the lace-work of steel at the broad sweep of the magnificent harbor. The dark blue hills of Staten Island framed the picture.

He was right. She had never seen New York before. Never before had its immense panorama been swept within two hours. Never before had she realized its dimensions. She had always felt stunned and crushed in the effort to conceive it.

Today she had wings. The city lay at her feet, conquered. She was mistress of Time and Space.

Again her sidelong glance swept the lines of Jim Anthony's massive jaw. She laughed softly.

"What's the matter?" he asked.

"Nothing. I'm just happy."

She blushed and wondered if he had read her thoughts by some subtle power of clairvoyance. She was speculating on the effects of love at first sight on such a man. Would he hesitate, back and fill and hang on for months trying in vain to gain the courage to speak? Or would he spring with the leap of a young tiger the moment he realized what he wanted?

Her own attitude was purely one of joyous expectancy. It would, of course, be a long time before her feelings could take any definite attitude toward a man. For the moment she was supremely happy. It was enough. She made no effort to probe her feelings. She might return to earth tomorrow. Today she was in Heaven. She would make the most of it.

They skimmed the wooded cliffs of Bay Ridge, her heart beating in ecstasy at the revelation of beauty of whose existence she had not dreamed.

"I bet you never saw this drive before, now did you?" he asked with boyish enthusiasm.

"No - it's wonderful."

"Some view - eh?"

"Entrancing!"

"You know when I make my pile, I'd like a palace of white marble perched on this cliff with the windows on the south looking out over Sandy Hook, and the windows on the west looking over that fort on the top of Staten Island with its black eyes gazing over the sea. How would you like that?"

She turned away to mask the smile she couldn't repress.

"That would be splendid, wouldn't it?"

"I like the water, don't you?"

"I love it."

"Water and hills both right together! I reckon my father must 'a' been a sea-captain and my mother from the mountains -"

He said this with a pathos that found the girl's heart. What a pitiful, lonely life, a boy's without even the memory of a mother or father! The mother instinct rose in a resistless flood of pity. Her eyes grew suddenly dim.

"Well," he said briskly, "now for the dainty job! I've got to jump my way through that Coney Island bunch. You see my low speed's a racing pace for an everyday car. All I can do in a crowd is to jump from one crossing to the next and cut her power off every time. You can bet I'll make a guy or two jump with me -"

"You won't hurt anyone?" she pleaded.

"Lord, no! I wouldn't dare to put her through that mob in the afternoon. I'd kill a regiment of 'em. But it's early - just the shank of the morning. There's nobody down here yet."

The car suddenly leaped into the Avenue that runs through the heart of Coney Island, the deep-throated horn screaming its warning. The crowd scattered like sheep before a lion.

The girl laughed in spite of her effort at self-control.

"Watch 'em hump!" Jim grunted.

"It's funny, isn't it?"

"When you're in the car - yes. It don't seem so funny when you're on foot. Well, some people were made to walk and some to ride. I had to hoof it at first. I like riding better - don't you?"

"To be perfectly honest - yes!"

The car leaped forward again, the horn screaming. The wheel passed within a foot of a fat woman's skirt. With a cry of terror she fled to the sidewalk and shook her fist at Jim, her face purple with anger.

He waved his hand back at her:

"Never touched you, dearie! Never touched you!"

Mary lost all fear of accident and watched him handle the machine with the skill of a master. She could understand now the spirit of deviltry in a chauffeur who knows his business. It seemed a wicked, cruel thing from the ground - this swift plunge of a car as if bent on murder. But now that she felt the sure, velvet grip of the brake in a master's hand, she saw that the danger was largely a myth.

It was fun to see people jump at the approach of an avalanche of steel that always stopped just short of harm. Of course, it took a steady nerve and muscle to do the trick. The man by her side had both. He was always smiling. Nothing rattled him.

Her trust was now implicit. She relaxed the tension of the first two hours of doubt and fear, and yielded to the spell of his strength. It seemed inseparable from the throbbing will of the giant machine. He was its incarnate spirit. She was being swept through space now on the wings of omnipotent power - but power always obedient to her whim.

With steady, even pulse they glided down the long, broad Avenue to Prospect Park, swung through its winding lanes, on through the streets of Brooklyn and once more into the open road.

"Now for Long Beach and a good lunch!" he cried. "I'll show you something - but you'll have to shut your eyes to see it."

With a sudden bound, the car leaped into the air, and shot through the sky with the hiss and shriek of a demon.

The girl caught her breath and instinctively gripped his arm.

"Look out, Kiddo!" he shouted. "Don't touch me - or we'll both land in Kingdom Come. I ain't ready for a harp just yet. I'd rather fool with this toy for a while down here."

She braced her feet and gripped the sides of the car, gasping for breath, steadied herself at last and crouched low among the furs to guard her throat from the icy daggers of the wind.

The landscape whirled in a circle of trees and sky, while above the dark line of hills hung the boiling cauldron of cloud-banked heavens.

"Are you game?" he called above the roar.

"Yes," she gasped. "Don't stop -"

Her soul had risen at last to the ecstasy of the mania for speed that fired the man's spirit and nerved his hand. It was inconceivable until experienced - this awful joy! Her spirit sank with childish disappointment as he slowly lowered the power.

"Got to take a sharp curve down there," he explained. "We turn to the right for the meadows and the Beach - how was that?"

"Wonderful," she cried, with dancing eyes. "Let her go again if you want to - I'm game - now."

Jim laughed.

"A little rattled at first?"

"Yes -"

"Well, we can't let her out on this road. It's too narrow - have to take a ditch sometimes to pass. That wouldn't do for an eighty-mile clip, you know - now would it?"

"Hardly."

"I might risk it alone - but my first name's `Old Man Caution' today - you get me?"

Mary nodded and turned her head away again.

"I got you the first time, sir," she answered playfully taking his tone.

He ran the car into the garage at the Beach, sprang out and lifted Mary to the ground with quick, firm hand. They threw off their heavy coats and left them.

"Look out for this junk now, sonny," he cried to the attendant, tossing him a half dollar.

"Sure, Mike!"

"Fill her up to the chin by the time we get back."

"Righto!"

Quickly they walked to the hotel and in five minutes were seated beside a window in the dining-room, watching the lazy roll of the sea sweep in on the sands at low tide.

"I'm hungry as a wolf!" he whispered.

"So am I -"

"We'll eat everything in sight - start at the top and come down."

He handed her the menu card and watched her from the depths beneath the drooping eyelids.

Conscious of his gaze and rejoicing in its frank admiration, she ordered the dinner with instinctive good taste. No effort at conversation was made by either. They were both too hungry. As Jim lighted his cigarette when the coffee was served, he leaned back in his chair and watched the breakers in silence.

"That's the best dinner I ever had in my life," he said slowly.

"It was good. We were hungry."

"I've been hungry before, many a time. It was something else, too." He paused and rose abruptly. "Let's walk up the Beach."

"I'd love to," she answered, slowly rising.

Thomas Dixon

CHAPTER VI

BESIDE THE SEA

They strolled leisurely along the board-walk, found the sand, walked in the firm, dry line of the high-water mark for a mile to the east, and sat down on a clump of sea-grass on the top of a sand dune.

"I like this!" she cried joyously.

"So do I," he answered soberly, and lapsed into silence.

The sun was warm and genial. The wind had died, and the waves of the rising tide were creeping up the long, sloping stretches of the sand with a lazy, soothing rush. A winter gull poised above their heads and soared seaward. The smoke of an ocean liner streaked the horizon as she swept toward the channel off Sandy Hook.

Jim looked at the girl by his side and tried to speak. She caught the strained expression in his strong face and lowered her eyes.

He began to trace letters in the sand.

She knew with unerring instinct that he had made his first desperate effort to speak his love and failed. Would he give it up and wait for weeks and possibly months - or would he storm the citadel in one mad rush at the beginning?

He found his voice at last. He had recovered from the panic of his first impulse.

"Well, how do you like my idea of a good day as far as you've gone?" he asked lightly.

She met his gaze with perfect frankness. "The happiest day I ever spent in my life," she confessed.

"Honest?"

"Honest."

"Oh, shucks - what's the use!" he cried, with sudden fierce resolution. "You've got me, Kiddo, you've got me! I've been eatin' out of your hand since the minute I laid my eyes on you in that big room. I'm all yours. You can do anything you want with me. For God's sake, tell me that you like me a little."

The blood slowly mounted to her cheeks in red waves of tremulous emotion.

"I like you very much," she said in low tones.

He seized her hand and held it in a desperate grip.

"I love you, Kiddo," he went on passionately. "You don't mind me calling you Kiddo? You're so dainty and pretty and sweet, and that dimple keeps coming in your cheek, it just seems like that's the word - you don't mind?"

"No -"

"You don't know how I've been starvin' all my life for the love of a pure girl like you. You're the first one I ever spoke to. I was scared to death yesterday when I saw you. But I'd 'a' spoke to you if it killed me in my tracks. I couldn't help it. It just looked like an angel had dropped right down out of the gold clouds from that ceilin'. I was afraid I'd lose you in the crowd and never see you again. It didn't seem you were a stranger anyhow - I didn't seem strange to you, did I?"

Her lips quivered, and she was silent.

"Didn't you feel like you'd known me somewhere before?" he pleaded.

"Yes."

"I just felt you did, and that's what give me courage. Oh, Kiddo, you've got to love me a little - I've never been loved by a human soul in all my life. The first thing I remember was hidin' under a stoop from a brute who beat me every night. I ran away and slept in barrels and crawled into coal shutes till I was big enough to earn a livin' sellin' papers. For years I never knew what it meant to have enough to eat. I just scratched and fought my way through the streets like a little hungry wolf till I got in a blacksmith's shop down on South Street and learned to handle tools. I was quick and smart, and the old man liked me and let me sleep in the shop. I had enough to eat then and got strong as an ox. I went to the night schools and learned to read and write. I don't know anything, but I'm quick and you can teach me - you will, won't you?"

"I'll try," was the low answer.

"You do like me, Kiddo? Say it again!"

She rose to her feet and looked out over the sea, her face scarlet.

"Yes, I do," she said at last.

With a sudden resistless sweep he clasped her in his arms and kissed her lips.

Her heart leaped in mad response to the first kiss a lover had ever given. Her body quivered and relaxed in his embrace. It was sweet - it was wonderful beyond words.

He kissed her again, and she clung to him, lifting her eyes to his at last in a long, wondering gaze and then pressed her own lips to his.

"Oh, my God, Kiddo, you love me! It beats the world, don't it? Love at first sight for both of us!

I've heard about it, but I didn't think it would ever happen to me like this - did you?"

She shook her head and bit her lips as the tears slowly dimmed her eyes.

"It takes my breath," she murmured. "I can't realize what it all means. It seems too wonderful to be true."

"And you won't turn me down because I don't know who my father and mother was?"

"No - my heart goes out to you in a great pity for your lonely, wretched boyhood."

"I couldn't help that - now could I?"

"Of course not. It's wonderful that you've made your way alone and won the fight of life."

He gripped her hands and held her at arms' length, devouring her with his deep, slumbering eyes.

"Gee, but you're a brick, little girl! I thought you were an angel when I first saw you. Now I know it. Just watch me work for you! I'll show you a thing or two. You'll marry me right away, won't you?"

He bent close, his breath on her lips.

Her eyes drooped under his passionate gaze, and the tears slowly stole down her cheeks. Her hour of life had struck! So suddenly, so utterly unexpectedly, it rang a thunderbolt from the clear sky.

"You will, won't you?" he pleaded.

She smiled at him through her tears and slowly said:

"I can't say yes today."

"Why - why?"

"You've swept me off my feet - I - I can't think."

"I don't want you to think - I want you to marry me right now."

"I must have a little time."

His face fell in despair.

"Say, little girl, don't turn me down - you'll kill me."

"I'm not turning you down," she protested tenderly. "I only want time to see that I'm not crazy. I have to pinch myself to see if I'm awake. It all seems a dream" - she paused and lifted her radiant face to his - "a beautiful dream - the most wonderful my soul has ever seen. I must be sure it's real!"

He drew her into his arms, and her body again relaxed in surrender as his lips touched hers.

"Isn't that the real thing?" he laughed.

She lay very still, her eyes closed, her face a scarlet flame. She was frightened at the swift realization of its overwhelming reality. The touch of his hand thrilled to the last fiber and nerve of her body. Her own trembling fingers clung to him with desperate longing tenderness. She roused herself with an effort and drew away.

"That's enough now. I must have a little common-sense. Let's go -"

He clung to her hand.

"You'll let me come to see you, tomorrow night?"

"Yes -"

"And the next night - and every night this week - what's the difference? There's nobody to say no, is there?"

"No one."

"You'll let me?"

"Tomorrow sure. Maybe you won't want to come the next night."

"Maybe I won't! Just wait and see!"

He seized both hands again and held her at arms' length.

"Don't go yet - just let me look at you a minute more! The only girl I ever had in my life - and she's the prettiest thing God ever made on this earth. Ain't I the lucky boy?"

"We must go now," she cried, blushing again under his burning eyes.

He dropped her hands suddenly and saluted military fashion.

"All right, teacher! I'm the little boy that does exactly what he's told."

They strolled leisurely along the shining sands in silence. Now and then his slender hand caught hers and crushed it. The moment he touched her a living flame flashed through her body - and through every moment of contact her nerves throbbed and quivered as if a musician were sweeping the strings of a harp. If this were not love, what could it be?

Her whole being, body and soul, responded to his. Her body moved instinctively toward his, drawn by some hidden, resistless power. Her hands went out to meet his; her lips leaped to his.

She must test it with time, of course. And yet she knew by a deep inner sense that time could only fan the flame that had been kindled into consuming fire that must melt every barrier between them.

She had asked him nothing of himself, his business or his future, and knew nothing except what he had told her in the first impetuous rush of his confession of love. No matter. The big thing today was the fact of love and the new radiance with which it was beginning to light the world. The effect was stunning. Their conversation had been the simplest of commonplace questions and answers - and yet the day was the one miracle of her life - her happiness something unthinkable until realized.

She had not asked time in order to know him better. She had only asked time to see herself more clearly in the new experience. Not for a moment did she raise the question of the worthiness of the man she loved. It was inconceivable that she should love a man not worthy of her. The only questions asked were soul-searching ones put to herself.

Through the sweet, cool drive homeward, a hundred times she asked within:

"Is this love?"

And each time the answer came from the depths:

"Yes - yes - a thousand times yes. It's the voice of God. I feel it and I know it."

He throttled the racer down to the lowest speed and took the longest road home.

Again and again he slipped his left hand from the wheel and pressed hers.

"You won't let anybody knock me behind my back, now will you, little girl?"

She pressed his hand in answer.

"I ain't got a single friend in all God's world to stand up for me but just you."

"You don't need anyone," she whispered.

"You'll give me a chance to get back at 'em if any of your friends knock me, won't you?"

"Why should they dislike you?"

He shrugged his shoulders.

"Well, I ain't exactly one o' the high-flyers now am I?"

"I'm glad you're not."

"Sure enough?"

"Yes."

"Then it's me for you, Kiddo, for this world and the next."

The car swung suddenly to the curb and Mary lifted her eyes with a start to find herself in front of her home.

Jim sprang to the ground and lifted her out.

"Keep this coat," he whispered. "We'll need it tomorrow. What time is your school out?"

"At three o'clock."

"I can come at four?"

"You don't have to work tomorrow?"

He hesitated a moment.

"No, I'm on a vacation till after Christmas. They're putting through my new patent."

He followed her inside the door and held her hand in the shadows of the hall.

"All right, at four," she said.

"I'll be here."

He stooped and kissed her, turned and passed quickly out.

She stood for a moment in the shadows and listened to the throb of the car until it melted into the roar of the city's life, her heart beating with a joy so new it was pain.

CHAPTER VII

A VAIN APPEAL

A week passed on the wings of magic.

Every day at four o'clock the car was waiting at her door. The drab interior of the school-room had lost its terror. No annoyance could break the spell that reigned within. Her patience was inexhaustible, her temper serene.

Walking with swift step down the Avenue to her home she wondered vaguely how she could have been lonely in all the music and the wonder of New York's marvelous life. The windows of the stores were already crowded with Christmas cheer, and busy thousands passed through their doors. Each man or woman was a swift messenger of love. Somewhere in the shadows of the city's labyrinth a human heart would beat with quickened joy for every step that pressed about these crowded counters. Love had given new eyes to see, new ears to hear and a new heart to feel the joys and sorrows of life.

She hadn't given her consent yet. She was still asking her silly heart to be sure of herself. Of her lover, the depth and tenderness, the strength and madness of his love, there could be no doubt. Each day he had given new tokens.

For Saturday afternoon she had told him not to bring the car.

When they reached Fifth Avenue, across the Square, he

stopped abruptly and faced her with a curious, uneasy look:

"Say, tell me why you wanted to walk?"

"I had a good reason," she said evasively.

"Yes, but why? It's a sin to lay that car up a day like this. Look here -"

He stopped and tried to gulp down his fears.

"Look here - you're not going to throw me down after leading me to the very top of the roof, are you?"

She looked up with tender assurance.

"Not today -"

"Then why hoof it? Let me run round to the garage and shoot her out. You can wait for me at the Waldorf. I've always wanted to push my buzz-wagon up to that big joint and wait for my girl to trip down the steps."

"No. I've a plan of my own today. Let me have my way."

"All righto - just so you're happy."

"I am happy," she answered soberly.

At the foot of the broad stairs of the Library she paused and looked up smilingly at its majestic front.

"Come in a moment," she said softly.

He followed her wonderingly into the vaulted hall and climbed the grand staircase to the reading-room. She walked slowly to the shelf on which the Century Dictionary rested and looked laughingly at the seat in which she sat Saturday afternoon a week ago at exactly this hour.

Jim smiled, leaned close and whispered:

"I got you, Kiddo - I got you! Get out of here quick or I'll grab you and kiss you!"

She started and blushed.

"Don't you dare!"

"Beat it then - beat it - or I can't help it!"

She turned quickly and they passed through the catalogue room and lightly down the stairs.

He held her soft, round arm with a grip that sent the blood tingling to the roots of her brown hair.

"You understand now?" she whispered.

"You bet! We walk the same way up the Avenue, through the Park to the little house on the laurel hill. And you're goin' to be sweet to me today, my Kiddo - I just feel it. I -"

"Don't be too sure, sir!" she interrupted, solemnly.

He laughed aloud.

"You can't fool me now - and I'm crazy as a June bug! You know I like to walk - if I can be with you!"

At the Park entrance she stopped again and smiled roguishly.

"We'll find a seat in one of the summer houses along the Fifty-ninth Street side."

"All right," he responded.

"No - we'll go on where we started!"

With a laugh, she slipped her hand through his arm.

"You were a little scared of me last Saturday about this time, weren't you?"

"Just a little -"

"It hurt me, too, but I didn't let you know."

"I'm sorry."

"It's all right now - it's all right. Gee I but we've traveled some in a week, haven't we?"

"I've known you more than a week," she protested gayly.

"Sure - I've known you since I was born."

They walked through the stately rows of elms on the Mall in joyous silence. Crowds of children and nurses, lovers and loungers, filled the seats and thronged the broad promenade.

Scarcely a word was spoken until they reached the rustic house nestling among the trees on the hill.

"Just a week by the calendar," she murmured. "And I've lived a lifetime."

"It's all right then - little girl? You'll marry me right away? When - tonight?"

"Hardly!"

"Tomorrow, then?"

She drew the glove from her hand and held the slender fingers up before him.

"You can get the ring -"

"Gee! I do have to get a ring, don't I?"

"Yes -"

"Why didn't you tell me? You know I never got married before."

"I should hope not!"

He seized her hand and kissed it, drew her into his arms, held her crushed and breathless and released her with a quick, impulsive movement.

"You'll help me get it?" he asked eagerly.

"If you like."

"A big white sparkler?"

"No - no -"

"No?"

"A plain little gold band."

"Let me get you a big diamond!"

"No - a plain gold band."

"It's all settled then?"

"We're engaged. You're my fiance."

"But for God's sake, Kiddo - how long do I have to be a fiance?"

A ripple of laughter rang through the trees.

"Don't you think we've done pretty well for seven days?"

"I could have settled it in seven minutes after we met," he answered complainingly. "You won't tell me the day yet?"

"Not yet -"

"All right, we'll just have to take blessings as they come, then."

Through the beautiful afternoon they sat side by side with close-pressed hands and planned the future which love had given. A modest flat far up among the trees on the cliffs overlooking the Hudson, they decided on.

"We'll begin with that," he cried enthusiastically, "but we won't stay there long. I've got big plans. I'm going to make a million. The white house down by the sea for me, a yacht out in the front yard and a half-dozen thundering autos in the garage. If this deal I'm on now goes through, I'll make my pile in a year -"

They rose as the shadows lengthened.

"I must go home and feed my pets," she sighed.

"All right," he responded heartily. "I'll get the car and be there in a jiffy. We'll take a spin out to a road-house for dinner."

She lifted her eyes tenderly.

"You can come right up to my room - now that we're engaged."

He swept her into his arms again, and held her in unresisting happiness.

It was dark when he swung the gray car against the curb and sprang out. He didn't blow his horn for her to come down. The privilege she had granted was too sweet and wonderful. He wouldn't miss it for the world.

The stairs were dark. Ella was late this afternoon getting back to her work. His light footstep scarcely made a sound. He found each step with quick, instinctive touch. The building seemed deserted. The tenants were all on trips to the country and the seashore. The day was one of rare beauty and warmth. Someone was fumbling in the dark on the third floor back.

He made his way quickly to her room, and softly knocked, waited a moment and knocked again. There was no response. He couldn't be mistaken. He had seen her lean out of that window every day the past week.

Perhaps she was busy in the kitchenette and the noise from the street made it impossible to hear.

He placed his hand on the doorknob.

From the darkness of the hall, in a quick, tiger leap, Ella threw herself on him and grappled for his throat.

"What are you doing at that door, you dirty thief?" she growled.

"Here! Here! What'ell - what's the matter with you?" he gasped, gripping her hands and tearing them from his neck. "I'm no thief!"

"You are! You are, too!" she shrieked. "I heard you sneak in the door downstairs - heard you slippin' like a cat upstairs! Get out of here before I call a cop!"

She was savagely pushing him back to the landing of the stairs. With a sudden lurch, Jim freed himself and gripped her hands.

"Cut it! Cut it! Or I'll knock your block off! I've come to take my girl to ride -"

He drew a match and quickly lighted the gas as Mary's footstep echoed on the stairs below.

"Well, she's coming now - we'll see," was the sullen answer.

Ella surveyed him from head to foot, her one eye gleaming in angry suspicion.

Mary sprang up the last step and saw the two confronting each other. She had heard the angry voices from below.

"Why, Ella, what's the matter?" she gasped.

"He was trying to break into your room -"

Jim threw up his hands in a gesture of rage, and Mary broke into a laugh.

"Why, nonsense, Ella, I asked him to come! This is Mr. Anthony," - her voice dropped, - "my fiance."

Ella's figure relaxed with a look of surprise.

"Oh, ja?" she murmured, as if dazed.

"Yes - come in," she said to Jim. "Sorry I was out. I had to run to the grocer's for the Kitty."

Ella glared at Jim, turned and began to light the other hall lamps without any attempt at apology.

Jim entered the room with a look of awe, took in its impression of sweet, homelike order and recovered quickly his composure.

"Gee, you're the dandy little housekeeper! I could stay here forever."

"You like it?"

"It's a bird's nest " He glanced in the mirror and saw the print of Ella's fingers on his collar. "Will you look at that?" he growled.

"It's too bad," she said, sympathetically.

"You know I thought a she-tiger had got loose from the Bronx and jumped on me."

"I'm awfully sorry," she apologized. "Ella's very fond of me. She was trying to protect me. She couldn't see who it was in the dark."

"No; I reckon not," Jim laughed.

"I've changed our plans for the evening," she announced. "We won't go to ride tonight. I want you to bring my best friend to dinner with us at Mouquin's. Go after her in the car. I want to impress her -"

"I got you, Kiddo! She's goin' to look me over - eh? All right, I'll stop at the store and get a clean collar. I wouldn't like her to see the print of that tiger's claw on my neck."

"There's her address the Gainsborough Studios. Drop me at Mouquin's and I'll have the table set in one of the small rooms upstairs. I'll meet you at the door."

Jim glanced at the address, put it in his pocket and helped her draw on her heavy coat.

"You'll be nice to Jane? I want her to like you. She's the only real friend I've ever had in New York."

"I'll do my best for you, little girl," he promised.

He dropped her at the wooden cottage-front on Sixth Avenue near Twenty-eighth Street, and returned in twenty minutes with Jane.

As the tall artist led the way upstairs, Jim whispered:

"Say, for God's sake, let me out of this!"

"Why?"

"She's a frost. If I have to sit beside her an hour I'll catch cold and die. I swear it; save me! Save my life!"

"Sh! It's all right. She's fine and generous when you know her."

They had reached the door and Mary pushed him in. There was no help for it. He'd have to make the most of it.

The dinner was a dismal failure.

Jane Anderson was polite and genial, but there was a straight look of wonder in her clear gray eyes that froze the blood in Jim's veins.

Mary tried desperately for the first half-hour to put him at his ease. It was useless. The attack of Ella had upset his nerves, and the unexpressed hostility of Jane had completely crushed his spirits. He tried to talk once, stammered and lapsed into a sullen silence from which nothing could stir him.

The two girls at last began to discuss their own affairs and the dinner ended in a sickening failure that depressed and angered Mary.

The agony over at last, she rose and turned to Jim:

"You can go now, sir - I'll take Jane home with me for a friendly chat."

"Thank God!" he whispered, grinning in spite of his effort to keep a straight face.

"Tomorrow?" he asked in low tones.

"At eight o'clock."

Jim bowed awkwardly to Jane, muttered something inarticulate and rushed to his car.

The two girls walked in silence through Twenty-eighth Street to Broadway and thence across the Square.

Seated in her room, Mary could contain her pent-up rage no longer.

"Jane Anderson, I'm furious with you! How could you be so rude - so positively insulting!"

"Insulting?"

"Yes. You stared at him in cold disdain as if he were a toad under your feet!"

"I assure you, dear -"

"Why did you do it?"

The artist rose, walked to the window, looked out on the Square for a moment, extended her hand and laid it gently on Mary's shoulder.

"You've made up your mind to marry this man, honey?"

"I certainly have," was the emphatic answer.

Jane paused.

"And all in seven days?"

"Seven days or seven years - what does it matter? He's my mate - we love - it's Fate."

"It's incredible!"

"What's incredible?"

"Such madness."

"Perhaps love is madness - the madness that makes life worth the candle. I've never lived before the past week."

"And you, the dainty, cultured, pious little saint, will marry this - this -"

"Say it! I want you to be frank -"

"Perfectly frank?"

"Absolutely."

"This coarse, ugly, illiterate brute -"

"Jane Anderson, how dare you!" Mary sprang to her feet, livid with rage.

"I asked if I might be frank. Shall I lie to you? Or shall I tell you what I think?"

"Say what you please; it doesn't matter," Mary interrupted angrily.

"I only speak at all because I love you. Your common-sense should tell you that I speak with reluctance. But now that I have spoken, let me beg of you for your father's sake, for your dead mother's sake, for my sake - I'm your one disinterested friend and you know that my love is real - for the sake of your own soul's salvation in this world and the next - don't marry that brute! Commit suicide if you will - jump off the bridge - take poison, cut your throat, blow your brains out - but, oh dear God, not this!"

"And why, may I ask?" was the cold question.

"He's in no way your equal in culture, in character, in any of the essentials on which the companionship of marriage must be based -"

"He's a diamond in the rough," Mary staunchly asserted.

"He's in the rough, all right! The only diamond about him is the one in his red scarf - `Take it from me, Kiddo! Take it from me!'"

Her last sentence was a quotation from Jim, her imitation of his slang so perfect Mary's cheeks flamed anew with anger.

"I'll teach him to use good English - never fear. In a month he'll forget his slang and his red scarf."

"You mean that in a month you'll forget to use good English and his style of dress will be yours. Oh, honey, can't you see that such a man will only drag you down, down to his level? Can it be possible that you - that you really love him?"

"I adore him and I'm proud of his love!"

"Now listen! You believe in an indissoluble marriage, don't you?"

"Yes -"

"It's the first article of your creed - that marriage is a holy sacrament, that no power on earth or in hell can ever dissolve its bonds? Fools rush in where angels fear to tread, my dear! They always have - they always will, I suppose. This is peculiarly true of your type of woman - the dainty, clinging girl of religious enthusiasm. You're peculiarly susceptible to the physical power of a brutal lover. Your soul glories in submission to this force. The more coarse and brutal its attraction the more abject and joyful the surrender. Your religion can't save you because your religion is purely emotional - it is only another manifestation of your sex emotions."

"How can you be so sacrilegious!" the girl interrupted with a look of horror.

"It may shock you, dear, but I'm telling you one of the simplest truths of Nature. You'd as well know it now as later. The moment you wake to realize that your emotions have been deceived and bankrupted, your faith will collapse. At least keep, your grip on common-sense. Down in the cowardly soul of every weak woman - perhaps of every woman - is the insane desire to be dominated by a superior brute force. The woman of the lower classes - the peasant of Russia, for example, whose sex impulses are of all races the most violent - refuses with scorn the advances of the man who will not strike her. The man who can't beat his wife is beneath contempt - he is no man at all -"

Mary broke into a laugh.

"Really, Jane, you cease to be serious you're a joke. For Heaven's sake use a little common-sense yourself. You can't be warning me that my lover is marrying me in order to use his fists on me?"

"Perhaps not, dear," - the artist smiled; "there might be greater depths for one of your training and character. I'm just telling you the plain truth about the haste with which you're rushing into this marriage. There's nothing divine in it. There's no true romance of lofty sentiment. It's the simplest and most elemental of all the brutal facts of animal life. That it is resistless in a woman of your culture and refinement makes it all the more pathetic -"

The girl rose with a gesture of impatience.

"It's no use, Jane dear; we speak a different language. I don't in the least know what you're talking about, and what's more, I'm glad I don't. I've a vague idea that your drift is indecent. But we're different. I realize that. I don't sit in judgment on you. You're wasting your breath on me. I'm going into this marriage with my eyes wide open. It's the fulfillment of my brightest hopes and aspirations. That I shall be happy with this man and make him supremely happy I know by an intuition deeper and truer than reason. I'm going to trust that intuition without reservation."

"All right, honey," the artist agreed with a smile. "I won't say anything more, except that you're fooling yourself about the depth of this intuitive knowledge. Your infatuation is not based on the verdict of your deepest and truest instincts."

"On what, then?"

"The crazy ideals of the novels you've been reading - that's all."

"Ridiculous!"

"You're absolutely sure, for instance, that God made just one man the mate of one woman, aren't you?"

"As sure as that I live."

"Where did you learn it?"

"So long ago I can't remember."

"Not in your Bible?"

"No."

"The Sunday school?"

"No."

"Craddock didn't tell you that, did he?"

"Hardly -"

"I thought not. He has too much horse-sense in spite of his

emotional gymnastics. You learned it in the first dime-novel you read."

"I never read a dime-novel in my life," she interrupted, indignantly.

"I know - you paid a dollar and a quarter for it - but it was a dime-novel. The philosophy of this school of trash you have built into a creed of life. How can you be so blind? How can you make so tragic a blunder?"

"That's just it, Jane: I couldn't if your impressions of his character were true. I couldn't make a mistake about so vital a question. I couldn't love him if he really were a coarse,illiterate brute. What you see is only on the surface. He hasn't had his chance yet -"

"Who is he? What does he do? Who are his people?"

"He has no people -"

"I thought not."

"I love him all the more deeply," she went on firmly, "because of his miserable childhood. I'll do my best to make up for the years of cruelty and hunger and suffering through which he passed. What right have you to sit in judgment on him without a hearing? You've known him two hours -"

Jane shrugged her shoulders.

"Two minutes was quite enough."

"And you judge by what standard?"

"My five senses, and my sixth sense above all. One look at his square bulldog jaw, his massive neck and the deformity of his delicate hands and feet! I hear the ignorant patois of the East Side underworld. I smell the brimstone in his suppressed rage at my dislike. There's something uncanny in the sensuous droop of his heavy eyelids and the glitter of his steel-blue eyes. There's something incongruous in his whole personality. I was afraid of him the moment I saw him."

Mary broke into hysterical laughter.

"And if my five senses and my intuitions contradict yours? Who is to decide? If I loved him on sight - If I looked into his eyes and saw the soul of my mate? If their cold fires thrill me with inexpressible passion? If I see in his massive neck and jaw the strength of an irresistible manhood, the power to win success and to command the world? If I see in his slender hands and small feet lines of exquisite beauty - am I to crush my senses and strangle my love to please your idiotic prejudice?"

Jane threw up her hands in despair.

"Certainly not! If you're blind and deaf I can't keep you from committing suicide. I'd lock you up in an asylum for the insane if I had the power to save you from the clutches of the brute."

Mary drew herself erect and faced her friend.

"Please don't repeat that word in my hearing - there's a limit to friendship. I think you'd better go -"

Jane rose and walked quickly to the door, her lips pressed firmly.

"As you like - our lives will be far apart from tonight. It's just as well."

She closed the door with a bang and reached the head of the stairs before Mary threw her arms around her neck.

"Please, dear, forgive me - don't go in anger."

The older woman kissed her tenderly, glad of the dim light to hide her own tears.

"There, it's all right, honey - I won't remember it. Forgive me for my ugly words."

"I love him, Jane - I love him! It's Fate. Can't you understand?"

"Yes, dear, I understand, and I'll love you always - good-by."

"You'll come to my wedding?"

"Perhaps -"

"I'll let you know -"

Another kiss, and Jane Anderson strode down the stairs and out into the night with a sickening, helpless fear in her heart.

CHAPTER VIII

JIM'S TRIAL

The quarrel had left Mary in a quiver of exalted rage. How dare a friend trample her most sacred feelings! She pitied Jane Anderson and her tribe - these modern feminine leaders of a senseless revolution against man - they were crazy. They had all been disappointed in some individual and for that reason set themselves up as the judges of mankind.

"Thank God my soul has not been poisoned!" she exclaimed aloud with fervor. "How strange that these women who claim such clear vision can be so stupidly blind!"

She busied herself with her little household, and made up her mind once and for all time to be done with such friendships. The friendship of such women was a vain thing. They were vicious cats at heart - not like her gentle Persian kitten whose soul was full of sleepy sunlight. These modern insurgents were wild, half-starved stray cats that had been hounded and beaten until they had lapsed into their elemental brute instincts. They were so aggravating, too, they deserved no sympathy.

Again she thanked God that she was not one of them - that her heart was still capable of romantic love - a love so sudden and so overwhelming that it could sweep life before it in one mad rush to its glorious end.

She woke next morning with a dull sense of depression. The

room was damp and chilly. It was storming. The splash of rain against the window and the muffled roar from the street below meant that the wind was high and the day would be a wretched one outside.

They couldn't take their ride.

It was a double disappointment. She had meant to have him dash down to Long Beach and place the ring on her finger seated on that same bright sand-dune overlooking the sea. Instead, they must stay indoors. Jim was not at his best indoors. She loved him behind the wheel with his hand on the pulse of that racer. The machine seemed a part of his being. He breathed his spirit into its steel heart, and together they swept her on and on over billowy clouds through the gates of Heaven.

There was no help for it. They would spend the time together in her room planning the future. It would be sweet - these intimate hours in her home with the man she loved.

Should she spend a whole day alone there with him? Was it just proper? Was it really safe? Nonsense! The vile thoughts which Jane had uttered had poisoned her, after all. She hated her self that she could remember them. And yet they filled her heart with dread in spite of every effort to laugh them off.

"How could Jane Anderson dare say such things?" she muttered angrily. "`A coarse, illiterate brute!' It's a lie! a lie! a lie!" She stamped her foot in rage. "He's strong and brave and masterful - a man among men - he's my mate and I love him!"

And yet the frankness with which her friend had spoken had in reality disturbed her beyond measure. Through every hour of the day her uneasiness increased. After all she was utterly alone and her life had been pitifully narrow. Her knowledge of men she had drawn almost exclusively from romantic fiction.

It was just a little strange that Jim persisted in living so completely in the present and the future. He had told her of his pitiful childhood. He had told her of his business. It had been definite - the simple statement he made - and she accepted it without question until Jane Anderson had dropped these ugly suspicions. She hated the meddler for it.

In the light of such suspicions the simplest, bravest man might seem a criminal. How could her friend be blind to the magnetism of this man's powerful personality? Bah! She was jealous of their perfect happiness. Why are women so contemptible?

She began a careful study of every trait of her lover's character, determined to weigh him by the truest standards of manhood. Certainly he was no weakling. The one abomination of her soul was the type of the city degenerate she saw simpering along Broadway and Fifth Avenue at times. Jim was brave to the point of rashness. No man with an ounce of cowardice in his being could handle a car in every crisis with such cool daring and perfect control. He was strong. He could lift her body as if it were a feather. His arms crushed her with terrible force. He could earn a living for them both. There could be no doubt about that. His faultless clothes, the ease with which he commanded unlimited credit among the automobile manufacturers and dealers - every supply store on Broadway seemed to know him - left no doubt on that score.

There was just a bit of mystery and reserve about his career as an inventor. His first success that had given him a start he had not explained. The big deal about the new carburetor she could, of course, understand. He had a workshop all his own. He had told her this the first day they met. She would ask him to take her to see it this afternoon. The storm would prevent the trip to the Beach. She would ask this, not because she doubted his honesty, but because she really wished to see the place in which he worked. It was her workshop now, as well as his.

For a moment her suspicions were sickening. Suppose he had

romanced about his workshop and his room? Supposed he lived somewhere in the squalid slums of the lower East Side and his people, after all, were alive? Perhaps a drunken father and a coarse, brutal mother - and sisters -

She stopped with a frown and clenched her fists.

She would ask Jim to show her his workshop. That would be enough. If he had told her the truth about that she would make up to him in tender abandonment of utter trust for every suspicion she harbored.

The car was standing in front of her door. He waved for her to come down.

"Jump right in!" he called gayly. "I've got an extra rubber blanket for you."

"In the storm, Jim?" she faltered.

"Surest thing you know. It's great to fly through a storm. You can just ride on its wings. Throw on your raincoat and come on quick! I'm going to run down to the Beach. Who's afraid of an old storm with this thing under us?"

Her heart gave a bound. Her longing had reached her lover and brought him through the storm to do her bidding. It was wonderful - this oneness of soul and body.

She was happy again - supremely, divinely happy. The man by her side knew and understood. She knew and understood. She loved this daring spirit that rose to the wind - this iron will that brooked no interference with his plans, even from Nature, when it crossed his love.

The sting of the raindrops against her cheek was exhilarating. The car glided over the swimming roadway like a great gray gull skimming the beach at low tide. Her soul rose. The sun of a perfect faith and love was shining now behind the clouds.

She nestled close to his side and watched him tenderly from the corners of her half-closed eyes, her whole being content in his strength. The idea of dashing through a blinding rain to the Beach on such a day would have been to her mind an unthinkable piece of madness. She was proud of his daring. It would be hers to shield from the storms of life. She loved the rugged lines of his massive jaw in profile. How could Jane be such a fool as to call him ugly!

The weather, of course, prevented them from walking up the Beach to their sand-dune. The walk would have been all right - but it was out of the question to sit down there and give her the ring in the pouring rain. She knew this as well as he. She knew, too, that he had the ring in his pocket, though he had carefully refrained from referring to it in any way.

He led her to a secluded nook behind a pillar in the little parlor. The hotel was deserted. They had the building almost to themselves. A log fire crackled in the open fireplace, and he drew a settee close. The wind had moderated and the rain was pouring down in straight streams, rolling in soft music on the roof.

He drew the ring from his pocket. "Well, Kiddo, I got it. The fellow said this was all right."

He held the tiny gold band before her shining eyes.

"Slip it on!" she whispered.

"Which one?"

"This one, silly!"

She extended her third finger, as he pressed the ring slowly on.

"Seems to me a mighty little one and a mighty cheap one, but he said it was the thing."

"It's all right, dear," she whispered. "Kiss me!"

He pressed his lips to hers and held them until she sank back and lifted her hand in warning.

"Be careful!"

"Whose afraid?" Jim muttered, glancing over his shoulder toward the door. "Now tell me what day - tomorrow?"

"Nonsense, man!" she cried. "Give me time to breathe -"

"What for?"

"Just to realize that I'm engaged - to plan and think and dream of the wonderful day."

"We're losing time -"

"We'll never live these wonderful hours over again, dear."

Jim's face fell and his voice was pitiful in its funereal notes: "Lord, I thought the ring settled it."

"And so it does, dear - it does -"

"Not if that long-legged spider that took dinner with us the other night gets in her fine work. I'll bet that she handed me a few when you got home?"

Mary was silent.

"Now didn't she?"

"To the best of her ability - yes - but I didn't mind her silly talk."

"Gee, but I'd love to give her a bouquet of poison ivy!"

"We had an awful quarrel -"

"And you stood up for me?"

"You know I did!"

"All right, I don't give a tinker's damn what anybody says if you stand by me! In all this world there's just you - for me. There's never been anybody else - and there never will be. I'm that kind."

"And I love you for it!" she cried, with rapture pressing his hand in both of hers.

"What did she say about me, anyhow?"

"Nothing worth repeating. I've forgotten it."

Jim held her gaze.

"It's funny how you love anybody the minute you lay eyes on 'em - or hate 'em the same way. I wanted to choke her the minute she opened her yap to me."

"Forget it, dear," she broke in briskly. "I want you to take me to see your workshop tomorrow - will you?"

A flash of suspicion shot from the depths of his eyes.

"Did she tell you to ask me that?"

"Of course not! I'm just interested in everything you do. I want to see where you work."

"It's no place for a sweet girl to go - that part of town."

"But I'll be with you."

"I don't want you to go down there," he sullenly maintained.

"But why, dear?"

"It's a low, dirty place. I had to locate the shop there to get the room I needed for the rent I could pay. It's not fit for you. I'm going to move uptown in a little while."

"Please let me go," she pleaded.

He shook his head emphatically.

"No."

She turned away to hide the tears. The first real, hideous fear she had ever had about him caught her heart in spite of every effort to fight it down. His workshop might be a myth after all. He had failed in the first test to which she had put him. It was horrible. All the vile suggestions of Jane Anderson rushed now into her memory.

She struggled bravely to keep her head and not break down. It was beyond her strength. A sob strangled her, and she buried her face in her hands.

Jim looked at her in helpless anguish for a moment, started to gather her in his arms and looked around the room in terror.

He leaned over her and whispered tensely:

"For God's sake, Kiddo - don't - don't do that! I didn't mean to hurt you - honest, I didn't. Don't cry any more and I'll take you right down to the black hole, and let you sleep on the floor if you want to. Gee! I'll give you the whole place, tools, junk and all -"

She lifted her head.

"Will you, Jim?"

"Sure I will! We start this minute if you want to go."

She glanced over his shoulder to see that no one was looking, threw her arms around his neck and kissed him again and again.

"It was the first time you ever said no, dear, and it hurt. I'm happy again now. If you'll just let me see you in the shop for five minutes I'll never ask you again."

"All right - tomorrow when you get out of school. I'll take you down. Holy Mike, that was a dandy kiss! Let's quarrel again - start something else."

She rose laughing and brushed the last trace of tears from her eyes.

"Let's eat dinner now - I'm hungry."

"By George, I'd forgot all about the feed!"

By eight o'clock the storm had abated; the rain suddenly stopped, and the moon peeped through the clouds.

He drove the big racer back at a steady, even stride on her lowest notch of speed - half the time with only his right hand on the wheel and his left gripping hers.

As the lights of Manhattan flashed from the hills beyond the Queensborough Bridge, he leaned close and whispered:

"Happy?"

"Perfectly."

The car was waiting the next day at half-past three.

"It's not far," he said, nodding carelessly. "You needn't put on the coat. Be there in a jiffy."

Down Twenty-third Street to Avenue A, down the avenue to

Eighteenth Street, and then he suddenly swung the machine through Eighteenth into Avenue B and stopped below a low, red brick building on the corner.

He set his brakes with a crash, leaped out and extended his hands.

"I didn't like to take you up these stairs at the back of that saloon, little girl, but you would come. Now don't blame me -"

She pressed his arm tenderly.

"Of course I won't blame you. I'm proud and happy to share your life and help you. I'm surprised to see everything so quiet down here. I thought all the East Side was packed with crowded tenements."

"No," he answered, in a matter-of-fact way. "About the only excitement we have in this quarter is an occasional gas explosion in the plant over there, and the noise of the second-hand material men unloading iron. The tenements haven't been built here yet."

He led her quickly past the back door of the saloon and up two narrow flights of stairs to the top of the building, drew from his pocket the key to a heavy padlock and slipped the crooked bolt from the double staples. He unlocked the door with a second key and pushed his way in.

"All righto," he cried.

The straight, narrow hall inside was dark. He fumbled in his pocket and lit the gas.

"The workshop first, or my sleeping den?"

"The workshop first!" she whispered excitedly.

She had made the reality of this shop the supreme test of Jim's word and character. She was in a fever of expectant uncertainty as to its equipment and practical use.

He unlocked the door leading to the front.

"That's my den - we'll come back here."

He passed quickly to the further end of the hall and again used two keys to open the door, and held it back for her to enter.

"I'm sorry it's so dirty - if you get your pretty dress all ruined - it's not my fault, you know."

Mary surveyed the room with an exclamation of delight.

"Oh, what a wonderful place! Why, Jim, you're a magician!"

There could be no doubt about the practical use to which the shop was being put. Its one small window opened on a fire escape in the narrow court in the rear. A skylight in the middle opened with a hinge on the roof and flooded the space with perfect light. An iron ladder swung from the skylight and was hooked up against the ceiling by a hasp fastened to a staple over a work-bench. On one side of the room was a tiny blacksmith's forge, an anvil, hammers and a complete set of tools for working in rough iron. A small gasoline engine supplied the power which turned his lathe and worked the drills, saw and plane. On the other side of the room was arranged a fairly complete chemical laboratory with several retorts, and an oxyhydrogen blow-pipe capable of developing the powerful heat used in the melting and brazing of metals. Beneath the benches were piled automobile supplies of every kind.

"You know how to use all these machines, Jim?" she asked in wonder.

"Sure, and then some!" he answered with a wave of his slender hand.

"You're a wizard -"

"Now the den?" he said briskly.

She followed him through the hall and into the large front corner room overlooking Avenue B and Eighteenth Street. The morning sun flooded the front and the afternoon sun poured into the side windows. The furniture was solid mahogany - a bed, bureau, chiffonier, couch and three chairs. The windows were fitted with wood-paneled shutters, shades and heavy draperies. A thick, soft carpet of faded red covered the floor.

"It's a nice room, Jim, but I'd like to dust it for you," she said with a smile.

"Sure. I'm for giving you the right to dust it every morning, Kiddo, beginning now. Let's find a preacher tonight!"

She blushed and moved a step toward the door.

"Just a little while. You know it's been only ten days since we met -"

"But we've lived some in that time, haven't we?"

"An eternity, I think," she said reverently.

"I want to marry right now, girlie!" he pleaded desperately. "If that spider gets you in her den again, I just feel like it's good night for me."

"Nonsense. You can't believe me such a silly child. I'm a woman. I love you. Do you think the foolish prejudice of a friend could destroy my love for the man whom I have chosen for my mate?"

"No, but I want it fixed and then it's fixed - and they can say what they please. Marry me tonight! You've got the ring. You're going to in a little while, anyhow. What's the use to wait and lose these days out of our life? What's the sense of it? Don't you know me by this time? Don't you trust me by this time?"

She slipped her hand gently into his.

"I trust you utterly. And I feel that I've known you since the day I was born -"

"Then why - why wait a minute?"

"You can't understand a girl's feelings, dear - only a little while and it's all right."

He sat down on the couch in silence, rose and walked to the window. She watched him struggling with deep emotion.

He turned suddenly.

"Look here, Kiddo, I've got to leave on that trip to the mountains of North Carolina. I've got to get down there before Christmas. I must be back here by the first of the year. Gee - I can't go without you! You don't want to stay here without me, do you?"

A sudden pallor overspread her face. For the first time she realized how their lives had become one in the sweet intimacy of the past ten days.

"You must go now?" she gasped.

"Yes. I've made my arrangements. I've business back here the first of the year that can't wait. Marry me and go with me. We'll take our honeymoon down there. By George, we'll go together in the car! Every day by each other's side over hundreds and hundreds of miles! Say, ain't you game? Come on! It's a crime to send me away without you. How can you do it?"

"I can't - I'm afraid," she faltered.

"You'll marry me, then?"

"Yes!" she whispered. "What is the latest day you can start?"

"Next Saturday, if we go in the car -"

"All right," - she was looking straight into the depths of his soul now - "next Saturday."

He clasped her in his arms and held her with desperate tenderness.

CHAPTER IX

ELLA'S SECRET

The consummation of her life's dream was too near, too sweet and wonderful for Jane's croakings to distress Mary Adams beyond the moment. She had, of course, wished her friend to be present at the wedding - yet the curt refusal had only aroused anew her pity at stupid prejudices. It was out of the question to ask her father to leave his work in the Kentucky mountains and come all the way to New York. She would surprise him with the announcement. After all, she was the one human being vitally concerned in this affair, and the only one save the man whose life would be joined to hers.

In five minutes after the painful scene with Jane she had completely regained her composure, and her face was radiant with happiness when she waved to Jim. He was standing before the door in the car, waiting to take her to the City Hall to get the marriage license.

"Gee!" he cried, "you're the prettiest, sweetest thing that ever walked this earth, with those cheeks all flaming like a rose! Are you happy?"

"Gloriously."

She motioned him to keep his seat and sprang lightly to his side.

"Aren't you happy, sir?" she added gayly.

"I am, yes - but to tell you the truth, I'm beginning to get scared. You know what to do, don't you, when we get before that preacher?"

"Of course, silly -"

"I never saw a wedding in my life."

She pressed his hand tenderly.

"Honestly, Jim?"

"I swear it. You'll have to tell me how to behave."

"We'll rehearse it all tonight. I'll show you. I've seen hundreds of people married. My father's a preacher, you know."

"Yes, I know that," he went on solemnly; "that's what gives me courage. I knew you'd understand everything. I'm counting on you, Kiddo - if you fall down, we're gone. I'll run like a turkey."

"It's easy," she laughed.

"And this license business - how do we go about that? What'll they do to us?"

"Nothing, goose! We just march up to the clerk and demand the license. He asks us a lot of questions -"

"Questions! What sort of questions?"

"The names of your father and mother - whether you've been married before and where you live and how old you are -"

"Ask you about your business?" he interrupted, sharply.

"No. They think if you can pay the license fee you can support your wife, I suppose."

"How much is it?"

"I don't know, here. It used to be two dollars in Kentucky."

"That's cheap - must come higher in this burg. I brought along a hundred."

"Nonsense."

"There's a lot of graft in this town. I'll be ready. I've got to get 'em - don't care how high they come."

"There'll be no graft in this, Jim," she protested gayly.

"Well, it'll be the first time I ever got by without it - believe me!"

The ease with which the license was obtained was more than Jim could understand. All the way back from the City Hall he expected to be held up at every corner. He kept looking over his shoulder to see if they were being followed.

Arrived in her room, they discussed their plans for the day of days.

"I'll come round soon in the morning, and we'll spend the whole day at the Beach," he suggested.

She lifted her hands in protest.

"No - no!"

"No?"

"Not on our wedding-day, Jim!"

"Why?"

"It's not good form. The groom should not see the bride that day until they meet at the altar."

"Let's change it!"

"No, sir, the old way's the best. I'll spend the day in saying good-by to the past. You'll call for me at six o'clock. We'll go to Dr. Craddock's house and be married in time for our wedding dinner."

The lover smiled, and his drooping eyelids fell still lower as he watched her intently.

"I want that dinner here in this little place, Kiddo -"

She blushed and protested.

"I thought we'd go to the Beach and spend the night there."

"Here, girlie, here! I love this little place - it's so like you. Get the old wild-cat who cleans up for you to fix us a dinner here all by ourselves - wouldn't she?"

"She'd do anything for me - yes."

"Then fix it here - I want to be just with you - don't you understand?"

"Yes," she whispered. "But I'd rather spend that first day of our new life in a strange place - and the Beach we both love - hadn't you just as leave go there, Jim?"

"No. The waiters will stare at us, and hear us talk -"

"We can have our meals served in our room.

"This is better," he insisted. "I want to spend one day here alone with you, before we go - just to feel that you're all mine. You see, if I walk in here and own the place, I'll know that better than any other way. I've just set my heart on it, Kiddo - what's the difference?"

She lifted her lips to his.

"All right, dear. It shall be as you wish. Tomorrow I will be all yours - in life, in death, in eternity. Your happiness will be the one thing for which I shall plan and work."

Ella was very happy in the honor conferred on her. She was given entire charge of the place, and spent the day in feverish preparation for the dinner. She insisted on borrowing a larger table from the little fat woman next door, to hold the extra dishes. She dressed herself in her best. Her raven black hair was pressed smooth and shining down the sides of her pale temples.

The work was completed by three o'clock in the afternoon, and Mary lay in her window lazily watching the crowds scurrying home. The offices closed early on Saturday afternoons.

Ella was puttering about the room, adding little touches here and there in a pretense of still being busy. As a matter of fact, she was watching the girl from her one eye with a wistful tenderness she had not dared as yet to express in words. Twice Mary had turned suddenly and seen her thus. Each time Ella had started as if caught in some act of mischief and asked an irrelevant question to relieve her embarrassment.

Mary could feel her single eye fixed on her now in a deep, brooding look. It made her uncomfortable.

She turned slowly and spoke in gentle tones.

"You've been so sweet to me today, Ella - father and mother and best friend. I'll never forget your kindness. You'd better rest awhile now until we go to Dr. Craddock's. I want you to be there, too -"

"To see the marriage - ja?" she asked softly.

"Yes."

"Oh, no, my dear, no - I stay here and wait for you to come. I keep the lights burning bright. I welcome the bride and groom to their little home - ja."

A quick glance of suspicion shot from Mary's blue eyes. Could it be possible that this forlorn scrubwoman would carry her hostility to her lover to the same point of ungracious refusal to witness the ceremony? It was nonsense, of course. Ella would feel out of place in the minister's parlor, that was all. She wouldn't insist.

"All right, Ella; you can receive us here with ceremony. You'll be our maid, butler, my father, my mother and my friends!"

There was a moment's silence and still no move on Ella's part to go. The girl felt her single eye again fixed on her in mysterious, wistful gaze. She would send her away if it were possible without hurting her feelings.

Mary lifted her eyes suddenly, and Ella stirred awkwardly and smiled.

"I hope you are very happy, meine liebe - ja?"

"I couldn't be happier if I were in Heaven," was the quick answer.

"I'm so glad -"

Again an awkward pause.

"I was once young and pretty like you, meine liebe," she began dreamily, " - slim and straight and jolly - always laughing."

Mary held her breath in eager expectancy. Ella was going to lift the veil from the mystery of her life, stirred by memories which the coming wedding had evoked.

"And you had a thrilling romance - Ella? I always felt it."

Again silence, and then in low tones the woman told her story.

"Ja - a romance, too. I was so young and foolish - just a baby myself - not sixteen. But I was full of life and fun, and I had a way of doing what I pleased.

"The man was older than me - Oh, a lot older - with gray hairs on the side of his head. I was wild about him. I never took to kids. They didn't seem to like me -"

She paused as if hesitating to give her full confidence, and quickly went on:

"My folks were German. They couldn't speak English. I learned when I was five years old. They didn't like my lover. We quarrel day and night. I say they didn't like him because they could not speak his language. They say he was bad. I fight for him, and run away and marry him -"

Again she paused and drew a deep breath.

"Ah, I was one happy little fool that year! He make good wages on the docks - a stevedore. They had a strike, and he got to drinking. The baby came -"

She stopped suddenly.

"You had a little baby, Ella?" the girl asked in a tender whisper.

"Ja - ja" she sobbed - "so sweet, so good - so quiet - so beautiful she was. I was very happy - like a little girl with a doll - only she laugh and cry and coo and pull my hair! He stop the drink a little while when she come, and he got work. And then he begin worse and worse. It seem like he never loved me any more after the baby. He curse me, he quarrel. He begin to strike me sometimes. I laugh and cry at first and make up and try again -"

Again she paused as if for courage to go on, and choked into silence.

"Yes - and then?" the girl asked.

"And then he come home one night wild drunk. He stumble and fall across the cradle and hurt my baby so she never cry - just lie still and tremble - her eyes wide open at first and then they droop and close and she die!

"He laugh and curse and strike me, and I fight him like a tiger. He was strong - he throw me down on the floor and gouge my eye out with his big claw -"

"Oh, my God," Mary sobbed.

Ella sprang to her feet and bent over the girl with trembling eagerness.

"You keep my secret, meine liebe?"

"Yes - yes -"

"I never tell a soul on earth what I tell you now - I just eat my heart out and keep still all the years, I can tell you - ja?"

"Yes, I'll keep it sacred - go on -"

"When I know he gouge my eye out, I go wild. I get my hand on his throat and choke him still. I drag him to the stairs and throw him head first all the way down to the bottom. He fall in a heap and lie still. I run down and drag him to the door. I kick his face and he never move. He was dead. I kick him again - and again. And then I laugh - I laugh - I laugh in his dead face - I was so glad I kill him!"

She sank in a paroxysm of sobs on the floor, and the girl touched her smooth black hair tenderly, strangled with her own emotions.

Ella rose at last and brushed the tears from her hollow cheeks.

"Now, you know, meine liebe! Why I tell you this today, I don't know - maybe I must! I dream once like you dream today -"

The girl slipped her arms around the drooping, pathetic figure and stroked it tenderly.

"The sunshine is for some, maybe," Ella went on pathetically; "for some the clouds and the storms. I hope you are very, very happy today and all the days -"

"I will be, Ella, I'm sure. I'll always love you after this."

"Maybe I make you sad because I tell you -"

"No - no! I'm glad you told me. The knowledge of your sorrow will make my life the sweeter. I shall be more humble in my joy."

It never occurred to the girl for a moment that this lonely, broken woman had torn her soul's deepest secret open in a last pathetic effort to warn her of the danger of her marriage. The wistful, helpless look in her eye meant to Mary only the anguish of memories. Each human heart persists in learning the big lessons of life at first hand. We refuse to learn any other way. The tragedies of others interest us as fiction. We make the application to others - never to ourselves.

Jim's familiar footstep echoed through the hall, and Mary sprang to the door with a cry of joy.

Thomas Dixon

CHAPTER X

THE WEDDING

Ella hurried into the kitchenette and busied herself with dinner. Jim's unexpectedly early arrival broke the spell of the tragedy to which Mary had listened with breathless sympathy. Her own future she faced without a shadow of doubt or fear.

Her reproaches to Jim were entirely perfunctory, on the sin of his early call on their wedding-day.

"Naughty boy!" she cried with mock severity. "At this unseemly hour!"

He glanced about the room nervously.

"Anybody in there?"

He nodded toward the kitchenette.

"Only Ella -"

"Send her away."

"What's the matter?"

"Quick, Kiddo - quick!"

Mary let Ella out from the little private hall without her seeing

Jim, and returned.

"For heaven's sake, man, what ails you?" she asked excitedly.

"Say - I forgot that thing already. We got to go over it again. What if I miss it?"

"The ceremony?"

"Yep -"

He mopped his brow and looked at his watch.

"By the time we get to that preacher's house, I won't know my first name if you don't help me."

Mary laughed softly and kissed him.

"You can't miss it. All you've got to do is say, `I will' when he asks you the question, put the ring on my finger when he tells you, and repeat the words after him - he and I will do the rest."

"Say my question over again."

"`Wilt thou have this woman to thy wedded wife, to live together after God's ordinance, in the holy estate of matrimony? Wilt thou love her, comfort her, honor, and keep her in sickness and in health; and, forsaking all others, keep thee only unto her, so long as ye both shall live?'"

She looked at him and laughed.

"Why don't you answer?"

"Now?"

"Yes - that's the end of the question. Say, `I will.'"

"Oh, I will all right! What scares me is that I'll jump in on him and say `I will' before he gets halfway through. Seems to me when he says, `Wilt thou have this woman to be thy wedded wife?' I'll just have to choke myself there to keep from saying, `You bet your life I will, Parson!'"

"It won't hurt anything if you say, `I will' several times," she assured him.

"It wouldn't queer the job?"

"Not in the least. I've often heard them say, `I will' two or three times. Wait until you hear the words, `so long as ye both shall live -'"

"`So long as ye both shall live,'" he repeated solemnly.

"The other speech you say after the minister."

"He won't bite off more than I can chew at one time, will he?"

"No, silly - just a few words -"

"Because if he does, I'll choke."

Jim drew his watch again, mopped his brow, and gazed at Mary's serene face with wonder.

"Say, Kiddo, you're immense - you're as cool as a cucumber!"

"Of course. Why not? It's my day of joy and perfect peace - the day I've dreamed of since the dawn of maidenhood. I'm marrying the man of my choice - the one man God made for me of all men on earth. I know this - I'm content."

"Let me hang around here till time - won't you?" he asked helplessly.

"We must have Ella come back to fix the table."

"Sure. I just didn't want her to hear me tell you that I had cold feet. I'm better now."

Ella moved about the room with soft tread, watching Jim with sullen, concentrated gaze when he was not looking.

The lovers sat on the couch beside the window, holding each other's hands and watching in silence the hurrying crowds pass below. Now that his panic was over, Jim began to breathe more freely, and the time swiftly passed.

As the shadows slowly fell, they rang the bell at the parson's house beside the church, and his good wife ushered them into the parlor. The little Craddocks crowded in - six of them, two girls and four boys, their ages ranging from five to nineteen.

Sweet memories crowded the girl's heart from her happy childhood. She had never missed one of these affairs at home. Her father was a very popular minister and his home the Mecca of lovers for miles around.

Craddock, like her father, was inclined to be conservative in his forms. Marriage he held with the old theologians to be a holy sacrament. He never used the new-fangled marriage vows. He stuck to the formula of the Book of Common Prayer.

When she stood before the preacher in this beautiful familiar scene which she had witnessed so many times at home, Mary's heart beat with a joy that was positively silly. She tried to be serious, and the dimple would come in her cheek in spite of every effort.

As Craddock's musical voice began the opening address, the memory of a foolish incident in her father's life flashed through her mind, and she wondered if Jim in his excitement had forgotten his pocket-book and couldn't pay the preacher.

"Dearly beloved," he began, "we are gathered together here in the sight of God -"

Mary tried to remember that she was in the sight of God, but she was so foolishly happy she could only remember that funny scene. A long-legged Kentucky mountain bridegroom at the close of the ceremony had turned to her father and drawled:

"Well, parson, I ain't got no money with me - but I want to give ye five dollars. I've got a fine dawg. He's worth ten. I'll send him to ye fur five - if it's all right?"

The children had giggled and her father blushed.

"Oh, that's all right," he had answered. "Money's no matter. Forget the five. I hope you'll be very happy."

Two weeks later a crate containing the dog had come by express. On the tag was scrawled:

Dear Parson: - I like Nancy so well, I send ye the hole dawg, anyhow.

She hadn't a doubt that Jim would feel the same way - but she hoped he hadn't forgotten his pocketbook.

The scene had flashed through her mind in a single moment. She had bitten her lips and kept from laughing by a supreme effort. Not a word of the solemn ceremonial, however, had escaped her consciousness.

"And in the face of this company," the preacher's rich voice was saying, "to join together this Man and this Woman in holy Matrimony; which is commended of St. Paul to be honorable among all men: and therefore is not by any to be entered into unadvisedly or lightly; but reverently, discreetly, advisedly, soberly, and in the fear of God. Into this holy estate these two persons present come now to be joined. If any man can show just cause, why they may not lawfully be joined together, let him now speak, or else hereafter for ever hold his peace."

Craddock paused, and his piercing eyes searched the man and woman before him.

"I require to charge you both, as ye will answer at the dreadful day of judgment, when the secrets of all hearts shall be disclosed, that if either of you know any impediment, why ye may not be lawfully joined together in Matrimony, ye do now confess it -"

Again he paused. The perspiration stood in beads on Jim's forehead, and he glanced uneasily at Mary from the corners of his drooping eyes. A smile was playing about her mouth, and Jim was cheered.

"For be ye well assured," the preacher continued, "that if any persons are joined together otherwise than as God's Word doth allow, their marriage is not lawful."

He turned with deliberation to Jim and transfixed him with the first question of the ceremony. The groom was hypnotized into a state of abject terror. His ears heard the words; the mind recorded but the vaguest idea of what they meant.

"Wilt thou have this Woman to thy wedded wife, to live together after God's ordinance in the holy estate of Matrimony? Wilt thou love her, comfort her, honor, and keep her in sickness and in health; and, forsaking all others, keep thee only unto her, so long as ye both shall live?"

Jim's mouth was open; his lower jaw had dropped in dazed awe, and he continued to stare straight into the preacher's face until Mary pressed his arm and whispered:

"Jim!"

"I will - yes, I will - you bet I will!" he hastened to answer.

The children giggled, and the preacher's lips twitched.

Thomas Dixon

He turned quickly to Mary.

"Wilt thou have this Man to thy wedded husband, to live together after God's ordinance, in the holy estate of Matrimony? Wilt thou obey him, and serve him, love, honor, and keep him in sickness and in health; and, forsaking all others, keep thee only unto him, so long as ye both shall live?"

With quick, clear voice, Mary answered:

"I will."

"Please join your right hands and repeat after me:"

He fixed Jim with his gaze and spoke with deliberation, clause by clause:

"I, James, take thee, Mary, to my wedded wife, to have and to hold from this day forward, for better, for worse, for richer, for poorer, in sickness and in health, to love and to cherish, till death us do part, according to God's holy ordinance; and thereto I plight thee my troth."

Jim's throat at first was husky with fear, but he caught each clause with quick precision and repeated them without a hitch.

He smiled and congratulated himself: "I got ye that time, old cull!"

The preacher's eyes sought Mary's:

"I, Mary, take thee, James, to my wedded husband, to have and to hold from this day forward, for better for worse, for richer for poorer, in sickness and in health, to love, cherish, and to obey, till death do us part, according to God's holy ordinance; and thereto I give thee my troth."

In the sweetest musical voice, quivering with happiness, the girl repeated the words.

Again the preacher's eyes sought Jim's:

AND THE MAN SHALL GIVE UNTO THE WOMAN A RING -

The groom fumbled in his pocket and found at last the ring, which he handed to Mary. The minister at once took it from her hand and handed it back to Jim.

The bride lifted her left hand, deftly extending the fourth finger, and the groom slipped the ring on, and held it firmly gripped as he had been instructed.

"With this ring I thee wed -"

"With this ring I thee wed -" Jim repeated firmly.

" - and with all my worldly goods I thee endow -"

" - and with all my worldly goods I thee endow -"

"In the Name of the Father -"

"In the Name of the Father -"

" - and of the Son -"

"- and of the Son -"

"- and of the Holy Ghost -"

"- and of the Holy Ghost -"

"Amen!"

"Amen!"

The voice of the preacher's prayer that followed rang far-away and unreal to the heart of the girl. Her vivid imagination had

Thomas Dixon

leaped the years. Her spirit did not return to earth and time and place until the minister seized her right hand and joined it to Jim's.

"Those whom God hath joined together let no man put asunder!

"Forasmuch as James Anthony and Mary Adams have consented together in holy wedlock, and have witnessed the same before God and this company, and thereto have given and pledged their troth, each to the other, and have declared the same by giving and receiving a Ring, and by joining hands; I pronounce that they are Man and Wife, In the Name of the Father, and of the Son, and of the Holy Ghost. Amen."

The preacher lifted his hands solemnly above their heads.

"God the Father, God the Son, God the Holy Ghost, bless, preserve, and keep you; the Lord mercifully with His favor look upon you, and fill you with all spiritual benediction and grace; that ye may so live together in this life, that in the world to come ye may have life everlasting. AMEN."

The preacher took Mary's hand.

"Your father is my friend, child. This is for him -"

He bent quickly and kissed her lips, while Jim gasped in astonishment.

The minister's wife congratulated them both. The two older children smilingly advanced and added their voices in good wishes.

Mary whispered to Jim:

"Don't forget the preacher's fee!"

"Lord, how much? Will fifty be enough? It's all I've got."

"Give him twenty. We'll need the rest."

It was not until they were seated in the waiting cab and sank back among the shadows, that Jim crushed her in his arms and kissed her until she cried for mercy.

"The gall of that preacher, kissing you!" he muttered savagely. "You know, I come within an ace of pasting him one on the nose!"

CHAPTER XI

"UNTIL DEATH"

The lights burned in the hall with unusual brightness. Ella stood in the open door of the room, through which the light was streaming. With its radiance came the perfume of roses - the scrub-woman's gift of love. The room was a bower of gorgeous flowers. She had spent her last cent in this extravagance. Mary swept the place with a look of amazement.

"Oh, Ella," she cried, "how could you be so silly!"

"You like them, ja?" Ella asked softly.

"They're glorious - but you should not have made such a sacrifice for me."

"For myself, maybe, I do it - all for myself to make me happy, too, tonight."

She dismissed the subject with a wave of her hand and placed the chairs beside the beautifully set table.

"Dinner is all ready," she announced cheerfully. "And shall I go now and leave you? Or will you let me serve your dinner first?"

A sudden panic seized the bride.

"Stay and serve the dinner, Ella, if you will," she quickly answered.

Jim frowned, but seated himself in business-like fashion.

"All right; I'm ready for it, old girl!"

With soft tread and swift, deft touch, Ella served the dinner, standing prim and stiff and ghost-like behind Jim's chair between the courses.

The bride watched her, fascinated by the pallor of her haggard face and the queer suggestion of Death which her appearance made in spite of the background of flowers. She had dressed herself in a simple skirt and shirtwaist of spotless white. The material seemed to be draped on her tall figure, thin to emaciation. The chalk-like pallor of her face brought out with startling sharpness the deep, hollow caverns beneath her straight eyebrows. Her single eye shone unusually bright.

Gradually the grim impression grew that Death was hovering over her bridal feast - a foolish fancy which persisted in her highly-wrought nervous state. Yet the idea, once fixed, could not be crushed. In vain she used her will to bring her wandering mind back to the joyous present. Each time she lifted her eyes they rested upon the silent, white figure with its single eye piercing the depths of her soul.

She could endure it no longer. She nodded and smiled wanly at Ella.

"You may go now!"

The woman gazed at the bride in surprise.

"I shall come again - yes?"

"Tomorrow morning, Ella, you may help me."

The white figure paused uncertainly at the door, and her drawling voice breathed her parting word tenderly:

"Good night!"

The bride closed her eyes and answered.

"Good night, Ella!"

The door closed. Jim rose quickly and bolted it.

"Thank God!" he exclaimed fervently. He fixed his slumbering eyes on his wife for a moment, saw the frightened look, walked quickly back to the table and took his seat.

"Now, Kiddo, we can eat in peace."

"Yes, I'd rather be alone," she sighed.

"I must say," Jim went on briskly, "that parson of yours did give us a run for our money."

"I like the old, long ceremony best."

"Well, you see, I ain't never had much choice - but do you know what I thought was the best thing in it?"

"No - what?"

"UNTIL DEATH DO US PART! Gee how he did ring out on that! His voice sounded to me like a big bell somewhere away up in the clouds. Did you hear me sing it back at him?"

Mary smiled nervously.

"You had found your voice then."

"You bet I had! I muffed that first one, though, didn't I?"

"A little. It didn't matter." She answered mechanically.

He fixed his eyes on her again.

"Hungry, Kiddo?"

"No," she gasped.

"What's the use!" he cried in low, vibrant tones, springing to his feet. "I don't want to eat this stuff - I just want to eat you!"

Mary rose tremblingly and moved instinctively to meet him.

He clasped her form in his arms and crushed with cruel strength.

"Until death do us part!" he whispered passionately.

She answered with a kiss.

CHAPTER XII

THE LOTOS-EATERS

It was eleven o'clock next morning before Ella ventured to rap softly on the door. They had just finished breakfast. The bride was clearing up the table, humming a song of her childhood.

Jim caught her in his arms.

"Once more before she comes!"

"Don't kill me!" she laughed.

Jim lounged in the window and smoked his cigarette while Ella and Mary chattered in the kitchenette.

In half an hour the scrub-woman had made her last trip with the extra dishes, and the little home was spick and span.

Mary sprang on the couch and snuggled into Jim's arms.

"I've changed our plans -" he began thoughtfully.

"We won't give up our honeymoon trip?" she cried in alarm. "That's one dream we MUST live, Jim, dear. I've set my heart on it."

"Sure we will - sure," he answered quickly. "But not in that car."

"Why?"

Jim grinned.

"Because I like you better - you get me, Kiddo?"

She pressed close and whispered:

"I think so."

"You see, that fool car might throw a tire or two. Believe me, it'll be a job to have her on my hands for a thousand miles. Of course, if I didn't know you, little girl, it would be all sorts of fun. But, honest to God, this game beats the world."

He bent low and kissed her again.

"Where'll we go, then?" she murmured.

"That's what I'm tryin' to dope out. I like the sea. It lulls me just like whisky puts a drunkard to sleep. I wish we could get where it's bright and warm and the sun shines all the time. We could stay two weeks and then jump on the train and be in Asheville the day before Christmas."

Mary sprang up excitedly.

"I have it! We'll go to Florida - away down to the Keys. It's the dream of my life to go there!"

"The Keys what's that?" he asked, puzzled.

"The Keys are little sand islands and reefs that jut out into the warm waters of the Gulf of Mexico. The railroad takes us right there."

"It's warm and sunny there now?"

"Just like summer up here. We can go in bathing in the surf

every day."

Jim sprang to his feet.

"Got a bathing suit?"

Yes - a beauty. I've never worn it here."

"Why?"

"It seemed so bold."

"All right. Maybe we can get a Key all by ourselves for two weeks."

"Wouldn't it be glorious!"

"We'll try it, anyhow. I'll buy the doggoned thing if they don't ask too much. Pack your traps. I'll go down to the shop and get my things. We'll be ready to start in an hour."

By four o'clock they were seated in the drawing-room of a Pullman car on the Florida Limited, gazing entranced at the drab landscape of the Jersey meadows.

Three days later, Jim had landed his boat on a tiny sand reef a half-mile off the coast of Florida with a tent and complete outfit for camping. Like two romping children, they tied the boat to a stake and rushed over the sand-dunes to the beach. They explored their domain from end to end within an hour. Not a tree obscured the endless panorama of sea and bay and waving grass on the great solemn marshes. Piles of soft, warm seaweed lay in long, dark rows along the high-tide mark.

Mary selected a sand-dune almost exactly the height and shape of the one on which they sat at Long Beach the day he told her of his love.

"Here's the spot for our home!" she cried. "Don't you

recognize it?"

"Can't say I've ever been here before. Oh, I got you - I got you! Long Beach - sure! What do you think of that?"

He hurried to the boat and brought the tent. Mary carried the spade, the pole and pegs.

In half an hour the little white home was shining on the level sand at the foot of their favorite dune. The door was set toward the open sea, and the stove securely placed beneath an awning which shaded it from the sun's rays.

"Now, Kiddo, a plunge in that shining water the first thing. I'll give you the tent. I'll chuck my things out here."

In a fever of joyous haste she threw off her clothes and donned the dainty, one-piece bathing suit. She flew over the sand and plunged into the water before Jim had finished changing to his suit.

She was swimming and diving like a duck in the lazy, beautiful waters of the Gulf when he reached the beach.

"Come on! Come on!" she shouted.

He waved his hand and finished his cigarette.

"It's glorious! It's mid-summer!" she called.

With a quick plunge he dived into the water, disappeared and stayed until she began to scan the surface uneasily. With a splash he rose by her side, lifting her screaming in his arms. Her bathing-cap was brushed off, and he seized her long hair in his mouth, turned and with swift, strong beat carried her unresisting body to the beach.

He drew her erect and looked into her smiling face.

"That's the way I'd save you if you had called for help. How'd you like it?"

"It was sweet to give up and feel myself in your power, dear!"

His drooping eyes were devouring her exquisite figure outlined so perfectly in the clinging suit.

"I was afraid to wear this in New York," she said demurely.

"I can't blame you. If you'd ever have gone on the beach at Coney Island in that, there'd have been a riot."

He lifted her in his arms and kissed her.

"And you're all mine, Kiddo! It's too good to be true! I'm afraid to wake up mornings now for fear I'll find I've just been dreaming."

They plunged again in the water, and side by side swam far out from the shore, circled gracefully and returned.

Hours they spent snuggling in the warm sand. Not a sound of the world beyond the bay broke the stillness. The music of the water's soft sighing came on their ears in sweet, endless cadence. The wind was gentle and brushed their cheeks with the softest caress. Far out at sea, white-winged sails were spread - so far away they seemed to stand in one spot forever. The deep cry of an ocean steamer broke the stillness at last.

"We must dress for dinner, Jim!" she sighed.

"Why, Kiddo?"

"We must eat, you know."

"But why dress? I like that style on you. It's too much trouble to dress."

"All right!" she cried gayly. "We'll have a little informal dinner this evening. I love to feel the sand under my feet."

He gathered the wood from the dry drifts above the waterline and kindled a fire. The salt-soaked sticks burned fiercely, and the dinner was cooked in a jiffy - a fresh chicken he had bought, sweet potatoes, and delicious buttered toast.

They sat in their bathing suits on camp-stools beside the folding table and ate by moonlight.

The dinner finished, Mary cleared the wooden dishes while Jim brought heaps of the dry, spongy sea grass and made a bed in the tent. He piled it two feet high, packed it down to a foot, and then spread the sheets and blankets.

"All ready for a stroll down the avenue, Kiddo?" he called from the door.

"Fifth Avenue or Broadway?" she laughed.

"Oh, the Great White Way - you couldn't miss it! Just look at the shimmer of the moon on the sands! Ain't it great?"

Hand in hand, they strolled on the beach and bathed in the silent flood of the moonlit night - no prying eyes near save the stars of the friendly southern skies.

"The moon seems different down here, Jim!" she whispered.

"It is different," he answered with boyish enthusiasm. "It's all so still and white!"

"Could we stay here forever?"

He shook his head emphatically.

"Not on your life. This little boy has to work, you know. Old man John D. Rockefeller might, but it's early for a young financier to retire."

"A whole week, then?"

"Sure! For a week we'll forget New York."

They sat down on the sand-dune behind the tent and watched the waters flash in the silvery light, the world and its fevered life forgotten.

"You're the only thing real tonight, Jim!" she sighed.

"And you're the world for me, Kiddo!"

She waked at dawn, with a queer feeling of awe at the weird, gray light which filtered through the cotton walls. A sense of oneness with Nature and the beat of Her eternal heart filled her soul. The soft wash of the water on the sands seemed to be keeping time to the throb of her own pulse.

She peered curiously into the face of her sleeping lover. She had never seen him asleep before. She started at the transformation wrought by the closing of his heavy eyelids and the complete relaxation of his features. The strange, steel-blue coloring of his eyes had always given his face an air of mystery and charm. The complete closing of the heavy lids and the slight droop of the lower jaw had worked a frightful change. The romance and charm had gone, and instead she saw only the coarse, brutal strength.

She frowned like a spoiled child, put her dainty hand under his chin and pressed his mouth together.

"Wake up, sir!" she whispered. "I don't like your expression!"

He refused to stir, and she drew the tips of her fingers across his ears and eyelids.

He rubbed his eyes and muttered:

"What t'ell?"

"Let's take a bath in the sea before sunrise - come on!"

The sleeper groaned heavily, turned over, and in a moment was again dead to the world.

Mary's eyes were wide now with excitement. The hours were too marvelous to be lost in sleep. She could sleep when they must return to the tiresome world with its endless crowds of people.

She rose softly, ran barefoot to the beach, threw her night-dress on the sand and plunged, her white, young body trembling with joy, into the water.

It was marvelous - this wonderful hush of the dawn over the infinite sea. The air and water melted into a pearl gray. Far out toward the east, the waters began to blush at the kiss of the coming sun. The pearl gray slowly turned into purple. So startling was the vision, she swam in-shore and stood knee-deep in the shallows to watch the magic changes. In breathless wonder she saw the sea and sky and shore turn into a trembling cloud of dazzling purple. A moment before, she had caught the water up in her hand and poured it out in a stream of pearls. She lifted a handful and poured it out now, each drop a dazzling amethyst. And even while she looked, the purple was changing to scarlet - the amethyst into rubies!

A great awe filled her in the solemn hush. She stood in Nature's vast cathedral, close to God's heart - her life in harmony with His eternal laws.

How foolish and artificial were the ways of the far-away, drab, prosaic world of clothes and houses and furnishings! If she could only live forever in this dream-world!

Even while the thought surged through her heart, she lifted her head and saw the red rim of the sun suddenly break through the sea, and started lest the white light of day had revealed her to some passing boatman hurrying to his nets.

Her keen eye quickly swept the circle of the wide, silent world of sand-dunes, marsh and waters. No prying eye was near. Only the morning star still gleaming above saw. And they were twin sisters.

Four days flew on velvet wings before the first cloud threw its shadow across her life. Jim always slept until nine o'clock, and refused with dogged good-natured indifference to stir when she had asked him to get the wood for breakfast. It was nothing, of course, to walk a hundred yards to the beach and pick up the wood, and she did it. The hurt that stung was the feeling that he was growing indifferent.

She felt for the first time an impulse to box his lazy jaws as he yawned and turned over for the dozenth time without rising. He looked for all the world like a bulldog curled up on his bed of grass.

She shook him at last.

"Jim, dear, you must get up now! Breakfast is almost ready and it won't be fit to eat if you don't come on."

He opened his heavy eyelids and gazed at her sleepily.

"All righto - ! Just as you say - just as you say."

"Hurry! Breakfast will be ready before you can dress."

"Gee! Breakfast all ready! You're one smart little wifie, Kiddo."

The compliment failed to please. She was sure that he had been fully awake twice before and pretended to be asleep from sheer laziness and indifference.

The thought hurt.

When they sat down at last to breakfast, she looked into his half-closed eyes with a sudden start.

"Why, Jim, your eyes are red!"

"Yes?"

"What's the matter?"

"Nothing."

"You're ill - what is it?"

He grinned sheepishly.

"You couldn't guess now, could you?"

"You haven't been drinking!" she gasped.

"No," he drawled lazily, "I wouldn't say drinking - I just took one big swallow last night - makes you sleep good when you're tired. Good medicine! I always carry a little with me."

A sickening wave went over her. Not that she felt that he was going to be a drunkard. But the utter indifference with which he made the announcement was a painful revelation of the fact that her opinion on such a question was not of the slightest importance. That he was now master of the situation he evidently meant that she should see and understand at once.

She refused to accept the humiliating position without a struggle and made up her mind to try at once to mold his character. She would begin by getting him to cut the slang from his conversation.

"You remember the promise you made me one day before we were married, Jim?" she asked brightly.

"Which one? You know a fellow's not responsible for what he

promises to get his girl. All's fair in love and war, they say -"

"I'm going to hold you to this one, sir," she firmly declared.

"All right, little bright eyes," he responded cheerfully as he lit a cigarette and sent the smoke curling above his red head.

She sat for a while in silence, studying the man before her. The task was delicate and difficult. And she had thought it a mere pastime of love! As her fiance, he had been wax in her hands. As her husband, he was a lazy, headstrong, obstinate young animal grinning good-naturedly at her futile protests. How long would he grin and bear her suggestions with patience? The transition from this lazy grin to the growl of an angry bulldog might be instantaneous.

She would move with the utmost caution - but she would move and at once. It would be a test of character between them. She edged her chair close to his, drew his head down in her lap and ran her fingers through his thick, red hair.

"Still love me, Jim?" she smiled.

"Crazier over you every day - and you know it, too, you sly little puss," he answered dreamily.

"You WILL make good your promises?"

"Sure, I will - surest thing you know!"

"You see, Jim dear," she went on tenderly, "I want to be proud of you -"

"Well, ain't you?"

"Of course I am, silly. I know you and understand you. But I want all the world to respect you as I do." She paused and breathed deeply. "They've got to do it, too, they've got to -"

"Sure, I'll knock their block off - if they don't!" he broke in.

She raised her finger reprovingly and shook her head.

"That's just the trouble: you can't do it with your fists. You can't compel the respect of cultured men and women by physical force. We've got to win with other weapons."

"All right, Kiddo - dope it out for me," he responded lazily. "Dope it out -"

Her lips quivered with the painful recognition of the task before her. Yet when she spoke, her voice was low and sweet and its tones even. She gave no sign to the man whose heavy form rested in her arms.

"Then from today we must begin to cut out every word of slang - it's a bargain?"

"Sure, Mike - I promised!"

"Cut `Sure Mike!'"

She raised her finger severely.

"All right, teacher," he drawled. "What'll we put in Sure Mike's place? I've found him a handy man!"

"Say `certainly.'"

Jim grinned good-naturedly.

"Aw hell, Kiddo - that sounds punk!"

"And HELL, Jim, isn't a nice word -"

"Gee, Kid, now look here - can't get along with out HELL - leave me that one just a little while."

She shook her head.

"No."

"No?"

"And PUNK is expressive, but not suited to parlor use."

"All right - t'ell with PUNK!" He turned and looked. "What's the matter now?" he asked.

"Don't you realize what you've just said?"

"What did I say?"

She turned away to hide a tear.

He threw his arms around her neck and drew her lips down to his.

"Ah, don't worry, Kiddo - I'll do better next time. Honest to God, I will. That's enough for today. Just let's love now. T'ell with the rest."

She smiled in answer.

"You promise to try honestly?"

He raised his hand in solemn vow.

"S'help me!"

Each day's trial ended in a laugh and a kiss until at last Jim refused to promise any more. He grinned in obstinate, good-natured silence and let her do the worrying.

She watched him with growing wonder and alarm. He gradually lapsed into little coarse, ugly habits at the table. She tried playfully to correct them. He took it good-naturedly at first and then ignored her suggestions as if she were a kitten complaining at his feet.

She studied him with baffling rage at the mystery of his personality. The long silences between them grew from hour to hour. She could see that he was restless now at the isolation of their sand-island home. The queer lights and shadows that played in his cold blue eyes told only too plainly that his mind was back again in the world of battle. He was fighting something, too.

She was glad of it. She could manage him better there. She would throw him into the company of educated people and rouse his pride and ambition. She heard his announcement of their departure on the eighth day with positive joy.

"Well, Kiddo," he began briskly, "we've got to be moving. Time to get back to work now. The old town and the little shop down in Avenue B have been calling me."

"Today, Jim?" she asked quickly.

"Right away. We'll catch the first train north, stop two days, Christmas Eve and Christmas, in Asheville, and then for old New York!"

The journey along the new railroad built on concrete bridges over miles of beautiful waters was one of unalloyed joy. They had passed over this stretch of marvelous engineering at night on their trip down and had not realized its wonders. For hours the train seemed to be flying on velvet wings through the ocean.

She sat beside her lover and held his hand. In spite of her enthusiasm, he would doze. At every turn of entrancing view she would pinch his arm:

"Look, Jim! Look!"

He would lift his heavy eyelids, grunt good-naturedly and doze again.

In the dining-car she was in mortal terror at first lest he should lapse into the coarse table manners into which he had fallen in camp. She laid his napkin conspicuously on his plate and saw that he had opened and put it in place across his lap before ordering the meals.

The moment he found himself in a crowd, the lights began to flash in his eyes, his broad shoulders lifted and his whole being was at once alert and on guard. He followed his wife's lead with unerring certainty.

She renewed her faith in his early reformation, though his character was a puzzle. He seemed to be forever watching out of the corners of his slumbering eyes. She wondered what it meant.

CHAPTER XIII

THE REAL MAN

They arrived in Asheville the night before Christmas Eve. Jim listened to his wife's prattle about the wonderful views with quiet indifference.

They stopped at the Battery Park Hotel, and she hoped the waning moon would give them at least a glimpse of the beautiful valley of the French Broad and Swannanoa rivers and the dark, towering ranges of mountains among the stars. She made Jim wait on the balcony of the room for half an hour, but the clouds grew denser and he persisted in nodding.

His head dipped lower than usual, and she laughed.

"Poor old sleepy-head!"

"For the love o' Mike, Kiddo - me for the hay. Won't them mountains wait till morning?"

"All right!" she answered cheerily. "I'll pull you out at sunrise. The sunrise from our window will be glorious."

He rose and stretched his body like a young, well fed tiger.

"I think it's prettier from the bed. But have it your own way - have it your own way. I'll agree to anything if you lemme go to sleep now."

She rose as the first gray fires of dawn began to warm the cloud-banks on the eastern horizon, stood beside her window and watched in silent ecstasy. Jim was sleeping heavily. She would not wake him until the glory of the sunrise was at its height. She loved to watch the changing lights and shadows in sky and valley and on distant mountain peaks as the light slowly filtered over the eastern hills.

She had recovered from the depression of the last days of their camp. The journey back into the world had improved Jim's manners. There could be no doubt about his ambitions. His determination to be a millionaire was the lever she now meant to work in raising his social aspirations.

Why should she feel depressed?

Their married life had just begun. The two weeks they had passed on their honeymoon had been happy beyond her dreams of happiness. Somehow her imagination had failed to give any conception of the wonder and glory of this revelation of life. His little lapses of selfishness on their sand island no doubt came from ignorance of what was expected of him.

For one thing she felt especially thankful. There had been no ugly confessions of a shady past to cloud the joy of their love. Her lover might be ignorant of the ways of polite society. He was equally free of its sinister vices. She thanked God for that. The soul of the man she had married was clean of all memories of women. The love he gave was fierce in its unrestrained passion - but it was all hers. She gloried in its strength.

She made up her mind, standing there in the soft light of the dawn, that she would bend his iron will to her own in the growing, sweet intimacy of their married life and threw her fears to the winds.

The thin, fleecy clouds that hung over the low range of the eastern foreground were all aglow now, with every tint of the rainbow, while the sun's bed beyond the hills was flaming in scarlet and gold.

She clapped her hands in ecstasy.

"Jim! Jim, dear!"

He made no response, and she rushed to his side and whispered:

"You must see this sunrise - get up quick, quick, dear. It's wonderful."

"What's the matter?" he muttered.

"The sunrise over the mountains - quick - it's glorious."

His heavy eyelids drooped and closed. He dropped on the pillow and buried his face out of sight.

"Ah, Jim dear, do come - just to please me."

"I'm dead, Kiddo - dead to the world," he sighed. "Don't like to see the sun rise. I never did. Come on back and let's sleep -"

His last words were barely audible. He was breathing heavily as his lips ceased to move.

She gave it up, returned to the window and watched the changing colors until the white light from the sun's face had touched with life the last shadows of the valleys and flashed its signals from the farthest towering peaks.

Her whole being quivered in response to the beauty of this glorious mountain world. The air was wine. She loved the sapphire skies and the warm, lazy, caressing touch of the sun of the South.

A sense of bitterness came, just for a moment, that the man she had chosen for her mate had no eye to see these wonders and no ear to hear their music. During the madness of his whirlwind courtship she had gotten the impression that his spirit was sensitive to beauty - to the waters of the bay, the sea and the wooded hills. She must face the facts. Their stay on the island had convinced her that he had eyes only for her. She must make the most of it.

It was ten o'clock before Jim could be persuaded to rise and get breakfast. She literally pulled him up the stairs to the observatory on the tower of the hotel.

"What's the game, Kiddo? What's the game?" he grumbled.

"Ask me no questions. But do just as I tell you; come on!"

Her face was radiant, her hair in a tangle of riotous beauty about her forehead and temples, her eyes sparkling.

"Don't look till I tell you!" she cried, as they emerged on the little minaret which crowns the tower.

"Now open and see the glory of the Lord!" she cried with joyous awe.

The day was one of matchless beauty. The clouds that swung low in the early morning had floated higher and higher till they hung now in shining billows above the highest balsam-crowned peaks in the distance.

In every direction, as far as the eye could reach, north, south, east, west, the dark ranges mounted in the azure skies until the farthest dim lines melted into the heavens.

"Oh, Jim dear, isn't it wonderful! We're lucky to get this view on our first day. It's such a good omen."

Jim opened his eyes lazily and puffed his cigarette in a calm, patronizing way.

"Tough sledding we'd have had with an automobile over those hills," he said. "We'll try it after lunch, though."

"We'll go for a ride?" she cried joyfully.

"Yep. Got to hunt up the folks. The mountains near Asheville!" he said with disgust. "I should say they are near - and far, too. Holy smoke, I'll bet we get lost!"

"Nonsense -"

"Where's the Black Mountains, I wonder?" he asked suddenly.

"Over there!" She pointed to the giant peaks projecting here and there in dim, blue waves beyond the Great Craggy Range in the foreground.

"Holy Moses! Do we have to climb those crags before we start?"

"To go to Black Mountain?"

"Yes. That's where the lawyer said they lived, under Cat-tail Peak in the Black Mountain Range - wherever t'ell that is."

"No, no! You don't climb the Great Craggy; you go around this end of it and follow the Swannanoa River right up to the foot of Mount Mitchell, the highest peak this side of the Rockies. The Cat-tail is just beyond Mount Mitchell."

"You've been there?" he asked in surprise.

"Once, with a party from Asheville. We spent three days and slept in caves."

"Suppose you'd know the way now?"

"We couldn't miss it. We follow the bed of the Swannanoa to its source -"

"Then that settles it. We'll go by ourselves. I don't want any mutt along to show us the way. We couldn't get lost nohow, could we?"

"Of course not - all the roads lead to Asheville. We can ask the way to the house you want, when we reach the little stopping place at the foot of Mount Mitchell."

"Gee, Kid, you're a wonder!" he exclaimed admiringly. "Couldn't get along without you, now could I?"

"I hope not, sir!"

"You bet I couldn't! We'll start right away. The roads will give us a jolt -"

He turned suddenly to go.

"Wait - wait a minute, dear," she pleaded. "You haven't seen this gorgeous view to the southwest, with Mount Pisgah looming in the center like some vast cathedral spire - look, isn't it glorious?"

"Fine! Fine!" he responded in quick, businesslike tones.

"You can look for days and weeks and not begin to realize the changing beauty of these mountains, clothed in eternal green! Just think, dear, Mount Pisgah, there, is forty miles away, and it looks as if you could stroll over to it in an hour's walk. And there are twenty-three magnificent peaks like that, all of them more than six thousand feet high -"

She paused with a frown. He was neither looking nor listening. He had fallen into a brown study; his mind was miles away.

"You're not listening, Jim - nor seeing anything," she said reproachfully.

"No - Kiddo, we must get ready for that trip. I've got a letter for a lawyer downtown. I'll find him and hire a car. I'll be back here for you in an hour. You'll be ready?"

"Right away, in half an hour -"

"Just pack a suit-case for us both. We'll stay one night. I'll take a bag, too, that I have in my trunk."

It was noon before he returned with a staunch touring car ready for the trip. He opened the little steamer trunk which he had always kept locked and took from it a small leather bag. He placed it on the floor, and, in spite of careful handling, the ring of metal inside could be distinctly heard.

"What on earth have you got in that queer black bag?" she asked in surprise.

"Oh, just a lot o' junk from the shop. I thought I might tinker with it at odd times. I don't want to leave it here. It's got one of my new models in it."

He carried the bag in his hand, refusing to allow the porter who came for the suit-case to touch it.

He threw the suit-case in the bottom of the tonneau. The bag he stowed carefully under the cushions of the rear seat. The moment he placed his hand on the wheel of the machine, he was at his best. Every trace of the street gamin fell from him. Again he was the eagle-eyed master of time and space. The machine answered his touch with more than human obedience. He knew how to humor its mood. He conserved its power for a hill with unerring accuracy and threw it over the grades with rarely a pause to change his speeds. He could turn the sharp curves with such swift, easy grace that he scarcely caused Mary's body to swerve an inch. He could sense a rough place in the road and glide over it with velvet touch.

A tire blew out, five miles up the stream from Asheville, and the easy, business-like deliberation with which he removed the old and adjusted the new, was a revelation to Mary of a new phase of his character.

He never once grunted, or swore, or lost his poise, or manifested the slightest impatience. He set about his task coolly, carefully, skillfully, and finished it quickly and silently.

His long silences at last began to worry her. An invisible barrier had reared itself between them. The impression was purely mental - but it was none the less real and distressing.

There was a look of aloof absorption about him she had never seen before. At first she attributed it to the dread of meeting his kinsfolk for the first time, his fear of what they might be like or what they might think of him.

He answered her questions cheerfully but mechanically. Sometimes he stared at her in a cold, impersonal way and gave no answer, as if her questions were an impertinence and she were not of sufficient importance to waste his breath on.

Unable at last to endure the strain, she burst out impatiently:

"What on earth's the matter with you, Jim?"

"Why?" he asked softly.

"You haven't spoken to me in half an hour, and I've asked you two questions."

"Just studying about something, Kiddo, something big. I'll tell you sometime, maybe - not now."

Slowly a great fear began to shape itself in her heart. The real man behind those slumbering eyes she had never known. Who was he?

CHAPTER XIV

UNWELCOME GUESTS

While she was yet puzzling over the strange mood of absorbed brooding into which Jim had fallen, his face suddenly lighted, and he changed with such rapidity that her uneasiness was doubled.

They had reached the stretches of deep forest at the foot of the Black Mountain ranges. The Swannanoa had become a silver thread of laughing, foaming spray and deep, still pools beneath the rocks. The fields were few and small. The little clearings made scarcely an impression in the towering virgin forests.

"Great guns, Kiddo!" he exclaimed, "this is some country! By George, I had no idea there was such a place so close to New York!"

She looked at him with uneasy surprise. What could be in his mind? The solemn gorge through which they were passing gave no entrancing views of clouds or sky or towering peaks. Its wooded cliffs hung ominously overhead in threatening shadows. The scene had depressed her after the vast sunlit spaces of sky, of shining valleys and cloud-capped, sapphire peaks on which they had turned their backs.

"You like this, Jim?" she asked.

"It's great - great!"

"I thought that waterfall we just passed was very beautiful."

"I didn't see it. But this is something like it. You're clean out of the world here - and there ain't a railroad in twenty miles!"

The deeper the shadows of tree and threatening crag, the higher Jim's strange spirit seemed to rise.

She watched him with increasing fear. How little she knew the real man! Could it be possible that this lonely, unlettered boy of the streets of lower New York, starved and stunted in childhood, had within him the soul of a great poet? How else could she explain the sudden rapture over the threatening silences and shadows of these mountain gorges which had depressed her? And yet his utter indifference to the glories of beautiful waters, his blindness at noon before the most wonderful panorama of mountains and skies on which she had ever gazed, contradicted the theory of the poetic soul. A poet must see beauty where she had seen it - and a thousand wonders her eyes had not found.

His elation was uncanny. What could it mean?

He was driving now with a skill that was remarkable, a curious smile playing about his drooping, Oriental eyelids. A wave of fierce resentment swept her heart. She was a mere plaything in this man's life. The real man she had never seen. What was he thinking about? What grim secret lay behind the mysterious smile that flickered about the corners of those eyes? He was not thinking of her. The mood was new and cold and cynical, for all the laughter he might put in it.

She asked herself the question of his past, his people, his real life-history. The only answer was his baffling, mysterious smile.

A frown suddenly clouded his face.

"Hello! Ye're running right into a man's yard!"

Mary lifted her head with quick surprise.

"Why yes, it's the stopping place for the parties that climb Mount Mitchell. I remember it. We stayed all night here, left our rig, and started next morning at sunrise on horseback to climb the trail."

"Pretty near the jumping-off place, then," he remarked. "We'll ask the way to Cat-tail Peak."

He stopped the car in front of the low-pitched, weather-stained frame house and blew the horn.

A mountain woman with three open-eyed, silent children came slowly to meet them.

She smiled pleasantly, and without embarrassment spoke in a pleasant drawl:

"Won't you 'light and look at your saddle?"

The expression caught Jim's fancy, and he broke into a roar of laughter. The woman blushed and laughed with him. She couldn't understand what was the matter with the man. Why should he explode over the simple greeting in which she had expressed her pleasure at their arrival?

Anyhow, she was an innkeeper's wife, and her business was to make folks feel at home - so she laughed again with Jim.

"You know that's the funniest invitation I ever got in a car," he cried at last. "We fly in these things sometimes. And when you said, `Won't you 'light,'" - he paused and turned to his wife - "I could just feel myself up in the air on that big old racer's back."

"Won't you-all stay all night with us?" the soft voice drawled again.

"Thank you, not tonight," Mary answered.

She waited for Jim to ask the way.

"No - not tonight," he repeated. "You happen to know an old woman by the name of Owens who lives up here?"

"Nance Owens?"

"That's her name."

"Lord, everybody knows old Nance!" was the smiling answer.

"She ain't got good sense!" the tow-headed boy spoke up.

"Sh!" the mother warned, boxing his ears.

"She's a little queer, that's all. Everybody knows her in Buncombe and Yancey counties. Her house is built across the county line. She eats in Yancey and sleeps in Buncombe -"

"Yes," broke in the boy joyously, "an' when the Sheriff o' Yancey comes, she moves back into Buncombe. She's some punkin's on a green gourd vine, she is - if she ain't got good sense."

His mother struck at him again, but he dodged the blow and finished his speech without losing a word.

"Could you tell us the way to her house?"

"Keep right on this road, and you can't miss it."

"How far is it?"

"Oh, not far."

"No; right at the bottom o' the Cat's-tail," the boy joyfully explained.

"He means the foot o' Cat-tail Peak!" the mother apologized.

"How many miles?"

"Just a little ways - ye can't miss it; the third house you come to on this road."

"You'll be there in three shakes of a sheep's tail - in that thing!" the boy declared.

Jim waved his thanks, threw in his gear, and the car shot forward on the level stretch of road beyond the house. He slowed down when out of sight.

"Gee! I'd love to have that kid in a wood-shed with a nice shingle all by ourselves for just ten minutes."

"The people spoil him," Mary laughed. "The people who stop there for the Mount Mitchell climb. He was a baby when I was there six years ago" - she paused and a rapt look crept into her eyes - "a beautiful little baby, her first-born, and she was the happiest thing I ever saw in my life."

Her voice sank to a whisper.

A vision suddenly illumined her own soul, and she forgot her anxiety over Jim's queer moods.

Deeper and deeper grew the shadows of crag, gorge, and primeval forest. The speedometer on the foot-board registered five miles from the Mount Mitchell house. They had passed two cabins by the way, and still no sign of the third.

"Why couldn't she tell us how many miles, I'd like to know?" Jim grumbled.

"It's the way of the mountain folk. They're noncommittal on distances."

He stopped the car and lighted the lamps.

"Going to be dark in a minute," he said. "But I like this place," he added.

He picked his way with care over the narrow road. They crossed the little stream they were trailing, and the car crawled over the rocks along the banks at a snail's pace.

An owl called from a dead tree-top silhouetted against an open space of sky ahead.

"Must be a clearing there," Jim muttered.

He stopped the car and listened for the sounds of life about a house.

A vast, brooding silence filled the world. A wolf howled from the edge of a distant crag somewhere overhead.

"For God's sake!" Jim shivered. "What was that?"

"Only a mountain wolf crying for company."

"Wolves up here?" he asked in surprise.

"A few - harmless, timid, lonesome fellows. It makes me sorry for them when I hear one."

"Great country! I like it!" Jim responded.

Again she wondered why. What a queer mixture of strength and mystery - this man she had married!

He started the car, turned a bend in the road, and squarely in front, not more than a hundred yards away, gleamed a light in a cabin window - four tiny panes of glass.

"By Geeminy, we come near stopping in the front yard

without knowing it!" he exclaimed. "Didn't we?"

"I'm glad she's at home!" Mary exclaimed. "The light shines with a friendly glow in these deep shadows."

"Afraid, Kiddo?" he asked lightly.

"I don't like these dark places."

"All right when you get used to 'em - safer than daylight."

Again her heart beat at his queer speech. She shivered at the thought of this uncanny trait of character so suddenly developed today. She made an effort to throw off her depression. It would vanish with the sun tomorrow morning.

He picked his way carefully among the trees and stopped in front of the cabin door. The little house sat back from the road a hundred feet or more.

He blew his horn twice and waited.

A sudden crash inside, and the light went out. He waited a moment for it to come back.

Only darkness and dead silence.

"Suppose she dropped dead and kicked over the lamp?" Jim laughed.

"She probably took the lamp into another room."

"No; it went out too quick - and it went out with a crash."

He blew his horn again.

Still no answer.

"Hello! Hello!" he called loudly.

Someone stirred at the door. Jim's keen ear was turned toward the house.

"I heard her bar the door, I'll swear it."

"How foolish, Jim!" Mary whispered. "You couldn't have heard it."

"All the same I did. Here's a pretty kettle of fish! The old hellion's not even going to let us in."

He seized the lever of his horn and blew one terrific blast after another, in weird, uncanny sobs and wails, ending in a shriek like the last cry of a lost soul.

"Don't, Jim!" Mary cried, shivering. "You'll frighten her to death."

"I hope so."

"Go up and speak to her - and knock on the door."

He waited again in silence, scrambled out of the car, and fumbled his way through the shadows to the dark outlines of the cabin. He found the porch on which the front door opened.

His light foot touched the log with sure step, and he walked softly to the cabin wall. The door was not yet visible in the pitch darkness. His auto lights were turned the other way and threw their concentrated rays far down into the deep woods.

He listened intently for a moment and caught the cat-like tread of the old woman inside.

"I say - hello, in there!" he called.

Again the sound of her quick, furtive step told him that she was on the alert and determined to defend her castle against all comers. What if she should slip an old rifle through a crack and blow his head off?

She might do it, too!

He must make her open the door.

"Say, what's the matter in there?" he asked persuasively.

A moment's silence, and then a gruff voice slowly answered:

"They ain't nobody at home!"

"The hell they ain't!" Jim laughed.

"No!"

"Who are you?"

She hesitated and then growled back:

"None o' your business. Who are you?"

"We're strangers up here - lost our way. It's cold - we got to stop for the night."

"Ye can't - they's nobody home, I tell ye!" she repeated with sullen emphasis.

Jim broke into a genial laugh.

"Ah! Come on, old girl! Open up and be sociable. We're not revenue officers or sheriffs. If you've got any good mountain whiskey, I'll help you drink it."

"Who are ye?" she repeated savagely.

"Ah, just a couple o' gentle, cooing turtle-doves - a bride and groom. Loosen up, old girl; it's Christmas Eve - and we're just a couple o' gentle cooin' doves -"

Jim kept up his persuasive eloquence until the light of the candle flashed through the window, and he heard her slip the heavy bar from the door.

He lost no time in pushing his way inside.

Nance threw a startled look at his enormous, shaggy fur coat - at the shining aluminum goggles almost completely masking his face. She gave a low, breathless scream, hurled the door-bar crashing to the floor and stared at him like a wild, hunted animal at bay, her thin hands trembling, the iron-gray hair tumbling over her forehead.

"Oh, my God!" she wailed, crouching back.

Jim gazed at her in amazement. He had forgotten his goggles and fur coat.

"What's the matter?" he asked in high-keyed tones of surprise.

Nance made no answer but crouched lower and attempted to put the table between them.

"What t'ell Bill ails you - will you tell me?" he asked with rising wrath.

"I THOUGHT you wuz the devil," the old woman panted. "Now I KNOW it!"

Jim suddenly remembered his goggles and coat, and broke into a laugh.

"Oh!"

He removed his goggles and cap, threw back his big coat and squared his shoulders with a smile.

"How's that?"

Nance glowered at him with ill-concealed rage, looked him over from head to foot, and answered with a snarl:

"'Tain't much better - ef ye ax ME!"

"Gee! But you're a sociable old wild-cat!" he exclaimed, starting back as if she had struck him a blow.

His eye caught the dried skin of a young wildcat hanging on the log wall.

"No wonder you skinned your neighbor and hung her up to dry," he added moodily.

He took in the room with deliberate insolence while the old woman stood awkwardly watching him, shifting her position uneasily from one foot to the other.

In all his miserable life in New York he could not recall a room more bare of comforts. The rough logs were chinked with pieces of wood and daubed with red clay. The door was made of rough boards, the ceiling of hewn logs with split slabs laid across them. An old-fashioned, tall spinning wheel, dirty and unused, sat in the corner. A rough pine table was in the middle of the floor and a smaller one against the wall. On this side table sat two rusty flat-irons, and against it leaned an ironing board. A dirty piece of turkey-red calico hung on a string for a portiere at the opening which evidently led into a sort of kitchen somewhere in the darkness beyond.

The walls were decorated at intervals. A huge bunch of onions hung on a wooden peg beside the wild-cat skin. Over the window was slung an old-fashioned muzzle-loading musket. The sling which held it was made of a pair of ancient home-made suspenders fastened to the logs with nails. Beneath the gun hung a cow's horn, cut and finished for powder, and with it a dirty game-bag. Strings of red peppers were strung along each of the walls, with here and there bunches of popcorn in the ears. A pile of black walnuts lay in one corner of the cabin and a pile of hickory nuts in another.

A three-legged wooden stool and a split-bottom chair stood beside the table, and a haircloth couch, which looked as if it had been saved from the Ark, was pushed near the wall beside the door.

Across this couch was thrown a ragged patchwork quilt, and a pillow covered with calico rested on one end, with the mark of a head dented deep in the center.

Jim shrugged his shoulders with a look of disgust, stepped quickly to the door and called:

"Come on in, Kid!"

Nance fumbled her thin hands nervously and spoke with the faintest suggestion of a sob in her voice.

"I ain't got nothin' for ye to eat -"

"We've had dinner," he answered carelessly.

He stepped to the door and called:

"Bring that little bag from under the seat, Kiddo."

He held the door open, and the light streamed across the yard to the car. He watched her steadily while she raised the cushion of the rear seat, lifted the bag and sprang from the car. His keen eye never left her for an instant until she placed it in his hands.

"Mercy, but it's heavy!" she panted, as she gave it to him.

He took it without a word and placed it on the table in the center of the room.

Nance glared at him sullenly.

"There's no place for ye, I tell ye -"

Jim faced her with mock politeness.

"For them kind words - thanks!"

He bowed low and swept the room with a mocking gesture.

"There ain't no room for ye," the old woman persisted.

Jim raised his voice to a squeaking falsetto with deliberate purpose to torment her.

"I got ye the first time, darlin'!" he exclaimed, lifting his hands above her as if to hold her down. "We must linger awhile for your name - anyhow, we mustn't forget that. This is Mrs. Nance Owens?"

The old woman started and watched him from beneath her heavy eyebrows, answering with sullen emphasis:

"Yes."

Again Jim lifted his hands above his head and waved her to earth.

"Well! Don't blame me! I can't help it, you know -"

He turned to his wife and spoke with jolly good humor.

"It's the place, all right. Set down, Kiddo - take off your hat and things. Make yourself at home."

Nance flew at him in a sudden frenzy at his assumption of insolent ownership of her cabin.

"There's no place for ye to sleep!" she fairly shrieked in his face.

Again Jim's arms were over her head, waving her down.

"All right, sweetheart! We're from New York. We don't sleep. We've come all the way down here to the mountains of North Carolina just to see you. And we're goin' to sit up all night and look at ye -"

He sat down deliberately, and Nance fumbled her hands with a nervous movement.

Mary's heart went out in sympathy to the forlorn old creature in her embarrassment. Her dress was dirty and ragged, an ill-fitting gingham, the elbows out and her bare, bony arms showing through. The waist was too short and always slipping from the belt of wrinkled cloth beneath which she kept trying to stuff it.

Mary caught her restless eye at last and held it in a friendly look.

"Please let us stay!" she pleaded. "We can sleep on the floor - anywhere."

"You bet!" Jim joined in. "Married two weeks - and I don't care whether it rains or whether it pours or how long I have to stand outdoors - if I can be with you, Kid."

The old woman hesitated until Mary's smile melted its way into her heart.

Her lips trembled, and her watery blue eyes blinked.

"Well," she began grumblingly, "thar's a little single bed in that shed-room thar for you - ef he'll sleep in here on the sofy."

Jim leaped to his feet.

"What do ye think of that? Bully for the old gal! Kinder slow at first. As the poet sings of the little bed-bug, she ain't got no wings - but she gets there just the same!"

He drew the electric torch from his pocket and advanced on Nance.

"By Golly - I'll have another look at you."

Nance backed in terror at the sight of the revolver-like instrument.

"What's that?" she gasped.

"Just a little Gatlin' gun!" he cried jokingly. He pressed the button, and the light flashed squarely in the old woman's eyes.

"God 'lmighty - don't shoot!" she screamed.

Jim doubled with laughter.

"For the love o' Mike!"

Nance leaned against the side table and wiped the perspiration from her brow.

"Lord! I thought you'd kilt me!" she panted, still trembling.

"Ah, don't be foolish!" Jim said persuasively. "It can't hurt you. Here, take it in your hand - I'll show you how to work it. It's to nose round dark places under the buzz-wagon."

He held it out to Nance.

"Here, take it and press the button."

The old woman drew back.

"No - no - I'm skeered! No -"

Jim thrust the torch into her hand and forced her to hold it.

"Oh, come on, it's easy. Push your finger right down on the button."

Nance tried it gingerly at first, and then laughed at the ease with which it could be done. She flashed it on the floor again and again.

"Why, it's like a big lightnin' bug, ain't it?"

She turned the end of it up to examine more closely, pushed the button unconsciously, and the light flashed in her eyes. She jumped and handed it quickly to Jim.

"Or a jack o' lantern - here, take it," she cried, still trembling.

Jim threw his hands up with a laugh.

"Can you beat it!"

Backing quickly to the door, Nance called nervously to Mary:

"I'll get your room ready in a minute, ma'am." She paused and glanced at Jim.

"And thar's a shed out thar you can put your devil wagon in -"

She slipped through the dirty calico curtains, and Mary saw her go with wondering pity in her heart.

CHAPTER XV

A LITTLE BLACK BAG

Mary watched Nance, with a quick glance at Jim. Again he had forgotten that he had a wife. She had studied this strange absorption with increasing uneasiness. During the long, beautiful drive of the afternoon beside laughing waters, through scenes of unparalleled splendor, through valleys of entrancing peace, the still, sapphire skies bending above with clear, Southern Christmas benediction, he had not once pressed her hand, he had not once bent to kiss her.

Each time the thought had come, she fought back the tears. She had made excuses for him. He was absorbed in the memories of his miserable childhood in New York, perhaps. The approaching meeting with his relatives had awakened the old hunger for a mother's love that had been denied him. The scenes through which they were passing had perhaps stirred the currents of his subconscious being.

And yet why should such memories estrange his spirit from hers? The effect should be the opposite. In the remembrance of his loneliness and suffering, he should instinctively turn to her. The love with which she had unfolded his life should redeem the past.

He was standing now with his heavy chin silhouetted against the flickering light of the candle on the table. His hand closed suddenly on the handle of the bag with the swift clutch of an eagle's claw. She started at the ugly picture it made in the dim rays of the candle.

What were the thoughts seething behind the mask of his face? She watched him, spellbound by his complete surrender to the mood that had dominated him from the moment he had touched the deep forests of the Black Mountain range. A grim elation ruled even his silences. The man standing there rigid, his face a smiling, twitching mask, was a stranger. This man she had never known, or loved. And yet they were bound for life in the tenderest and strongest ties that can hold the human soul and body.

She tossed her head and threw off the ugly thought. It was morbid nonsense! She was just hungry for a kiss, and in his new environment he had forgotten himself as many thought-less men had forgotten before and would forget again.

"Jim!" she whispered tenderly.

He made no answer. His thick lips were drawn in deep, twisted lines on one side, as if he had suddenly reached a decision from which there could be no appeal.

She raised her voice slightly.

"Jim?"

Not a muscle of his body moved. The drawn lines of the mouth merely relaxed. His answer was scarcely audible.

"Yep -"

"She's gone!"

"Yep -"

She moved toward him wistfully.

"Aren't you forgetting something?"

His square jaw still held its rigid position silhouetted in sharp profile against the candle's light. He answered slowly and mechanically.

"What?"

His indifference was more than the sore heart could bear. The pent-up tears of the afternoon dashed in flood against the barriers of her will.

"You - haven't - kissed - me - today," she stammered, struggling with each word to save a break.

Still he stood immovable. This time his answer was tinged with the slightest suggestion of amusement.

"No?"

She staggered against the table beside the door and gripped its edge desperately.

"Oh -" she gasped. "Don't you love me any more?"

With his sullen head still holding its position of indifference, his absorption in the idea which dominated his mind still unbroken, he threw out one hand in a gesture of irritation.

"Cut it, Kid! Cut it!"

His tones were not only indifferent; they were contemptuously indifferent.

With a sob, she sank into the chair and buried her face in her arms.

"You're tired! I see it now; you've tired of me. Oh - it's not possible - it's not possible!"

The torrent came at last in a flood of utter abandonment.

Jim turned, looked at her and threw up his hands in temporary surrender.

"Oh, for God's sake!" he muttered, crossing deliberately to her side. He stood and let her sob.

With a quick change of mood, he drew her to her feet, swept her swaying form into his arms, crushed her and covered her lips with kisses.

"How's that?"

She smiled through her tears.

"I feel better -"

Jim laughed.

"For better or worse - `until Death do us part' - that's what you said, Kid, and you meant it, too, didn't you?"

He seized both of her arms, held them firmly and gazed into her eyes with steady, stern inquiry.

She looked up with uneasy surprise.

"Of course - I meant it," she answered slowly.

He held her arms gripped close and said:

"Well - we'll see!"

His hands relaxed, and he turned away, rubbing his square chin thoughtfully.

She watched him in growing amazement. What could be the mystery back of this new twist of his elusive mind?

He laid his hand on the black bag again, smiled, and turned and faced her with expanding good humor.

"Great scheme, this marryin', Kid! And you believe in it exactly as I do, don't you?"

"How do you mean?" she faltered.

"That it binds and holds both our lives as only Almighty God can bind and hold?"

"Yes - nothing else IS marriage."

"That's what I say, too!"

He placed his hands on her shoulders.

"Great scheme!" he repeated. "I get a pretty girl to work for me for nothing for the balance of my life." He paused and lifted the slender forefinger of his right hand. "And you pledged your pious soul - I memorized the words, every one of them: 'I, Mary, take thee, James, to my wedded husband - TO HAVE AND TO HOLD from this day forward, FOR BETTER, FOR WORSE, for richer, for poorer, in sickness and in health, to love, cherish AND OBEY, TIL DEATH DO US PART, ACCORDING TO GOD'S HOLY ORDINANCE; AND THEREUNTO I GIVE THEE MY TROTH -'"

He paused, lifted his head and smiled grimly: "That's some promise, believe me, Kiddo! 'AND OBEY' - you meant it all, didn't you?"

She would have hedged lightly over that ugly old word which still survived in the ceremony Craddock had used, but for the sinister suggestion in his voice back of the playful banter. He had asked it half in jest, half in earnest. She had caught by the subtle sixth sense the tragic idea in that one word that he was going to hold her to it. The thought was too absurd!

"OBEY - you meant it, didn't you?" he repeated grimly.

A smile played about the corners of her mouth as she answered dreamily:

"Yes - I - I - PROMISED!"

"That's why I set my head on you from the first - you're good and sweet - you're the real thing."

Again she caught the sinister suggestion in his tone and threw him a startled look.

"What has come over you today, Jim?" she asked.

He hesitated and answered carelessly.

"Oh, nothing, Kiddo - just been thinking a little about business. Got to go to work, you know." He returned to the table and touched the bag lightly.

"Watch out now for this bag while I put up the car - and don't forget that curiosity killed the cat."

Quick as a flash, she asked:

"What's in it?"

Jim threw up his hands and laughed.

"Didn't I tell you that curiosity killed a cat?" He pointed to the skin on the wall. "That's what stretched that wild-cat's hide up there! She got too near the old musket!"

"Anyhow, I'm not afraid of her end - what's in it?"

Jim scratched his red head and looked at her thoughtfully.

"You asked me that once before today, didn't you?"

"Yes -"

"Well, it's a little secret of mine. Take my advice - put your hand on it, but not in it."

Again the sinister look and tone chilled her.

"I don't like secrets between us, Jim," she said.

She looked at the bag reproachfully, and he watched her keenly - then laughed.

"I'd as well tell you and be done with it; you'll go in it anyhow."

She tossed her head with a touch of angry pride. He took her hand, led her across the room and placed it on the valise.

"I've got five thousand dollars in gold in that bag."

She drew back, surprised beyond the power of speech.

"And I'm going to give it to this old woman -"

To her - why?" she gasped.

"She's my mother."

"Your MOTHER?"

"Yes."

"I - I - thought - you told me she was dead."

"No. I said that I didn't know who she was."

He paused, and a queer brooding look crept into his face.

"I haven't seen her since I was a little duffer three years old.

This room and these wild crags and trees come back to me now - just a glimpse of them here and there. I've always remembered them. I thought I'd dreamed it -"

"You remember - how wonderful!" she breathed reverently. She understood now, and the clouds lifted.

"The skunk I called my daddy," Jim went on thoughtfully, "took me to New York. He said that my mother deserted me when I was a kid. I believed him at first. But when he beat me and kicked me into the streets, I knew he was a liar. When I got grown I began to think and wonder about her. I hired a lawyer that knew my daddy, and he found her here -"

With a cry of joy, she seized his arms:

"Tell her quick! Oh, you're big and fine and generous, Jim - and I knew it! They said that you were a brute. I knew they lied. Tell her quick!"

He lifted his hand in protest.

"Nope - I'm going to put up a little job on the old girl - show her the money tonight, get her wild at the sight of it - and give it to her Christmas morning. We've only a few hours to wait -"

"Oh, give it to her now - Jim! Give it to her now!"

He shook his head and walked to the door.

"I want to say something to her first and give her time to think it over. Look out for the bag, and I'll bring in the things."

He swung the rough board door wide, slammed it and disappeared in the darkness.

The young wife watched the bag a moment with consuming curiosity. She had fiercely resented his insulting insinuations at her curiosity, and yet she was wild to look at that glowing pile of gold inside and picture the old woman's joyous surprise.

Her hand touched the lock carelessly and drew back as if her finger had been burned. She put her hands behind her and crossed the room.

"I won't be so weak and silly!" she cried fiercely.

She heard Jim cranking the car. It would take him five minutes more to start it, get it under the shed and bring in the suit-case and robes.

"Why shouldn't I see it!" she exclaimed. "He has told me about it." She hesitated and struggled for a moment, quickly walked back to the bag and touched the spring. It yielded instantly.

"Why, it's not even locked!" she cried in tones of surprise at her silly scruples.

Her hand had just touched the gold when Nance entered.

She snapped the bag and smiled at the old woman carelessly. What a sweet surprise she would have tomorrow morning!

Nance crossed slowly, glancing once at the girl wistfully as if she wanted to say something friendly, and then, alarmed at her presumption, hurried on into the little shed-room.

Mary waited until she returned.

"Room's all ready in thar, ma'am," she drawled, passing into the kitchen without a pause.

"All right - thank you," Mary answered.

She quickly opened the bag, thrust her hand into the gold and withdrew it, holding a costly green-leather jewelry-case of

Thomas Dixon

exquisite workmanship. There could be no mistake about its value.

With a cry of joy, she started back, staring at the little box.

"Another surprise! And for me! Oh, Jim, man, you're glorious! My Christmas present, of course! I mustn't look at it - I won't!"

She pushed the case from her toward the bag and drew it back again.

"What's the difference? I'll take one little, tiny peep."

She touched the spring and caught her breath. A string of pearls fit for the neck of a princess lay shining in its soft depths. She lifted them with a sigh of delight. Her eye suddenly rested on a stanza of poetry scrawled on the satin lining in the trembling hand of an old man she had known.

She dropped the pearls with a cry of terror. Her face went white, and she gasped for breath. The jewel- case in her hand she had seen before. It had belonged to the old gentleman who lived in the front room on the first floor of her building in the days when it was a boarding house. The wife he had idolized was long ago dead. This string of pearls from her neck the old man had worshiped for years. The stanza from "The Rosary" he had scrawled in the lining one day in Mary's presence. He had moved uptown with the landlady. Two months ago a burglar had entered his room, robbed and shot him.

"It's impossible - impossible!" she gasped. "Oh, dear God - it's impossible! Of course the burglar pawned them, and Jim bought them without knowing. Of course! My nerves are on edge today - how silly of me -"

Jim's footsteps suddenly sounded on the porch, and she thrust the jewel-case back into the bag with desperate effort to pull herself together.

CHAPTER XVI

THE AWAKENING

For a moment she felt the foundations of the moral and physical world sinking beneath her feet. Dizziness swept her senses. She gripped the table, leaning heavily against it, her eye watching the door with feverish terror for Jim's appearance.

She had never fainted in her life. It was absurd, but the room was swimming now in a dim blur. Again she gripped the table and set her teeth. She simply would not give up. Why should she leap to the worst possible explanation of the jewels? The hatred of old Ella for Jim and the furious antagonism of Jane Anderson had poisoned her mind, after all. It was infamous that she could suspect her husband of crime merely because two silly women didn't like him.

He could explain the jewels. He, of course, asked no questions of the pawn-broker. They were probably sold at auction and he bought them.

It seemed an eternity from the time Jim's foot step echoed on the little porch until he pushed the door open and hastily entered, his arms piled with lap-robes, coats and the dress-suit case in his hand.

He walked with quick, firm step, threw the coats and robes on the couch and placed the suit-case at its head. He hadn't turned toward her and his face was still in profile while he removed the gloves from his pockets, threw them on the robes, and drew the scarlet woolen neckpiece from his throat.

She was studying him now with new terror-stricken eyes. Never had she seen his jaw look so big and brutal. Never had the droop of his eyelids suggested such menace. Never had the contrast of his slender hands and feet suggested such hideous possibilities.

"Merciful God! No! No!" she kept repeating in her soul while her dilated eyes stared at him in sheer horror of the suggestion which the jewels had roused.

She drew a deep breath and strangled the idea by her will.

"I'll at least be as fair as a jury," she thought grimly. "I'll not condemn him without a hearing."

Jim suddenly became aware of the menace of her silence. She had not moved a muscle, spoken or made the slightest sound since he had entered. He had merely taken in the room at a glance and had seen her standing in precisely the same place beside the table.

He saw now that she was leaning heavily against it.

He raised his head and faced her with a sudden, bold stare, and his voice rang in tones of sharp command.

"Well?"

She tried to speak and failed. She had not yet sufficiently mastered her emotions.

"What's the matter?" he growled.

"Jim -" she gasped.

He took a step toward her with set teeth.

"You've been in that bag - Well?"

Her face was white, her voice husky.

"Those jewels, Jim -"

A cunning smile played about his mouth and he shook his head.

"I tried to keep my little secret from you till Christmas morning; but you're on to my curves now, Kiddo, and I'll have to 'fess up -"

"You bought them for me?" she asked with trembling eagerness.

"Who else do you reckon I'd buy 'em for? I was going to surprise you, too, tomorrow morning. You've spoiled the fun."

She had slipped close to his side and he could hear her quick intake of breath.

"That's - so - sweet of you, Jim. I'm sorry - I - spoiled the surprise - you'd - planned -"

"Oh, what's the difference!" he broke in carelessly. "It's all the same five minutes after, anyhow. Well, don't you like 'em? Why don't you say something?"

"They're wonderful, Jim. Where - where - did you buy them?"

He held her gaze in silence for an instant and fenced.

"Isn't that a funny question, Kiddo?" he said in low tones. "I once heard the old man I worked with in the shop say that you shouldn't look a gift horse in the mouth."

"I just want to know," she insisted.

"I'm not going to tell you!" he said with a dry laugh.

"Why not?"

"Because you keep asking."

"You wish to tease me?"

"Maybe."

"Please!"

"Why do you want to know? Are you afraid they're fakes?"

"No, they're beautiful - they're wonderful."

"Well, if you don't want them," he broke in angrily, "I'll keep them. I'll sell them."

"Don't tease me, Jim!" she begged. "I don't mind if you bought them at a pawn-shop - if that's why you won't tell me. That is the reason, isn't it? Honestly, isn't it?"

She asked the question with eager intensity. She had persuaded herself that it was so and the horror had been lifted. She pressed close with smiling, trembling lips:

"I don't mind that, Jim! You got them from a pawn-broker, of course, didn't you?"

He looked at her with a puzzled expression and hesitated.

"Didn't you?" she repeated.

"No - I didn't!" was the curt answer.

"You didn't?" she echoed feebly.

"No!"

With a quick breath she unconsciously drew back and he glared at her angrily.

"Say, what'ell's the matter with you, anyhow? Have you gone crazy?"

"You - won't - tell me - where you bought them?" she asked slowly.

He faced her squarely and spoke with deliberate contempt:

"It's - none - of your business!"

She held his gaze with steady determination.

"That string of pearls belongs to the man who once lived in the front room of my old building in New York. He moved uptown with my landlady. A few months ago a burglar robbed and shot him -"

She stopped, seized his arm and cried with strangling horror:

"Jim! Jim! Where did you get them?"

"Now I know you've gone crazy! You don't suppose that's the only string of pearls in the world, do you? Did you count 'em? Did you weigh 'em?"

"Where did you get them?" she demanded.

"What put it into your head that that string of pearls belonged to your old boarder?"

"I saw him write the stanza of poetry on the satin lining of that case. I've heard him recite it over and over again in his piping voice: `Each bead a pearl - my rosary!' I KNOW that they belonged to him!"

His mouth twitched angrily and he faced her, speaking with

cold, brutal frankness.

"I might keep on lying to you, Kiddo, and get away with it. But what's the use? You've got to know. It's just as well now - I did that job - Yes!"

Her face blanched.

"You - a - burglar - a murderer!"

Jim followed her with quick, angry gestures.

"All I wanted was his money! He fought - it was his life or mine -"

"A murderer!"

"I just went after his money - I tell you - besides, he didn't die; he got well. If he'd kept still he wouldn't have lost his pearls and he wouldn't have been hurt -"

"And I stood up for you against them all!" she answered in a dazed whisper. "They told me - Jane Anderson with brutal frankness, Ella with the heart-rending, timid confession of her own tragic life - they told me that you were bad. I said they were liars. I said that they envied our happiness. I believed that you were big and brave and fine. I stood by you and married you!"

She paused and looked at him steadily. In a rush of suppressed passion she seized his arm with a violence that caused his heavy eyelids to lift in amused surprise.

"Oh, Jim - it's not true! It's not true - it's not true! For God's sake, tell me that you're joking! - that you're teasing me! You can't mean it! I won't believe it - I won't believe it!"

Her head sank until it rested piteously against his breast. He stood with his face turned awkwardly away and then moved his body until she was forced to stand erect.

He touched her shoulder gently and spoke soothingly:

"Come, now, Kid, don't take on so. I'll quit the business when I make my pile."

She drew back instinctively and he followed:

"I'll never touch another penny of yours. There's blood on it!"

"Rot!" he went on soothingly. "It's good Wall Street cash - got it exactly like they got theirs - got it because I was quicker and smarter than the fellow that had it. I use a jimmy, they use a ticker - that's all the difference."

She drew her figure to its full height.

"I'm going - Jim -"

"Where?"

His voice rasped like a file against steel.

"Home!"

"Your home's with me."

"I won't live with a thief!"

He stepped squarely before her and spoke with deliberate menace.

"You're - not - going!"

"Get out of my way!" she cried defiantly.

His big jaw closed with a snap and his figure became rigid. The candle's yellow light threw a strange glare on his face, convulsed. The blue flames of hell were in the glitter of his steel eyes.

Her heart sank in a dull wave of terror. She tried to gauge the depth of his brutal rage. There was no standard by which to measure it. She had never seen that look in his face before. His whole being was transformed by some sinister power.

She was afraid to move, but her mind was alert in this moment of supreme trial. She hadn't used her last weapon yet. The fact that he held her with such terrible determination was proof of the spell she had cast over him. She might save him. He couldn't have been a criminal long. She formed her new battle-line with quick decision.

CHAPTER XVII

THE SURRENDER

How long she gazed into the convulsed face of the man who had squared himself before her, mattered little measured by the tick of the watch in her belt. Into the mental anguish endured a life's agony had been pressed. It could not have been more than twenty seconds, and yet it marked the birth of a new being within the soul of a woman. She had been searching only for her own happiness. The search had entangled another in the meshes of her life. Too much had been lived in the past two weeks to be undone by a word and forgotten in a day. She had attempted, coward-like, to run.

She saw now in the consuming flame of a great sorrow that the man before her had some rights which the purest woman must reckon with. He might be a burglar. At least it was her duty to try to save him from himself. Her surrender of the past weeks was a tie that would bind them through all eternity. There was no chemistry of earth or heaven or hell that could erase its memories. Her life was no longer her own - this man's was bound with hers. She must face the facts. She would make one honest, brave effort to save him. To do this she would give all without reservation - pride must be cast to the winds.

Her voice suddenly changed to tears.

"Oh, Jim, you do love me, don't you?"

　　　　Thomas Dixon

His body slowly relaxed, his eyes shifted, and he shrugged his square shoulders.

"What'ell did I marry you for?"

"Tell me - do you?" she demanded.

"You know that I love you. What do you ask me such a fool question for? I love you with a love that can kill. Do you hear me? That's why you're not going anywhere without me."

There was no mistaking the depth of his passion. She trembled to realize its power and yet it was the lever by which she must move him.

"Then you've got to give this life up. You're young and brave and strong. You can earn an honest living. You haven't been in this long - I feel it, I know it. Have you?"

"No!"

"How long?"

"Eight months."

"Oh, Jim, dear, you must give it up now for my sake. I'll work with you and work for you. I'll teach, I'll sew, I'll scrub, I'll slave for you day and night - if you're only clean and honest."

He turned on her fiercely.

"Cut it, Kid - cut it! I'm out for the stuff now. I'm going to get rich and I'm going to get rich QUICK - that's all that's the matter with me!"

"But, Jim," she broke in tenderly - "you did earn an honest living. Your workshop proves that."

"I've used that to improve my tools and melt the swag the past year. The shop's all right."

"But you did make a successful invention?"

"You bet I did," he answered savagely, "and that's why I quit the business. Three years ago I took down a big automobile and worked out an improvement in the transmission that settled the question of heavy draft machines. I took it to a lawyer in Wall Street and he took it to a man that had money. Between the two of 'em, they didn't do a thing to me! They were going to put my patent on the market and make me a millionaire. God, I was crazy -"

He paused and squared his shoulders with a deep breath.

"They put it on the market all right and they made some millionaires - but I wasn't one of 'em, Kiddo! They got me to sign a paper that skinned me out of every dollar as slick as you can pull an eel through your fingers. I hired another lawyer and gave him half he could get to beat 'em. He fought like a tiger and two days before I met you he got his verdict and they paid it - just ten thousand dollars. Think of it - ten thousand dollars! And each of them got a million cash. They sold it outright for two millions and a half. My lawyer got five thousand dollars, and I got five thousand dollars. That's mine, anyhow. It's in that bag there. I'm working on a new set of tools now in my shop. I'm going to get that money back from the two thieves who stole it from me by law. I'll take it by force, the way they took it. If I can croak them both in the fight - well, there'll be two thieves less to rob honest men and women, that's all."

"Oh, Jim!" Mary gasped, lifting a trembling hand to her throat as if to tear open her collar. "You're mad. You don't know what you're saying -"

"Don't fool yourself, Kiddo," he interrupted fiercely. "My eyes are open now, and I've got a level head back of 'em, too. I've doped it all out. You ought to 'a' heard that lawyer give me a few lessons in business when he'd skinned me and salted my hide. He was good-natured and confidential. He seemed to love me. `Business is war, sonny,' he piped, between the puffs of the big Havana cigar he was smoking - `war! war to the knife! We got you off your guard and put the knife into you at the right minute - that's all. Don't take it so hard! Invent something else and keep your eyes peeled. You ought to love us for giving you an education in business early in life. You're young. You won't have to learn your lesson again. Go to work, sonny, in your shop, and turn out another new tool for the advancement of trade!'"

He paused and smiled grimly.

"I've done it, too! I've just finished a little invention that'll crack any safe in New York in twenty minutes after I touch it."

He broke into a dry laugh, sat down and deliberately lighted a fresh cigarette.

She studied his face with beating heart. Was he lost beyond all hope of reformation? Or was this the boyish bravado of an amateur criminal poisoned by the consciousness of wrong? She tried to think. She felt the red blood pounding through her heart and beating against her brain in suffocating waves of despair.

In vivid flashes the scene of her marriage but two weeks ago, came back in tormenting memories. The solemn words she had spoken kept ringing like the throb of a funeral bell far up in the star-lit heavens -

"I, MARY ADAMS, TAKE THEE, JAMES ANTHONY, TO MY WEDDED HUSBAND, TO HAVE AND TO HOLD . . . FOR BETTER FOR WORSE, FOR RICHER FOR POORER, IN SICKNESS AND IN HEALTH, TO LOVE, CHERISH, AND TO OBEY, TILL DEATH DO US PART, ACCORDING TO GOD'S HOLY ORDIN-ANCE; AND THERETO I GIVE THEE MY TROTH."

The last solemn prayer kept ringing its deep-toned message over all -

"GOD THE FATHER, GOD THE SON, GOD THE HOLY GHOST, BLESS, PRESERVE, AND KEEP YOU; THE LORD MERCIFULLY WITH HIS FAVOR LOOK UPON YOU, AND FILL YOU WITH ALL SPIRITUAL BENEDICTION AND GRACE; THAT YE MAY SO LIVE TOGETHER IN THIS LIFE, THAT IN THE WORLD TO COME YE MAY HAVE LIFE EVERLASTING. AMEN."

In a sudden rush of desperate pity for herself and the man to whom she was bound, she dropped on her knees by his side, slipped her arms about his neck and clung to him, sobbing.

"Oh, Jim, Jim, man," she whispered hoarsely. "I can't see you sink into hell like this! Have you no real love in your heart for the woman who has given all? Have mercy on me! Have mercy! You can't mean the hideous things you've just said! You've been crazed by your losses. You're just a boy yet. Life is all before you. You're only twenty-four. I'm just twenty-four. We can both begin anew. I've never lived until these past weeks - neither have you. You couldn't drag me down into a life of crime -"

Her head sank and her voice choked into silence. He made no movement of his hand to soothe her. His voice was not persuasive. It was hard and cold.

"I'm not asking you to help me on any of my jobs," he said. "I'm the financier of the family. You can say the prayers and keep house."

"Knowing that you are a criminal? That your hands are stained with human blood?"

"Why not?" he snapped, the blue blaze flashing again in his eyes. "Suppose you were the wife of the gentlemanly lawyer-thief who robbed me, using the law instead of a jimmy - would you bother your little head about my business? Does his wife ask him where he got it? Does anybody know or care? He lives on Fifth Avenue now. He bought a palace up there the day after he got my money. We passed it on the way to the Park the day I met you. A line of carriages was standing in front and finely dressed women were running up the red carpet that led down the stoop and under the canopy to the curb. Did any of the gay dames who smiled and smirked at that thief's wife ask how he got the money to buy the house? Not much. Would they have cared if they had known? They'd have called him a shrewd lawyer - that's all! Do you reckon his wife worries about such tricks of trade? Why should mine worry?"

She gripped his hand with desperate pleading.

"Oh, Jim, dear, you can't be a criminal at heart! I wouldn't have loved you if it had been true. I can't believe it! I won't believe it. You're posing. You don't mean this. You can't mean it. You're going to return every dishonest dollar that you've taken."

"You don't know what you're talking about!"

He closed his jaw with a snap and leaned close in eager, tense excitement.

"Do you know how much junk I've piled into a little box in my shop the past three months?"

"I don't care - I don't want to know!"

"You've got to care - you've got to know now! It's worth a hundred thousand dollars, do you hear? A hundred thousand dollars! It would take me a life-time to earn that on a salary. In two weeks after we get back to New York with my new invention that lawyer advised me to make, I'll go through his house - I'll open his safe, I'll take every diamond, every pearl and every scrap of stolen jewelry his wife's wearing. And I won't leave a fingerprint on the window sill. I've got two of his servants working for me.

"In six months I'll be worth half a million. In a year I'll pull off the big haul I'm planning and I'll be a millionaire. We'll retire from business then - just like they did. We'll build our marble palace down at Bay Ridge and our yacht will nod in the harbor. We'll spend our summers in Europe when we like and every snob and fool in New York will fall over himself to meet me. And every woman will envy my wife. I'm young, Kiddo, but I've cut my eye teeth. You've just been born. I'm running the business end of this thing. You think you can reform me. You can - AFTER I'VE MADE OUR PILE. I'll join the church then and sing louder than that lawyer. But if you think you're going to stop my business career at this stage of the game - forget it, forget it!"

He sprang up with a quick movement of his tense body and threw her off. She rose and watched his restless steps as he paced the floor. Her mind was numb as if from a mortal blow. She brushed the tangled ringlets of brown hair back from her forehead, drew the handkerchief from her belt and wiped the perspiration from her brow.

Before she could gather the strength to speak, he wheeled suddenly and confronted her:

"I've known from the first, Kiddo, that you're not the kind to help in this business. I don't expect it. I don't ask it. I need a ranch like this down here for storage. I'm going to take the old woman into partnership with me."

She started back in an instinctive recoil of horror.

"Your MOTHER?"

He nodded.

"Yep!"

She drew a step nearer and peered into his set face.

"YOU WILL MAKE YOUR OWN MOTHER A CRIMINAL?"

"Sure!" he growled. "That's what I came down here for."

"She won't do it!"

"She won't, eh?" he sneered. "Look at this hog pen!"

He swept the bare, wretched cabin with a gesture of contempt and shrugged his shoulders.

"Look at the rags she's wearing," he went on savagely. "When we talk it over tonight with that five thousand dollars in gold shining in her eyes - I'm going to show her a lot o' things she never saw before, Kiddo - take it from me!"

She answered in slow, even tones:

"I can't live with you, Jim."

The blue flames beneath the drooping eyelids were leaping now in the yellow glare of the candle's rays. The muscles of his body were knotted. His voice came from his throat a low growl.

"Do you know who you're fooling with?"

The blood of a clean life flamed in her cheeks and nerved her with reckless daring. Her figure stiffened and her voice rang with defiant scorn:

"Yes. I know at last - a thief who would drag his own mother down to hell with him!"

Not a muscle of his powerful body moved; his face was a stolid mask. He threw his words slowly through his teeth:

"Now you listen to me. You're my wife. I didn't invent this marriage game. I played it as I found it. And that's the way you're going to play it. You're good and sweet and clean - I like that kind, and I won't have no other. You're mine. MINE, do you hear! Mine for life - body and soul - 'FOR BETTER FOR WORSE, FOR RICHER FOR POORER, IN SICKNESS AND IN HEALTH, TO LOVE, CHERISH' -"

He paused and thrust his massive jaw squarely into her face:

"`- AND OBEY!'" he hissed, "`UNTIL DEATH DO US PART, ACCORDING TO GOD'S HOLY ORDINANCE' - you said it, didn't you?"

"Yes -"

"Well?"

She turned from him with sudden aversion:

"I didn't know what you were -"

"Nobody ever knows BEFORE they're married!" he broke in savagely. "You took your chances. I took mine - 'FOR BETTER FOR WORSE.' We'll just say now it's for worse and let it go at that!"

The little body stiffened.

"I'll die first!"

He held her gaze without words, searching the depths of her being with the cold, blue flame in his drooping eyes. If she were bluffing, it was easy. She could talk her head off for all he cared. If she meant it, he might have his hands full unless he mastered the situation at once and for all time.

There was no sign of yielding to his iron will. An indomitable soul had risen in her frail body and defied him. His decision was instantaneous.

"Oh, you'll die sooner than live with me - eh?"

There was something hideous in the cold venom with which he drawled the words. Her heart fairly stopped its beating. With the last ounce of courage left, she held her place and answered:

"Yes!"

With the sudden crouch of a tiger he drew his clenched fist to strike.

"Forget it!"

She sprang back with terror, her body trembling in pitiful weakness.

"You snivelling little coward!" he growled.

"Oh, Jim, Jim," she faltered, - "you - you - couldn't strike me!"

A step nearer and he stood over her, his big, flat head thrust forward, his eyes gleaming, his muscles knotted in blind rage.

"No - I won't STRIKE you," he whispered. "I'll just KILL you - that's all!"

With the leap of an infuriated beast he sprang on her and his sharp fingers gripped her throat.

The world went black and she felt herself sinking into a bottomless abyss. With maniac energy she tore his hands from her throat and the warm blood streamed from the gash his nails had torn.

Jim! Jim! For God's sake!" she moaned in abject terror.

With a sullen growl, his fingers, sharp as a leopard's claw, found her neck again and closed with a grip that sent the blood surging to her brain and her eyes starting from their sockets.

The one hideous thought that flashed through her mind was that he was going to plunge his claws into her eyes and blind her for life. He could hold her his prisoner then. She made a last desperate struggle for breath, her hands relaxed, she drooped and sank to the couch toward which he had hurled her in the first rush of his assault.

He lifted her and choked the slender neck again to make sure, loosed his hands and the limp body dropped on the couch and was still.

He stood watching her in silence, his arms at his side.

"Damned little fool!" he muttered. "I had to give you that lesson. The sooner the better!"

He waited with contemptuous indifference until she slowly recovered consciousness. She lay motionless for a long time and then slowly opened her eyes.

Thank God! They had not been gouged out as poor Ella's. She didn't mind the warm blood that soaked her collar and ran down her neck. If he would only spare her eyes. Blindness had been her one unspeakable terror. She closed her eyes again and silently prayed for strength. Her strength was gone. Wave after wave of sickening, cowardly terror swept her prostrate soul. She could feel his sullen presence - his body with its merciless strength towering above her. She dared not look. She knew that he was watching her with cruel indifference. A single cry, a single word and he might thrust his claw into her eyes and the light of the world would go out forever.

Her terror was too hideous; she could endure it no longer. She must move. She must try to save herself. She lifted her head and caught his steady, venomous gaze.

A quick, sliding movement of abject fear and she was erect, facing him and backing away silently.

He followed with even step, his gaze holding her as the eyes of a snake its victim. She would not let him know her terror of blindness. She preferred death a thousand times. If he would only kill her outright it was all the mercy she would ask.

"You - won't - kill - me - Jim!" she sobbed. "Please - please, don't kill me!"

He lifted his sharp finger and followed her toward the shed-room door, his voice the triumphant cry of an eagle above his prey.

"`FOR BETTER, FOR WORSE - UNTIL DEATH DO US PART!'"

Her heart gave a bound of cowardly joy. He had relented. He would not blind her. She could live. She was young and life was sweet.

She tried to smile her surrender through her tears as she backed slowly away from his ominous finger.

"Yes, I'll try - Jim. I'll try - `UNTIL DEATH DO US PART - UNTIL DEATH - UNTIL DEATH -'"

Her voice broke into a flood of tears as she blindly felt her way through the door and into the darkened room.

He paused on the threshold, held the creaking board shutter in his hand and broke into a laugh.

"The world ain't big enough for you to get away from me, Kiddo. Good night - a good little wife now and it's all right!"

CHAPTER XVIII

TO THE NEW GOD

Jim closed the door of the little shed-room with a bang, and stood listening a moment to the sobs inside.

"'UNTIL DEATH DO US PART,' Kiddo!" he laughed grimly.

He turned back into the room and saw Nance standing at the opposite entrance between the calico curtains, an old, battered, flickering lantern in her hand. A white wool shawl was thrown over the gray head and fell in long, filmy waves about her thin figure. Her deep-sunken eyes were exaggerated in the dim light of lantern and candle. She smiled wanly.

He stopped short at the apparition; a queer shiver of superstitious fear shook him. The white form of Death suddenly and noiselessly appearing from the darkness could not have been more uncanny. He had wondered vaguely while the quarrel with his wife was progressing, what had become of his mother. As the fight had reached its height, he had forgotten her.

She looked at him, blinking her eyes and trying to smile.

"Where the devil have you been, old gal?" he asked nervously.

"Nowhere," she answered evasively.

"You've been mighty quiet on the trip anyhow. I see you've brought something back from nowhere."

Nance glanced down at the jug she carried in her left hand and laughed.

"What is it?" he asked.

"Nothin' -"

"Nothin' from nowhere sounds pretty good to me when I see it in a brown jug on Christmas Eve. You're all right, old gal! I was just going to ask if you had a little mountain dew. You're a mind reader. I'll bet the warehouse you keep that stored in is some snug harbor - eh?"

"They ain't never found it yit!" she giggled.

"And I'll bet they won't - bully for you!"

She took down a tin cup from a shelf and placed it beside the jug.

"Another glass, sweetheart -"

The old woman stared at him in surprise, walked to the shelf and brought another tin cup.

"What do ye want with two?" she asked in surprise.

Jim moved toward the stool beside the table.

"Sit down."

"Me?"

"Sure. Let's be sociable. It's Christmas Eve, isn't it?"

"Yeah!" Nance answered cheerfully, taking her seat and

glancing timidly at her guest.

Jim seized the jug, poured out two drinks of corn whiskey, handed her one and raised his:

"Well, here's lookin' at you, old girl."

He paused, lowered his cup and smiled.

"But say, give me a toast." He nodded toward the shed-room. "I'm on my honeymoon, you know."

His hostess laughed timidly and glanced at him from the corners of her eyes. She wished to be sociable and make up as best she could for her rudeness on their arrival.

"I ain't never heard but one fur honeymooners," she said softly.

"Let's have it. I've never heard a toast for honeymooners in my life. It'll be new to me - fire away!"

Nance fumbled her faded dress with her left hand and laughed again.

"'May ye live long and prosper an' all yer troubles be LITTLE ONES!'"

She laughed aloud at the old, worm-eaten joke and Jim joined.

"Bully! Bully, old girl - bully!"

He lifted his cup and drained it at one draught and Nance did the same.

He seized the jug and poured another drink for each.

"Once more -"

He leaned across the table.

"And here's one for you." He squared his body and lifted his cup:

"To all your little ones - no matter how big they are!"

Jim drained his liquor without apparently noticing her agitation, though he was watching her keenly from the corner of his eye.

The cup she held was lowered slowly until the whiskey poured over her dress and on the floor. Her thin figure drooped pathetically and her voice was the faintest sob:

"I - I - ain't got - none!"

"I heard you had a boy," Jim said carelessly.

The drooping figure shot upright as if a bolt of lightning had swept her. She stared at him in tense silence, trying to gather her wits before she answered.

"Who told you anything about me?" she demanded sternly.

"A fellow in New York," Jim continued with studied care-lessness - "said he used to live down here."

"He LIVED down here?" she repeated blankly.

"Yep - come now, loosen up and tell us about the kid."

"There ain't nuthin' ter tell - he's dead," she cried pathetically.

"He said you deserted the child and left him to starve."

"He said that?" she growled.

"Yep."

He was silent again and watched her keenly.

She fumbled her dress and glanced nervously across the table as if afraid to ask more. Unable to wait for him to speak, she cried nervously at last:

"Well - well - what else did he say?"

"That he took the little duffer to New York and raised him."

"RAISED him?"

She fairly screamed the words, springing to her feet trembling from head to foot.

"Till he was big enough to kick into the streets to shuffle for himself."

"The scoundrel said he was dead."

Her voice was far away and sank into dreamy silence. She was living the hideous, lonely years again with a heart starved for love.

Jim's voice broke the spell:

"Then you didn't desert him?" The man's eyes held hers steadily.

She stared at him blankly and spoke with rushing indignation:

"Desert him - my baby - my own flesh and blood? There's never been a minute since I looked into his eyes that I wouldn't 'a' died fur him."

She paused and sobbed.

"He had such pretty eyes, stranger. They looked like your'n - only they wuz puttier and bluer."

She lifted her faded dress, brushed the tears from her cheeks and went on rapidly:

"When I found his drunken brute of a daddy was a liar and had another wife, I wouldn't live with him. He tried to make me but I kicked him out of the house - and he stole the boy to get even with me." Her voice broke, she dropped her head and choked back the tears. "He did get even with me, too - he did," she sobbed.

Jim watched her in silence until the paroxysm had spent itself.

"You think you'd know this boy now if you found him?"

She bent close, her breath coming in quick gasps.

"My God, mister, do you think I COULD find him?"

"He lives in New York; his name is Jim Anthony."

"Yes - yes?" she said in a dazed way. "He called hisself Walter Anthony - he wuz a stranger from the North and my boy's name was Jim." She paused and bent eagerly across the table. "New York's an awful big place, ain't it?"

"Some town, old gal, take it from me."

"COULD I find him?"

"If you've got money enough. You said you'd know him. How?"

"I'd know him!" she answered eagerly. "The last quarrel we had was about a mark on his neck. He wuz a spunky little one. You couldn't make him cry. His devil of a daddy used to stick pins in him and laugh because he wouldn't cry. The last dirty trick he tried was what ended it all. He pushed a live cigar agin his little neck until I smelled it burnin' in the next room. I knocked him down with a chair, drove him from the house and told him I'd kill him if he ever put his foot inside the door agin.

He stole my boy the next night - but he'll carry that scar to his grave."

"You'd love this boy now if you found him in New York as bad as his father ever was?" Jim asked with a curious smile.

"Yes - he's mine!" was the quick, firm answer.

Jim watched her intently.

"I looked Death in the face for him," she went on fiercely. "I'd dive to the bottom o' hell to find him if I knowed he wuz thar - But what's the use to talk; that devil killed him! I've waked up many a night stranglin' with a dream when I seed the drunken brute burnin' an' beatin' an' torturin' him to death. The feller you've heard about ain't him. 'Tain't no use to make me hope an' then kill me -"

"He's not dead, I tell you. I know."

Jim's voice rang with conviction so positive the old woman's breath came in quick gasps and she smiled through her eager tears.

"And I MIGHT find him?"

"IF you've got money enough! Money can do anything in this world."

He opened the black bag, thrust both hands into it and threw out a handful of yellow coin which he allowed to pour through his fingers and rattle into a tin plate which had been left on the table.

Her eyes sparkled with avarice.

Thomas Dixon

"It's your'n - all your'n?" she breathed hungrily.

"I'm taking it down South to invest for a fool who thinks" - he stopped and laughed - "who thinks it's bad luck to keep money that's stained with blood -"

Nance started back.

"Got blood on it?"

Jim spoke in confidential appeal.

"That wouldn't make any difference to you, would it?"

She shook her gray locks and glanced at the pile of yellow metal, hungrily.

"I - I wouldn't like it with blood marks!"

He lifted a handful of coin, clinked it musically in his hands and held it in his open palms before her.

"Look! Look at it close! You don't see any blood marks on it, do you?"

Her eyes devoured it.

"No."

He seized her hand, thrust a half-dozen pieces into it and closed her thin fingers over it.

"Feel of it - look at it!"

Her hands gripped the gold. She breathed quickly, broke into a laugh, caught herself in the middle of it, and lapsed suddenly into silence.

"Feels good, don't it?" he laughed.

Nance grinned, her uneven, discolored gleaming ominously in the flicker of the candle.

"Don't it?" he repeated.

"Yeah!"

He lifted another handful and threw it in the air, catching it again.

"That's the stuff that makes the world go 'round. There's your only friend, old girl! Others promise well - but in the scratch they fail."

"Yeah - when the scratch comes they fail!" Nance echoed.

"Money never fails!" Jim continued eagerly. "It's the god that knows no right or wrong -"

He touched the pile in the plate and drew the bag close for her to see.

"How much do you guess is there?"

Nance gazed greedily into the open bag and looked again at the shining heap in the plate.

"I dunno - a million, I reckon."

The man laughed.

"Not quite that much! But enough to make you rich for life - IF you had it."

The old woman turned away pathetically and shook her gray head.

"I wouldn't have to work no more, would I?"

Her thin hands touched the faded, dirty dress.

"And I could buy me a decent dress," her voice sank to a whisper, "and I could find my boy."

"You bet you could!" Jim exclaimed. "There's just one god in this world now, old girl - the Almighty Dollar!"

He paused and leaned close, persuasively:

"Suppose now, the man that got that money had to kill a fool to take it - what of it? You don't get big money any other way. A burglar watches his chance, takes his life in his hands and drills his way into a house. He finds a fool there who fights. It's not his fault that the man was born a fool, now is it?"

"Mebbe not -"

"Of course not. A burglar kills but one to get his pile, and then only because he must, in self-defence. A big gambling capitalist corners wheat, raises the price of bread and starves a hundred thousand children to death to make his. It's not stained with blood. Every dollar is soaked in it! Who cares?"

"Yeah - who cares?" Nance growled fiercely.

Jim smiled at his easy triumph.

"It's dog eat dog and the devil take the hindmost now!"

"That's so - ain't it?" she agreed.

"You bet! Business is business and the best man's the man that gets there. Steal a hundred dollars, you go to the penitentiary - foolish! Don't do it. Steal a million and go to the Senate!"

"Yeah!" Nance laughed.

"Money - money for its own sake," he rushed on savagely -

"right or wrong. That's all there is in it today, old girl - take it from me!"

He paused and his smile ended in a sneer.

"Man shall eat bread in the sweat of his brow? Only fools SWEAT!"

Nance turned her face away, sighed softly, glancing back at Jim furtively.

"I reckon that's so, too. Have another drink, stranger?"

She poured another cup of whiskey and one for herself. She raised hers as if to drink and deftly threw the contents over her shoulder.

Jim seized the jug and poured again.

"Once more. Come, I've another toast for you. You'll drink this one I know."

He lifted his cup and rose a little unsteadily. Nance stood with uplifted cup watching him.

"As the poet sings," he began with a bow to the old woman:

"France has her lily, England the rose,

Everybody knows where the shamrock grows -

Scotland has her thistle flowerin' on the hill,

But the American Emblem - is a One Dollar Bill!"

He broke into a boisterous laugh.

"How's that, old girl?"

"That's bully, stranger!"

He lifted high his cup.

"We drink to the Almighty Dollar!"

"To the Almighty Dollar!" Nance echoed, clinking her cup against his."

He drained it while she again emptied hers over her shoulder.

"By golly, you're all right, old girl. You're a good fellow!" he cried jovially.

"Yeah - have another?" she urged.

She filled his cup and placed it on his side of the table. His eye had rested on the gold. He ignored the invitation, lifted a handful of gold and dropped it with musical clinking into the plate.

"Blood marks - tommyrot!" he sneered.

"Yeah - tommyrot!" she echoed. "That's what I say, too!"

Jim wagged his head sagely:

"Now you're talking sense, old girl!"

He leaned across the table and pointed his finger straight into her face.

"And don't you forget what I'm tellin' ye tonight - get money, get money!"

He stopped suddenly and a sneer curled his lips.

"Oh I Get it `fairly' - get it `squarely' - but whatever you do - by God! - GET IT!"

His uplifted hand crashed downward and gripped the gold. His fingers slowly relaxed and the coin clinked into the plate.

Nance watched him eagerly.

"Yeah, that's it - get it," she breathed slowly.

Jim lifted his drooping eyes to hers.

"If you've GOT it, you're a god - you can do no wrong. Nobody's goin' to ask you HOW you got it; all they want to know is HAVE you got it!"

"Yeah, nobody's goin' to ask you HOW you got it, Nance repeated, "they just want to know HAVE you got it! Yeah - yeah!"

"You bet!"

Jim's head sank in the first stupor of liquor and he dropped into the chair.

The old woman leaned eagerly over the plate of gold and clutched the coin with growing avarice. Her fingers opened and closed like a bird of prey. She touched it lovingly and held it in her hands a long time watching Jim's nodding head with furtive glances. She dropped a handful of coin into the plate and watched its effect on the drooping head.

He looked up and his eyes fell again.

"Bed-time, I reckon," Nance said.

"Yep - pretty tired. I'll turn in."

The old woman glided sidewise to the table near the kitchen door, picked up the lantern and started to feel her way backwards through the calico curtains.

"See you in the mornin', old gal," Jim drawled - "Christmas mornin' - an' I got somethin' else to tell ye in the mornin' -"

Again his head sank to the table.

"All right, mister - good night!" Nance answered, slowly feeling her way through the opening, watching him intently.

Jim lifted his head and nodded heavily for a moment. His hand slipped from the table and he drew himself up sharply and rose, holding to the table for support.

He picked up the plate of coin, poured it back in the bag, snapped the lock and walked with the bag unsteadily to the couch. He placed the bag under the pillow and pressed the soft feathers down over it, turned back to the table and extinguished the candle by a quick, square blow of his open palm on the flame.

He staggered to the couch, pushed the coats to the floor, dropped heavily, drew the lap-robe over him and in five minutes was sound asleep.

CHAPTER XIX

NANCE'S STOREHOUSE

The cabin was still. Only the broken sobbing of the woman in the little shed-room came faint and low on old Nance's ears.

She slipped from the kitchen into the shadows of a tree near the house and listened until the sobbing ceased.

She crept close to the shed and stood silent and ghost-like beside its daubed walls. Immovable as a cat crouching in the hedge to spring on her prey, she waited until the waning moon had sunk behind the crags. She laid her ear close to a crack in the logs from which she had once pushed the red mud to let in the light. All was still at last. The sobbing had stopped. The young wife was sound asleep.

She had wondered vaguely at first about the crying, but quickly made up her mind that it was only a lover's quarrel. She was glad of it. The girl would bar her door and sulk all night. So much the better. There would be no danger of her entering the living-room where Jim slept.

She would wait a little longer to make sure she was asleep. A half hour passed. The white-shrouded figure stood immovable, her keen ears tuned for the slightest sounds from within.

The stars were shining in unusual brilliance. She could see her way through the shadows even better than in full moon. A wolf was crying again for his mate from a distant crag. She had grown used to his howls. He had come close to her cabin once in the day-time. She had tried to creep on him and show her friendliness. But he had fled in terror at the first glimpse of her dress through the parting underbrush.

An owl was calling from his dead tree-top down the valley. She smiled at his familiar, tremulous call. Her own eyes were wide as his tonight. No sight or sound of Nature among the crags about her cabin had for her spirit any terror. The night was her mantle.

She added to the meager living which she had wrung from her mountain farm by trading with the illicit distillers of the backwoods of Yancey County. Too ignorant to run a distillery of her own, she had stored their goods with such skill that the hiding-place had never been discovered. She loved good whiskey herself. She had tried to find in its fiery depths the dreams of happiness life had so cruelly denied her.

The hiding-place of this whiskey had puzzled the revenue officers of every administration for years. They had watched her house day and night. Not one of them had ever struck the trail to her storehouse.

The game had excited her imagination. She loved its daring and danger. That there was the slightest element of wrong or crime in her association with the moonshiners of her native heath had never for a moment entered her mind. It was no crime to make whiskey. This was the first article of the creed of the true North Carolina mountaineer. They had from the first declared that the tax levied by the Federal Government on the product of their industry was an infamous act of tyranny. They had fought this tyranny for two generations. They would fight it as long as there was breath in their bodies and a single load of powder and buckshot for their rifles.

Nance considered herself a heroine in the pride of her soul for the shrewd and successful defiance she had given the revenue officers for so many years.

She had been too cunning to even allow one of her own people to know the secret of her store house. For that reason it had never been discovered. She always stored the whiskey temporarily in the potato shed or under the cabin floor until night and then alone carried it to the place she had discovered.

She laughed softly at the thought of this deep hiding-place tonight. Its temperature never varied winter or summer. Not a track had ever been left at its door. She might live a hundred years and, unless some spying eye should see her enter, its existence could never be suspected.

She tipped softly into the kitchen, walked to the door of the living-room and listened to the even, heavy breathing of the man on the couch.

Once more the faint echo of a sob in the shed beyond came to her keen ears. She stood for five minutes. It was not repeated. She had only imagined it. The girl was still asleep.

She turned noiselessly back into the kitchen, put a box of matches in her pocket, felt her way to the low shelf on which she had placed the battered lantern, picked it up and shook it to make sure the oil was sufficient.

She stepped lightly into the yard, pushed open the gate of the split-board garden fence, walked along the edge to the corner and selected a spade from the tools that leaned against the boards.

Carrying the spade and unlighted lantern in her left hand, she glided from the yard into the woods. Her right hand before her to feel for underbrush or overhanging bough, she made her way rapidly to the swift-flowing mountain brook.

Arrived at the water whose musical ripple had guided her steps, she removed her shoes and placed them beside a tree. She wore no stockings. The faded skirt she raised and tucked into her belt. She could wade knee deep now without hindrance.

Seizing the spade and lantern, she made her way slowly and carefully downstream for three hundred yards and paused beside a shelving ledge which projected half-way across the brook.

She paused and listened again for full ten minutes, immovable as the rock on which her thin, bony hand rested. The stars were looking, but they could only peep through the network of overhanging trees.

Feeling her way along the rock until the ledge rose beyond her reach, she bent low and waded through a still pool of eddying water straight under the mountain-side for more than a hundred feet. Her extended right hand had felt for the stone ceiling above her head until it ran abruptly out of reach.

She straightened her body and took a deep breath. Ten steps she counted carefully and placed her bare feet on the dry rock beyond the water.

Carefully picking her way up the sloping bank until she reached a stretch of soft earth, she sank to her hands and knees and crawled through an opening less than three feet in height.

"Thar now!" she laughed. "Let 'em find me if they can!"

She lighted her lantern and seated herself on a boulder to rest - one hundred and fifty feet in the depths of a mountain. The cavern was ten feet in height and fifty feet in length. The projecting ledges of rock made innumerable shelves on which a merchant might have displayed his wares.

The old woman was too shrewd for that. Her jugs were carefully planted in the ground behind two fallen boulders, and their hiding-place concealed by a layer of drift which she had gathered from the edge of the water. She had taken this precaution against the day when some curious explorer might stumble on her secret as she had found it hunting ginsing roots in the woods overhead. Her foot had slipped suddenly through a hole in the soft mould. She peered cautiously below and could see no bottom. She dropped a stone and heard it strike in the depths. She made her way down the side of the crag and found the opening through the still eddying waters. The hole through the roof she had long ago plugged and covered with earth and dry leaves.

She carried her lantern and spade to the further end of her storehouse and dug a hole in the earth about two feet in depth. The earth she carefully placed in a heap.

"That's the place!" she giggled excitedly.

She left her lantern burning, dropped again on the soft, mould-covered earth and quickly emerged on the stone banks of the wide, still pool. Her hand high extended above her head, she waded through the water until she touched the heavy ceiling, lowered her body again to a stooping position and rapidly made her way out into the bed of the brook.

She passed eagerly along the babbling path and stopped with sure instinct at the tree beside whose trunk she had placed her shoes.

In five minutes she had made her way through the woods and reached the house. She tipped into the kitchen and stood in the doorway or the living-room watching her sleeping guest. The even breathing assured her that all was well. Her plan couldn't fail. She listened again for the sobs in the shed-room.

She was sure once that she heard them. Five minutes passed and still she was uncertain. To avoid any possible accident she tipped back through the kitchen, circled the house and placed her ear against the crack in the logs.

The girl was sobbing - or was she praying? She crouched beside the wall, waited and listened. The night wind stirred the dead leaves at her feet. She lifted her head with a sudden start, laughed softly and bent again to listen.

CHAPTER XX

TRAPPED

The sobbing in the little room was the only sound that came from one of the grimmest battle-fields from which the soul of a woman ever emerged alive.

To the first rush of cowardly tears Mary had yielded utterly. She had fallen across the high-puffed feather mattress of the bed, shivering in humble gratitude at her escape from the horror of blindness. The grip of his claw-like fingers on her throat came back to her now in sickening waves. The blood was still trickling from the wound which his nails had made when she tore them loose in her first mad fight for breath.

She lifted her body and breathed deeply to make sure her throat was free. God in heaven! Could she ever forget the hideous sinking of body and soul down into the depths of the black abyss! She had seen the face of Death and it was horrible. Life, warm and throbbing, was sweet. She loved it. She hated Death.

Yes - she was a coward. She knew it now, and didn't care.

She sprang to her feet with sudden fear. He might attack her again to make sure that her soul had been completely crushed.

She crept to the door and felt its edges.

"Yes, thank God, there's a place for the bar!" She shivered.

She ran her trembling fingers carefully along the rough logs and found it in the corner. She slipped it cautiously into the iron sockets, staggered to the bed and dropped in grateful assurance of safety for the moment. She buried her face in the pillow to fight back the sobs. How great her fall! She could crawl on her hands and knees to Jane Anderson now and beg for protection. The last shred of pretense was gone. The bankrupt soul stood naked and shivering, the last rag torn from pride.

What a miserable fight she had made, too, when put to the test! Ella had at least proved herself worthy to live. The scrub-woman had risen in the strength of desperation and killed the beast who had maimed her. She had only sunk a limp mass of shivering, helpless cowardice and fled from the room whining and pleading for mercy.

She could never respect herself again. The scene came back in vivid flashes. His eyes, glowing like two balls of blue fire, froze the blood in her veins - his voice the rasping cold steel of a file. And this coarse, ugly beast had held her in the spell of love. She had clung to him, kissed him in rapture and yielded herself to him soul and body. And he had gripped her delicate throat and choked her into insensibility, dropping her limp form from his hands like a strangled rat. She could remember the half-conscious moment that preceded the total darkness as she felt his grip relax.

He would choke and beat her again, too. He had said it in the sneering laughter at the door.

"A good little wife now and it's all right!"

And if you're not obedient to my whims I'll choke you until you are! That was precisely what he meant. That he was capable of any depth of degradation, and that he meant to drag her with him, there could be no longer the shadow of a doubt.

She could not endure another scene like that. She sprang to her feet again, shivering with terror. She could hear the hum of the conversation in the next room. He was persuading his mother to join in his criminal career. He was busy with his oily tongue transforming the simple, ignorant, lonely old woman into an avaricious fiend who would receive his blood-stained booty and rejoice in it.

He was laughing again. She put her trembling hands over her ears to shut out the sound. He had laughed at her shame and cowardice. It made her flesh creep to hear it.

She would escape. The mountain road was dark and narrow and crooked. She would lose her way in the night, perhaps. No matter. She could keep warm by walking. At dawn she would find her way to a cabin and ask protection. If she could reach Asheville, a telegram would bring her father. She wouldn't lose a minute. Her hat and coat were in the living-room. She would go bareheaded and without a coat. In the morning she could borrow one from the woman at the Mount Mitchell house.

She crept cautiously along the walls of the room searching for a door or window. There must be a way out. She made the round without discovering an opening of any kind. There must be a window of some kind high up for ventilation. There was no glass in it, of course. It was closed by a board shutter - if she could reach it.

She began at the door, found the corner of the room and stretched her arms upward until they touched the low, rough joist. Over every foot of its surface she ran her fingers, carefully feeling for a window. There was none!

She found an open crack and peered through. The stars were shining cold and clear in the December sky. The twinkling heavens reminded her that it was Christmas Eve. The dawn she hoped to see in the woods, if she could escape, would be Christmas morning. There was no time for idle tears of self-pity.

The one thought that beat in every throb of her heart now was to escape from her cell and put a thousand miles between her body and the beast who had strangled her. She might break through the roof! As a rule the shed-rooms of these rude mountain cabins were covered with split boards lightly nailed to narrow strips eighteen inches apart. If there were no ceiling, or if the ceiling were not nailed down and she should move carefully, she might break through near the eaves and drop to the ground. The cabin was not more than nine feet in height.

She raised herself on the footrail of the bed and felt the ceiling. There could be no mistake. It was there. She pressed gently at first and then with all her might against each board. They were nailed hard and fast.

She sank to the bed again in despair. She had barred herself in a prison cell. There was no escape except by the door through which the beast had driven her. And he would probably draw the couch against it and sleep there.

And then came the crushing conviction that such flight would be of no avail in a struggle with a man of Jim's character. His laughing words of triumph rang through her soul now in all their full, sinister meaning.

"The world ain't big enough for you to get away from me, Kiddo!"

It wasn't big enough. She knew it with tragic and terrible certainty. In his blind, brutal way he loved her with a savage passion that would halt at nothing. He would follow her to the ends of the earth and kill any living thing that stood in his way. And when he found her at last he would kill her.

How could she have been so blind! There was no longer any mystery about his personality. The slender hands and feet, which she had thought beautiful in her infatuation, were merely the hands and feet of a thief. The strength of jaw and neck and shoulders had made him the most daring of all thieves - a burglar.

His strange moods were no longer strange. He laughed for joy at the wild mountain gorges and crags because he saw safety for the hiding-place of priceless jewels he meant to steal.

There could be no escape in divorce from such a brute. He was happy in her cowardly submission. He would laugh at the idea of divorce. Should she dare to betray the secrets of his life of crime, he would kill her as he would grind a snake under his heel.

A single clause from the marriage ceremony kept ringing its knell - "until DEATH DO US PART!"

She knelt at last and prayed for Death.

"Oh, dear God, let me die, let me die!"

Suicide was a crime unthinkable to her pious mind. Only God now could save her in his infinite mercy.

She lay for a long time on the floor where she had fallen in utter despair. The tears that brought relief at first had ceased to flow. She had beaten her bleeding wings against every barrier, and they were beyond her strength.

Out of the first stupor of complete surrender, her senses slowly emerged. She felt the bare boards of the floor and wondered vaguely why she was there.

The hum of voices again came to her ears. She lay still and listened. A single terrible sentence she caught. He spoke it with such malignant power she could see through the darkness the flames of hell leaping in his eyes.

"Nobody's going to ask you HOW you got it - all they want to know is HAVE you got it!"

She laughed hysterically at the idea of reformation that had stirred her to such desperate appeal in the first shock of discovery. As well dream of reforming the Devil as the man who expressed his philosophy of life in that sentence! Blood dripped from every word, the blood of the innocent and the helpless who might consciously or unconsciously stand in his way. The man who had made up his mind to get rich quick, no matter what the cost to others, would commit murder without the quiver of an eyelid. If she had ever had a doubt of this fact, she could have none after her experience of tonight.

She wondered vaguely of the effects he was producing on his ignorant old mother. Her words were too low and indistinct to be heard. But she feared the worst. The temptation of the gold he was showing her would be more than she could resist.

She staggered to her feet and fell limp across the bed. The iron walls of a life prison closed about her crushed soul. The one door that could open was Death and only God's hand could lift its bars.

CHAPTER XXI

THE DEVIL'S DISCIPLE

Hour after hour Nance stood beside the wall of the shed-room and with the patience of a cat waited for the sobs to cease and the girl to be quiet.

Mary had risen from the bed once and paced the floor in the dark for more than an hour, like a frightened, wild animal, trapped and caged for the first time in life. With growing wonder, Nance counted the beat of her foot-fall, five steps one way and five back - round after round, round after round, in ceaseless repetition.

"Goddlemighty, is she gone clean crazy!" she exclaimed.

The footsteps stopped at last and the low sobs came once more from the bed. The old woman crouched down on a stone beside the log wall and drew the shawl about her shoulders.

A rooster crowed for midnight. Still the restless thing inside was stirring. Nance rose uneasily. Her lantern was still burning in her storehouse under the cliff. The wick might eat so low it would explode. She had heard that such things happened to lamps. It was foolish to have left it burning, anyhow.

She glided noiselessly from the house into the woods, entered her hidden door exactly as she had done before, extinguished the lantern, placed it on a shelving rock and put a dozen matches beside it.

In ten minutes she had returned to the house and crouched once more against the wall of the shed.

The low, pleading voice was praying. She pressed her ear to the crack and heard distinctly. She must be patient. Her plan was sure to succeed if she were only patient. No woman could sob and pray and walk all night. She must fall down unconscious from sheer exhaustion before day.

The old woman slipped into the kitchen, took up the quilt which she had spread on the floor for her bed, wrapped it about her thin shoulders and returned to her watch.

Again and again she rose, believing her patience had won, and placed her ear to the crack only to hear a sound within which told her only too plainly that the girl was yet awake. Sometimes it was a sigh, sometimes she cleared her throat, sometimes she tossed restlessly. One spoken sentence she heard again and again:

"Oh, dear God, have mercy on my lost soul!"

"What can be the matter with the fool critter!" Nance muttered. "Is she moanin' for sin? To be shore, they don't have no revival meetings this time o' year!"

She had known sinners to mourn through a whole summer sometimes, but never in all her experience in religious revivals had a mourner carried it over into winter. The dancing had always eased the tension and brought a relapse to sinful thoughts.

The hours dragged until the roosters began to crow for day. It would soon be light.

She must act now. There was no time to lose. She pressed her ear to the crack once more and held it five minutes.

Not a sound came from within. The broken spirit had yielded to the stupor of exhaustion at last.

With swift, cat's tread Nance circled the cabin and entered the kitchen. The quilt she carefully spread on the floor leading to the entrance to the living-room, crossed it softly and stood in the doorway with her long hands on the calico hangings.

For five minutes she remained immovable and listened to the deep, regular breathing of the sleeping man. Her wits were keen, her eyes wide. She could see the dim outlines of the furniture by the starlight through the window. Small objects in the room were, of course, invisible. To light a candle was not to be thought of. It might wake the sleeper.

She knew how to make the light without a noise or its rays reaching his face. He had startled her with the electric torch because of its novelty. She was no longer afraid. She would know how to press the button. He had left the thing lying on the table beside the black bag. He might have hidden the gold. He would not remember in his drunken stupor to move the electric torch.

She glided ghost-like into the room. Her bare feet were velvet. She knew every board in the floor. There was one near the table that creaked. She counted her steps and cleared the spot without a sound.

Her thin fingers found the edge of the table and slipped with uncanny touch along its surface until her hand closed on the rounded form of the torch.

Without moving in her tracks she turned the light on the table and in every nook and corner of the room beyond. She slowly swung her body on a pivot, flashing the light into each shadow and over every inch of floor, turning always in a circle toward the couch.

Satisfied that the object she sought was nowhere in the circle she had covered, she moved a step from the table and winked the light beneath it. She squatted on the floor and flashed it carefully over every inch of its boards from one corner of the room to the other and under the couch.

She rose softly, glided behind the head of the sleeping man and stood back some six feet, lest the flash of the torch might disturb him. She threw its rays behind the couch and slowly raised them until they covered the dirty pillow on which Jim was sleeping. There beneath the pillow lay the bag with its precious treasure. He was sleeping on it. She had feared this, but felt sure that the whiskey he had drunk would hold him in its stupor until late next morning.

She crouched low and fixed the light's ray slowly on the bag that her hand might not err the slightest in its touch. She laid her bony fingers on it with a slow, imperceptible movement, held them there a moment and moved the bag the slightest bit to test the sleeper's wakefulness. To her surprise he stirred instantly.

"What'ell!" he growled sleepily.

She stood motionless until he was breathing again with deep, even, heavy throb. Gliding back to the table, she flashed the light again on the bag and studied its position. His big neck rested squarely across it. To move it without waking him was a physical impossibility.

Here was a dilemma she had not fully faced. She had not believed it possible for him to place the bag where she could not get it. Her only purpose up to this moment had been to take it and store it safely beneath the soft earth in the inner recess of the cave. He would miss it in the morning, of course. She would express her amazement. The bar would be down from the front door. Someone had robbed him. The money could never be found.

She had made up her mind to take it the moment he had

convinced her that his philosophy of life was true. His eloquence had transformed her from an ignorant old woman, content with her poverty and dirt, into a dangerous and daring criminal.

There was no such thing as failure to be thought of now for a moment. The spade in the inner room of her store-house could be put to larger use if necessary. With the strength of the madness now on her she could carry his body on her back through the woods. The world would be none the wiser. He had quarreled with his wife, and left her in a rage that night. That was all she knew. The sheriff of neither county could afford to bother his head long over an insolvable mystery. Besides, both sheriffs were her friends.

Her decision was instantaneous when once she saw that it was safe.

She smiled over the grim irony of the thing - his words kept humming in her ears, his voice, low and persuasive:

"Suppose now the man that got that money had to kill a fool to take it - what of it? You don't get big money any other way!"

On the shelf beside the door was a butcher knife which she also used for carving. She had sharpened its point that night to carve her Christmas turkey next day.

She raised the torch and flashed its rays on the shelf to guide her hand, crept to the wall, took down the knife and laid the electric torch in its place.

Steadying her body against the wall, her arms outspread, she edged her way behind the couch and bent over the sleeping man until by his breathing she had located his heart.

She raised her tall figure and brought the knife down with a crash into his breast. With a sudden wrench she drew it from the wound and crouched among the shadows watching him with wide-dilated eyes.

The stricken sleeper gasped for breath, his writhing body fairly leaped into the air, bounded on the couch and stood erect. He staggered backward and lurched toward her. The crouching figure bent low, gripping the knife and waiting for her chance to strike the last blow.

Strangling with blood, Jim opened his eyes and saw the old woman creeping nearer through the gray light of the dawn.

He threw his hands above his head and tried to shout his warning. She was on him, her trembling hand feeling for his throat, before he could speak.

Struggling, in his weakened condition, to tear her fingers away, he gasped:

"Here! Here! Great God! Do you know what you're doing?"

"I just want yer money," she whispered. "That's all, and I'm a-goin' ter have it!"

Her fingers closed and the knife sank into his neck.

She sprang back and watched him lurch and fall across the couch. His body writhed a moment in agony and was still.

Holding the knife in her hand, she tore open the bag and thrust her itching fingers into the gold, gripping it fiercely.

"Nobody's goin' to ask ye how ye got it - they just want to know HAVE ye got it - yeah! Yeah -"

The last word died on her lips. The door of the shed-room suddenly opened and Mary stood before her.

CHAPTER XXII

DELIVERANCE

The first dim noises of the tragedy in the living-room Mary's stupefied senses had confused with a nightmare which she had been painfully fighting.

The torch in Nance's hand had flashed through a crack into her face once. It was the flame of a revolver in the hands of a thief in Jim's den in New York. She merely felt it. Her eyes had been gouged out and she was blind. A gang of his coarse companions were holding a council, cursing, drinking, fighting. Jim had sprung between two snarling brutes and knocked the revolver into the air. The flame had scorched her face.

With an oath he had slapped her.

"Get out, you damned little fool!" he growled. "You're always in the way when you're not wanted. Nobody can ever find you when there's work to be done -"

"But I can't see, Jim dear," she pleaded. "I do not know when things are out of place -"

"You're a liar!" he roared. "You know where every piece of junk stands in this room better than I do. I can't bring a friend into that door that you don't know it. You can hear the swish of a woman's skirt on the stairs four stories below -"

"I only asked you who the woman was who came in with you, Jim -"

His fingers gripped her throat and stopped her breath. Through the roar of surging blood she could barely hear the vile words he was dinning into her ears.

"I know you just asked me, you nosing little devil, and it's none of your business! She's a pal of mine, if you want to know, the slickest thief that ever robbed a flat. She's got more sense in a minute than you'll ever have in a lifetime. She's going to live here with me now. You can sleep on the cot in the kitchen. And you come when she calls, if you know what's good for your lazy hide. I've told her to thrash the life out of you if you dare to give her any impudence."

She had cowered at his feet and begged him not to beat her again. The fumes of whiskey and stale beer filled the place.

Jim turned from her to quell a new fight at the other end of the room. Another woman was there, coarse, dirty, beastly. She drew a knife and demanded her share of the night's robberies. She was trying to break from the men who held her to stab Jim. They were all fighting and smashing the furniture -

She sprang from the bed with a cry of horror. The noise was real! It was not a dream. The beast inside was stumbling in the dark. His passions fired by liquor, he was fumbling to find his way into her room.

She rushed to the door and put her shoulder against the bar, panting in terror.

She heard his strangling cry:

"Here! Here! Great God! Do you know what you're doing?"

And then his mother's voice, mad with greed, cruel, merciless:

"I just want yer money - that's all, an' I'm goin' to have it!"

She heard the clinch in the struggle and the dull blow of the knife. In a sudden flash she saw it all. He had succeeded in rousing Nance's avarice and transforming her into a fiend. Without knowing it she was stabbing her own son to death in the room in which he had been born!

She tried to scream and her lips refused to move. She tried to hurry to the rescue and her knees turned to water.

Gasping for breath, she drew the bar from her prison door and walked slowly into the room.

Nance's tall, bony figure was still crouched over the open bag, her left hand buried in the gold, her right gripping the knife, her face convulsed with greed - avarice and murder blended into perfect hell-lit unity at last.

Jim lay on his back, limp and still, obliquely across the couch, his breast bared in the struggle, the blood oozing a widening scarlet blot on his white shirt. His head had fallen backward over the edge and could not be seen.

Without moving a muscle, her body crouching, Nance spoke:

"You wuz awake - you heered?"

"Yes!"

The gleaming eyes burned through the gray dawn, two points of scintillating, hellish light fixed in purpose on the intruder.

She had only meant to take the money. The fool had fought. She killed him because she had to. And now the sobbing, sniveling little idiot who had kept her waiting all night had stuck her nose into some thing that didn't concern her. If she opened her mouth, the gallows would be the end.

She would open it too. Of course she would. She was his wife. They had quarreled, but the simpleton would blab. Nance knew this with unerring instinct. It was no use to offer her half the money. She didn't have sense enough to take it. She knew those pious, baby faces - well, there was room for two in the cave under the cliff. It was daylight now. No matter; it was Christmas morning. No man or woman ever darkened her door on Christmas day. She could hide their bodies until dark, and then it was easy. She would be in New York herself before anyone could suspect the meaning of that automobile in the shed or the owners would trouble themselves to come after it.

Again her decision was quick and fierce. Her hand was on the bag. She would hold it against the world, all hell and heaven.

With the leap of a tigress she was on the girl, the bag gripped in her left hand, the knife in her right.

To her amazement the trembling figure stood stock still gazing at her with a strange look of pity.

"Well!" Nance growled. "I ain't goin' ter be took now I've got this money - I'm goin' to New York ter find my boy!"

She lifted the knife and stopped in sheer stupor of surprise at the girl's immovable body and staring eyes. Had she gone crazy? What on earth could it mean? No girl of her youth and beauty could look death in the face without a tremor. No woman in her right senses could see the body of her dead husband lying there red and yet quivering without a sign. It was more than even Nance's nerves could endure.

She lowered the knife and peered into the girl's set face and glanced quickly about the room. Could she have called help? Was the house surrounded? It was impossible. She couldn't have escaped. What did it mean?

The old woman drew back with a terror she couldn't understand.

"What are you looking at me like that for?" she panted.

Mary held her gaze in lingering pity. Her heart went out now to the miserable creature trembling in the presence of her victim. The blow must fall that would crush the soul out of her body at one stroke. The gray hair had tumbled over her distorted features, the ragged dress had been torn from her throat in the struggle and her flat, bony breast was exposed.

"You don't - have - to - go - to - New York - to - find - your - boy!" the strained voice said at last.

Nance frowned in surprise and flew back at her in rage.

"Yes I do, too - he lives thar!"

The little figure straightened above the crouching form.

"He's here!"

Nance sank slowly against the table and rested the bag on the edge of the chair. Its weight was more than she could bear. She tried to glance over her shoulder at the body on the couch and her courage failed. The first suspicion of the hideous truth flashed through her stunned mind. She couldn't grasp it at once.

"Whar?" she whispered hoarsely.

Mary lifted her arm slowly and pointed to the couch.

"There!"

Nance glared at her a moment and broke into a hysterical laugh.

"It's a lie - a lie - a lie!"

"It's true -"

"Yer're just a lyin' ter me ter get away an give me up - but ye won't do it - little Miss - old Nance is too smart for ye this time. Who told you that?"

"He told me tonight!"

"He told you?" she repeated blankly.

"Yes."

"You're a liar!" she growled. "And I'll prove it - you move out o' your tracks an' I'll cut your throat. My boy's got a scar on his neck - I know right whar to look for it. Don't you move now till I see - I know you're a liar -"

She turned and with the quick trembling fingers of her right hand tore the shirt back from the neck and saw the scar. She still held the bag in her left hand. The muscles slowly relaxed and the bag fell endwise to the floor, the gold crashing and rolling over the boards. She stared in stupor and threw both hands above her streaming gray hair.

"Lord God Almighty!" she shrieked. "Why didn't I think that he wuz somebody else's boy if he weren't mine!"

The thin body trembled and crumpled beside the couch.

The girl lifted her head in a look of awe as if in prayer.

"And God has set me free! free! free!"

CHAPTER XXIII

THE DOCTOR

Mary stood overwhelmed by the tragedy she had witnessed. For the time her brain refused to record sensations. She had seen too much, felt too much in the past eight hours. Soul and body were numb.

The first impressions of returning consciousness were fixed on Nance. She had risen suddenly from the floor and smoothed the hair back from Jim's forehead with tender touch as if afraid to wake him. She drew the quilt from the kitchen floor, spread it over the body, and lifted her eyes to Mary's. It was only too plain.

Reason had gone.

She tipped close and put her fingers on her lips.

"Sh! We mustn't wake him. He's tired. Let him sleep. It's my boy. He's come home. We'll fix him a fine Christmas dinner. I've got a turkey. I'll bake a cake -" she paused and laughed softly. "I've got eggs too, fresh laid yesterday. We'll make egg-nog all day and all night. I ain't had no Christmas since that devil stole him. We'll have one this time, won't we?"

The girl's wits were again alert. She must run for help. A minute to humor the old woman's delusion and she might return before any harm came to her. Jim had not moved a muscle. It was plain that he was beyond help.

"Yes," Mary answered cheerfully. "You fix the cake - and I'll get the wood to make a fire."

Nance laughed again.

"We'll have the dinner all ready for him when he wakes, won't we?"

"Yes. I'll be back in a few minutes."

Nance hurried into the kitchen humming an old song in a faltering voice that sent the cold chills down the girl's spine.

Mary slipped quietly through the door and ran with swift, sure foot down the narrow road along which the machine had picked its way the afternoon before. The cabin they had passed last could not be more than a mile.

She made no effort to find the logs for pedestrians when the road crossed the brook. She plunged straight through the babbling waters with her shoes, regardless of skirts.

Panting for breath, she saw the smoke curling from the cabin chimney a quarter of a mile away.

"Thank God!" she cried. "They're awake!"

She was so glad to have reached her goal, her strength suddenly gave way and she dropped to a boulder by the wayside to rest. In two minutes she was up and running with all her might.

She rushed to the door and knocked.

A mountaineer in shirt-sleeves and stockings answered with a look of mild wonder.

"For God's sake come and help me. I must have a doctor

quick. We spent the night at Mrs. Owens'. She's lost her mind completely - a terrible thing has happened - you'll help me?"

"Cose I will, honey," the mountaineer drawled. "Jest ez quick ez I get on my shoes."

"Is there a doctor near?" she asked breathlessly.

He answered without looking up:

"The best one that God ever sent to a sick bed. He don't charge nobody a cent in these parts. He just heals the sick because hit's his callin'. Come from somewhar up North and built hisself a fine log house up on the side of the mountains. Hit's full of all the medicines in the world, too -"

"Will you ask him to come for me?" Mary broke in.

"I'll jump on my hoss an' have him thar in half a' hour. You can run right back, honey, and look out for the po' ole critter till we get thar."

"Thank you! Thank you!" she answered grate fully.

"Not at all, not at all!" he protested as he swung through the door and hurried to the low-pitched sheds in which his horse and cow were stabled. "Be thar in no time!"

When Mary returned, Nance was still busy in the kitchen. She had built a fire and put the turkey in the oven.

Mary was counting the minutes now until the doctor should come. The old woman's prattle about the return of her lost boy, so big and strong and handsome, had become unendurable. She felt that she should scream and collapse unless help came at once. She looked at her watch. It was just thirty-five minutes from the time she had left the cabin in the valley below.

She sprang to her feet with a smothered cry of joy. The beat of a horse's hoof at full gallop was ringing down the road.

In two minutes the Doctor's firm footstep was heard at the kitchen door.

Nance turned with a look of glad surprise.

"Well, fur the land sake, ef hit ain't Doctor Mulford! Come right in!" she cried.

The Doctor seized her hand.

"And how is my good friend, Mrs. Owens, this morning?" he asked cheerfully.

Mary was studying him with deep interest. She had asked herself the question a hundred times how much she could tell him - what to say and what to leave unsaid. One glance at his calm, intellectual face was enough. He was a man of striking appearance, six feet tall, forty-five years of age, hair prematurely gray and a slight stoop to his broad shoulders. His brown eyes seemed to enfold the old woman in their sympathy.

Nance was chattering her answer to his greeting.

"Oh, I'm feelin' fine, Doctor -" she dropped her voice confidentially - "and you're just in time for a good dinner. My boy that was lost has come home. He's a great big fellow, wears fine clothes and come up the mountain all the way in a devil wagon." She put her hand to her mouth. "Sh! He's asleep! We won't wake him till dinner! He's all tired out."

The Doctor nodded understandingly and turned toward Mary.

"And this young lady?"

"Oh, that's his wife from New York - ain't she purty?"

The Doctor saw the delicate hands trembling and extended his.

No word was spoken. None was needed. There was healing in his touch, healing in his whole being. No man or woman could resist the appeal of his personality. Their secrets were yielded with perfect faith.

"Come with me quickly," Mary whispered.

"I understand," he answered carelessly.

Turning again to Nance, he said with easy confidence:

"I'll not disturb you with your cooking, Mrs. Owens. Go right on with it. I'll have a little chat with your son's wife. If she's from New York I want to ask her about some of my people up there -"

"All right," Nance answered, "but don't you wake HIM! Go with her inter the shed-room."

"We'll go on tip-toe!" the Doctor whispered.

Nance nodded, smiled and bent again over the oven.

Mary led him quickly through the living-room, head averted from the couch, and into the prison cell in which she had passed the night. The physician glanced with a startled look at the gold still scattered on the floor.

She seized his hand and swayed.

He touched the brown hair of her bared head gently and pressed her hand.

"Steady, now, child, tell me quickly."

"Yes, yes," she gasped, "I'll tell you the truth -"

He held her gaze.

"And the whole truth - it's best."

Mary nodded, tried to speak and failed. She drew her breath and steadied herself, still gripping his hand.

"I will," she began faintly. "He's dead -"

She paused and nodded toward the living-room.

"The man - her son?"

"Yes. We came last night from Asheville. We were on our honeymoon. We haven't been married but three weeks. I never knew the truth about his life and character until last night when he told me that this old woman was his mother. I found a case of jewels in the bag he carried - jewels that belonged to a man in New York who was robbed and shot. I recognized the case. He confessed to me at last in cold, brutal words that he was a thief. I couldn't believe it at first. I tried to make him give up his criminal career. He laughed at me. He gloried in it. I tried to leave him. He choked me into insensibility and drove me into this cell, where I spent the night. He brought the gold that you saw on the floor which he had honestly made to give to his old mother - but for a devilish purpose. He showed it to her last night to rouse her avarice and make her first agree to hide his stolen goods. He succeeded too well. Before he had revealed himself she slipped into the room at daylight while he slept in a drunken stupor, murdered him and took the money. The struggle waked me and I rushed in. She gripped her knife to kill me. I told her that she had murdered her own son and she went mad -"

She paused for breath and her lips trembled piteously.

"You know what to do, Doctor?"

"Yes!"

"And you'll help me?"

He smiled tenderly and nodded his head.

"God knows you need it, child!"

The nerves snapped at last, and she sank a limp heap at his feet.

CHAPTER XXIV

THE CALL DIVINE

The Doctor threw off his coat and took charge of the stricken house. He sent his waiting messenger for a faithful nurse, a mountain woman whom he had trained, and began the fight for Mary's life. The collapse into which she had fallen would require weeks of patient care. There was no immediate danger of death, and while he awaited the arrival of help, he turned into the living-room to examine the body of the slain husband.

The head had fallen backward over the side of the lounge and a pool of blood, still warm and red, lay on the floor in a widening circle beneath it. His quick eye took in its significance at a glance. He sprang forward, ripped the shirt wide open and applied his ear to the breast.

"He's still alive!" he cried excitedly.

He examined the ugly wound in the left side and found that the knife had penetrated the lung. The heart had not been touched. The blow on the neck had not been fatal. The shock of the final stroke had merely choked the wounded man into collapse from the hemorrhage of the left lung. The position into which the body had fallen across the couch had gradually cleared the accumulated blood. There was a chance to save his life.

In ten minutes he had applied stimulants and restored

respiration, but the deep wheeze from the stricken lung told only too plainly the dangerous character of the wound. It would be a bitter fight. His enormous vitality might win. The chances were against him.

Jim's lips moved and he tried to speak.

The Doctor placed his hand on his mouth and shook his head. The drooping eyelids closed in grateful obedience.

The beat of horses' hoofs echoed down the mountain road. His nurse and messenger were coming. He decided at once to move Mary to his own house. She must regain consciousness in new surroundings or her chance of survival would be slender. To awake in this miserable cabin, the scene of the tragedy she had witnessed, might be instantly fatal. Besides she must not yet know that the brute who had choked her was alive and might still hold the power of life and death over her frail body. She believed him dead. It was best so. He might be dead and buried before she recovered consciousness. The fever that burned her brain would completely cloud reason for days.

He hastily improvised a stretcher with a blanket and two strong quilting-poles which stood in the corner of the room. Nance helped him without question. She obeyed his slightest suggestion with childlike submission.

He placed Mary on the stretcher, wrapped her body in another warm blanket and turned to his nurse and messenger:

"Carry her to my house. Walk slowly and rest whenever you wish. Don't wake her. Tell Aunt Abbie to put her to bed in the south room overlooking the valley. Don't leave her a minute, Betty. She's in the first collapse of brain fever. You know what to do. I'll be there in an hour. You come back here, John. I want you."

The mountaineer nodded and seized one end of the stretcher. The nurse took up the other and the Doctor held wide the cabin door as they passed out.

For three weeks he fought the grim battle with Death for the two young lives the Christmas tragedy had thrust into his hands. He gave his entire time day and night to the desperate struggle.

When pneumonia had developed and Jim's life hung by a hair, he slept on the couch in the living-room of the cabin and had Nance make for herself a bed on the floor of the kitchen.

The old woman remained an obedient child. She cooked the Doctor's meals and did the work about the house and yard as if nothing had disturbed her habits of lonely plodding. She believed implicitly all that was told her. Her son had pneumonia from cold he had taken in the long drive from Asheville. The house must be kept quiet. John Sanders was helping her nurse him. She was sure the Doctor would save him.

Even the knife with which she had stabbed him made no impression on her numbed senses. The Doctor had scoured every trace of blood from the blade and put it back in its place on the shelf, lest she should miss it and ask questions. She used it daily without the slightest memory of the frightful story it might tell.

Each morning before going to the cabin the Doctor watched with patience for the first signs of returning consciousness in Mary's fever-wracked body. The day she lifted her grateful eyes to his and her lips moved in a tremulous question he raised his hand gently.

"Sh! Child - don't talk! It's all right. You're getting better. I've been with you every day. You're in my house now. You'll soon be yourself again."

She smiled wanly, put her delicate hand on his and pressed it gratefully.

"I understand. You thank me - you say that I am good to you. But I'm not. This is my life. I heal the sick because I must. I love this battle royal with Death. He beats me sometimes - but I never quit. I'm always tramping on his trail, and I've won this fight!"

The calm brown eyes held her in a spell and she smiled again.

"Sleep now," he said soothingly. "Sleep day and night. Just wake to take a little food - that's all and Nature will do the rest."

He stroked her hand gently until her eyelids closed.

Two days later Jim clung to the Doctor's hand and insisted on talking.

"Better wait a little longer, boy," the physician answered kindly. "You're not out of the woods yet -"

"I can't wait - Doc -" Jim pleaded. "I've just got to ask you something."

"All right. You can talk five minutes."

"My wife, Doc, how is she? You took her to your house, John told me. She'll get well?"

"Yes. She's rapidly recovering now."

"What does she say about me?"

"She thinks you're dead."

"You haven't told her?"

"No."

"Why?"

Thomas Dixon

"She had all she could stand -"

Jim stared in silence.

"You think she'd be sorry to know I am alive?" he asked slowly.

"It would be a great shock."

The steel blue eyes slowly filled with tears.

"God! I am rotten, ain't I?"

"There's no doubt about that, my son," was the firm answer.

"Why did you fight so hard to save me - I wonder?"

"An old feud between Death and me."

Jim suddenly seized the Doctor's hand.

"Say, you can't fool me - you're a good one, Doc. You've been a friend to me and you've got to help now - you've just got to. You're the only one on earth who can. You've a great big heart and you can't go back on a fellow that's down and out. Give me a chance! You will - won't you?"

The hot fingers gripped the Doctor's hand with pleading tenderness.

The brown eyes searched Jim's soul.

"If you can show me it's worth while -"

The fingers tightened their grip in silence.

"Just give me a chance, Doc," he said at last, "and I'll show you! I ain't never had a chance to really know what was right and what was wrong. If I'd a lived here with my old mother she'd have told me. You know what it is to be a stray dog on the streets of New York? Even then, I'd have kept straight if I hadn't been robbed by a lawyer and his pal. I didn't know what I was doin' till that night here in this cabin - honest to God, I didn't -"

He paused for breath and a tear stole down his cheek. He fought for control of his emotions and went on in low tones.

"I didn't know - till I saw my old mother creepin' on me in the shadows with that big knife gleamin' in her hand! I tried to stop her and I couldn't. I tried to yell and strangled with blood. I saw the flames of hell in her eyes and I had kindled them there - God! I never knew until that minute! I'm broken and bruised lyin' on the rocks now in the lowest pit - Give me your hand, Doc! You're my only friend - I'm goin' straight from now on - so help me God!"

He paused again for breath and sought the actor's eyes.

"You'll stand by me, won't you?"

A friendly grip closed on the trembling fingers.

"Yes - I'll help you - if I can."

CHAPTER XXV

THE MOTHER

Mary was resting in the chair beneath the southern windows of the sun-parlor of the Doctor's bungalow. He had built his home of logs cut from the mountainside. Its rooms were supplied with every modern convenience and comfort. Clear spring water from the cliff above poured into the cypress tank constructed beneath the roof. An overflow pipe sent a sparkling, bubbling and laughing through the lawn, refreshing the wild flowers planted along its edges.

The view from the window looking south was one of ravishing beauty and endless charm. Perched on a rising spur of the Black Mountain the house commanded a view of the long valley of the Swannanoa opening at the lower end into the wide, sunlit sweep of the lower hills around Asheville. Upward the balsam-crowned peaks towered among the clouds and stars.

No two hours of the day were just alike. Sometimes the sun was raining showers of diamonds on the trembling tree-tops of the valleys while the blackest storm clouds hung in ominous menace around Mount Mitchell and the Cat-tail. Sometimes it was raining in the valley - the rain cloud a level sheet of gray cloth stretching from the foot of the lawn across to the crags beyond, while the sun wrapped the little bungalow in a warm, white mantle.

Mary had never tired of this enchanted world during the days of her convalescence. The Doctor, with firm will, had lifted every care from her mind. She had gratefully submitted to his orders, and asked no questions.

She began to wonder vaguely about his life and people and why he had left the world in which a man of his culture and power must have moved, to bury himself in these mountain wilds. She wondered if he had married, separated from his wife and chosen the life of a recluse. He volunteered no information about himself.

When not attending his patients he spent his hours in the greenhouse among his flowers or in the long library extension of the bungalow. More than five thousand volumes filled the solid shelves. A massive oak table, ten feet in length and four feet wide, stood in the center of the room, always generously piled with books, magazines and papers. At the end of this table he kept the row of books which bore immediately on the theme he was studying.

Beside the window opening on the view of the valley stood his old-fashioned desk - six feet long, its top a labyrinth of pigeon-holes and tiny drawers.

He pursued his studies with boyish enthusiasm and chattered of them to Mary by the hour - with never a word passing his lips about himself.

Aunt Abbie, the cook, brought her a cup of tea, and Mary volunteered a question.

"Do you know the Doctor's people, Auntie?" she asked hesitatingly.

"Lord, child, he's a mystery to everybody! All we know is that he's the best man that ever walked the earth. He won't talk and the mountain folks are too polite to nose into his business. He saved my boy's life one summer, and when he was strong and well and went back to Asheville to his work, I had nothin' to do but to hold my hands, and I come here to cook for him. He tries to pay me wages but I laugh at him. I told him if he could save my boy's life for nothin' I reckon I could cook him a few good meals without pay -"

Her eyes filled with tears. She brushed them off, laughed and added:

"He lets me alone now and don't pester me no more about money."

Her tea and toast finished, Mary placed the tray on the table, rose with a sudden look of pain, and made her way slowly to the library.

A warm fire of hardwood logs sparkled in the big stone fireplace. The Doctor was out on a visit to a patient. He had given her the freedom of the place and had especially insisted that she use his books and make his library her resting place whenever her mind was fagged. She had spent many quiet hours in its inspiring atmosphere.

She seated herself at his desk and studied the calendar which hung above it. A sudden terror overwhelmed her; she buried her face in her arms and burst into tears.

She was still lying across the desk, sobbing, when the Doctor walked into the room.

He touched her hair reproachfully with his firm hand.

"Why, what's this? My little soldier has disobeyed orders?"

"I don't want to live now," she sobbed.

"And why not?"

"I - I - am going to be a mother," she whispered.

"So?"

"The mother of a criminal! Oh, Doctor, it's horrible! Why did you let me live? The hell I passed through that night was enough - God knows! This will be unendurable. I've made up my mind - I'll die first -"

"Rubbish, child! Rubbish!" he answered with a laugh. "Where did you get all this misinformation?"

"You know what my husband was. How can you ask?"

"Because I happen to know also his wife - the mother-to-be of this supposed criminal who has just set sail for the shores of our planet - and I know that she is one of the purest and sweetest souls who ever lost her way in the jungles of the world. If you were the criminal, dear heart, the case might be hopeless. But you're not. You are only the innocent victim of your own folly. That doesn't count in the game of Nature -"

"What do you mean?" she asked breathlessly.

"Simply this: The part which the male plays in the reproduction of the race is small in comparison with the role of the female. He is merely a supernumerary who steps on the stage for a moment and speaks one word announcing the arrival of the queen. The queen is the mother. She plays the star role in the drama of Heredity. She is never off the stage for a single moment. We inherit the most obvious physical traits from our male ancestors but even these may be modified by the will of the mother."

"Modified by the will of the mother?" she repeated blankly.

"Certainly. There are yet long days and weeks and months before your babe will be born - at least seven months. There's not a sight or sound of earth or heaven that can reach or influence this coming human being save through your eyes and ears and touch and soul. Almighty God can speak His message only through you. You are his ambassador on earth in this solemn hour. What your husband was, is of little importance. There is not a moment, waking or sleeping, day or night, that does not bring to you its divine opportunity. This human life is yours - absolutely to mold and fashion in body and mind as you will."

"You're just saying this to keep me from suicide," Mary interrupted.

"I am telling you the simplest truth of physical life. You can even change the contour of your baby's head if you like. You think in your silly fears that the bull neck and jaw of the father will reappear in the child. It might be so unless you see fit to change it. All any father can do is to transmit general physical traits unless modified by the will of the mother."

"You mean that I can choose even the personal appearance of my child?" she asked in blank amazement.

"Exactly that. Choose the type of man you wish your babe to be and it shall be so. Who in all the world would you prefer that he resemble?"

"You," she answered promptly.

He smiled gently.

"That pays me for all my trouble, child! No doctor ever got a bigger fee than that. Banks may fail, but I'll never lose it. Your choice simplifies that matter very much. You won't need a picture in your room -"

"A picture could determine the features of an unborn babe?" she asked incredulously.

"Beyond a doubt, and it will determine character sometimes. I knew a mother in the mountains of Vermont who hung the picture of a ship under full sail in her living-room. She bore seven sons. Not one of them ever saw the ocean until he was grown and yet all of them became sailors. This was not an accident. In her age and loneliness she blamed God for taking her children from her. Yet she had made sailors of them all by the selection of a single piece of furniture in her room. Nature has a way of starting her children on their journey through this world very nearly equal - each a bundle of possibilities in the hands of a mother. A father may transmit physical disease, if his body is unsound. Such marriages should be prohibited by law. But nine-tenths of the spiritual traits out of which character is formed are the work of the mother. A criminal mother will bring into the world only criminals. A criminal male may be the father of a saint. The responsibility of shaping the destiny of the race rests with the mother -"

The Doctor sprang to his feet and paced the floor, his arms gripped behind his back in deep thought. He paused before the enraptured listener and hesitated to speak the thought in his mind.

He lifted his hand suddenly, his decision apparently made.

"It is of the utmost importance to the race that our mothers shall be pure. Better certainly if both father and mother are so. It is indispensable that the mother shall be! On this elemental fact rests the dual standard of sex morals. On this fact rests the hope of a glorified humanity through the development of an intelligent motherhood. Stay here with me until your child is born and I'll prove the truth of every word I've spoken -"

"Oh, if I only could!"

"Why not?"

"I couldn't impose such a burden on you!" she faltered.

"You would confer on me the highest honor, if you will allow me to direct you in this experiment."

There was no mistaking his honesty and earnestness. There was no refusing the appeal.

"You really wish me to stay?" she asked.

"I beg of you to stay! You will bring to me a new inspiration - new faith - new courage to fight. Will you?"

She extended her hand.

"Yes."

"And you will agree to follow my instructions?"

"Absolutely."

"Good. We begin from this moment. I give you my first orders. Forget that James Anthony ever lived. Forget the tragedy of Christmas Eve. You are going to be a mother. All other events in life pale before this fact. God has conferred on you the highest honor He can give to mortal. Keep your soul serene, your body strong. You are to worry about nothing -"

"I must pay you for this extra expense I impose, Doctor. I have a thousand dollars in bank in New York," she interrupted.

"Certainly, if you will be happier. My home is now your sanitarium. You are my patient. Your board will cost me about eight dollars a week. All right. You can pay that if you wish.

"Take no thought now except on the business of being a mother. I will make myself your father, your brother, your guardian, your physician, your friend and companion. I will give you at once a course of reading. You are to think only beautiful thoughts, see beautiful things, dream beautiful dreams, hear beautiful music. I'm going to make you climb these mountain peaks with me for the next three months and live among the clouds. I'm going to refit your room with new furniture and pictures and place in it a phonograph with the best music. When you are strong enough you can work for me three hours a day as my secretary. You use the typewriter?"

"I'm an expert -"

"Good! I'm writing a book which I'm going to call 'The Rulers of the World.' It is a study of Motherhood. I am one who believes that the redemption of humanity awaits the realization by woman of her divine call. When woman knows that she is really a co-creator with God in the reproduction of the race, a new era will dawn for mankind. You promise me faithfully to obey my instructions?"

"Faithfully."

"You're a wonderful subject on which to make an experiment. You are young - in the first dawn of the glory of womanhood. Your body is beautiful, your mind singularly pure and sweet. You must give me at once the full power of your will in its concentration on Truth and Beauty. The success or failure of this experiment will depend almost entirely on your mentality and the use you make of it during these months in which your babe is being formed. Whatever the shape of the body there is one eternal certainty - only YOUR mind can reach the soul of this child. If the father were the veriest fiend who ever existedand should concentrate his mind to the task, not one thought from his darkened soul could reach your babe! YOUR mind will be the ever-brooding, enfolding spirit forming and fashioning character."

He paused and his deep brown eyes flashed with enthusiasm.

"Think of it! You are now creating an immortal being whose word may bend a million wills to his. And you are doing this mighty work solely by your mind. The physical processes are simple and automatic.

"The first lesson you must learn and hold with deathless grip is that thoughts are things. A thought can kill the body. A thought can heal the body. If I am successful as a physician it is because I use this power with my patients. With some I use drugs, with others none. With all I use every ounce of mental power which God has given me. You will remember this?"

"Yes."

He walked to the shelves and drew down a volume of poetry.

"Read these poems until you are tired today - then sleep. I'll give you a good novel tomorrow and when you've read it, a volume of philosophy. When we climb the peaks, I'll give you a study of these rocks that will tell you the story of their birth, their life, and their coming death. We'll learn something of the birds and flowers next spring. We'll dream great dreams and think great thoughts - you and I - in these wonderful days and weeks and months which God shall give us together."

She looked up at him through her tears:

"Oh, Doctor, you have not only saved a miserable life: you have saved my soul!"

CHAPTER XXVI

A SOUL IS BORN

It was more than a month after the experiment began before the Doctor ventured to hint of Jim's survival. He had waited patiently until Mary's strength had been fully restored and her mind filled with the new enthusiasm for motherhood. He could tell her now with little risk. And yet he ventured on the task with reluctance. He found her seated at her favorite window overlooking the deep blue valley of the Swannanoa, a volume of poetry in her lap.

He touched her shoulder and she smiled in cheerful response.

"You are content?" he asked.

"A strange peace is slowly stealing into my heart," she responded reverently. "I shall learn to love life again when my baby comes to help me."

"You remember your solemn promise?"

"Have I not kept it?" she murmured.

"Faithfully - and I remind you of it that you may not forget today for a moment that your work is too high and holy to allow a shadow to darken your spirit even for an hour. I have something to tell you that may shock a little unless I warn you -"

She lifted her eyes with a quick look of uneasiness, and studied his immovable face.

"You couldn't guess?" he laughed.

She shook her head in puzzled silence.

"Suppose I were to tell you," he went on evenly, "that I found a spark of life in your husband's body that morning and drew him back from the grave?"

Her eyes closed and she stretched her hand toward the Doctor.

He clasped the fingers firmly between both his palms, held and stroked them gently.

"You did save him?" she breathed.

"Yes."

"Thank God his poor old mother is not a murderer! But he is dead to me. I shall never see him again - never!"

"I thought you would feel that way," the Doctor quietly replied.

"You won't let him come here?" she asked suddenly.

"He won't try unless you consent -"

Mary shuddered.

"You don't know him -"

The Doctor smiled.

"I'm afraid you don't know him now, my child."

"He has changed?"

"The old, old miracle over again. He has been literally born again - this time of the spirit."

"It's incredible!"

"It's true. He's a new man. I think his reformation is the real thing. He's young. He's strong. He has brains. He has personality -"

Mary lifted her hand.

"All I ask of him is to keep out of my sight. The world is big enough for us both. The past is now a nightmare. If I live to be a hundred years old, with my dying breath I shall feel the grip of his fingers on my throat -"

She paused and closed her eyes.

"Forget it! Forget it!" the Doctor laughed. "We have more important things to think of now."

"He wishes to see me?"

"Begs every day that I ask you."

"And you have hesitated these long weeks?"

"Your strength and peace of mind were of greater importance than his happiness, my dear. Let him wait until you please to see him."

"He'll wait forever," was the firm answer.

Jim smiled grimly when his friend bore back the message.

"I'll never give up as long as there's breath in my body," he cried, bringing his square jaws together with a snap.

"That's the way to talk, my boy," the Doctor responded.

"Anyhow you believe in me, Doc, don't you?"

"Yes."

"And you'll help me a little on the way if it gets dark - won't you?"

"If I can - you may always depend on me."

Jim clasped his outstretched hand gratefully.

"Well, I'm going to make good."

There was something so genuine and manly in the tones of his voice, he compelled the Doctor's respect. A smaller man might have sneered. The healer of souls and bodies had come to recognize with unerring instinct the true and false note in the human voice.

His heart went out in a wave of sympathy for the lonely, miserable young animal who stood before him now, trembling with the first sharp pains of the immortal thing that had awaked within. He slipped his arm about Jim's shoulders and whispered:

"I'll tell you something that may help you when the way gets dark - the wife is going to bear you a child."

"No!"

"Yes."

"God! - - That's great, ain't it?"

Jim choked into silence and looked up at the Doctor with dimmed eyes.

"Say, Doc, you hit me hard when you brought what she said - but that's good news! Watch me work my hands to the bone -

you know it's my kid and she can't keep me from workin' for it if she tries now can she?"

"No."

"There's just one thing that'll hang over me like a black cloud," he mused sorrowfully.

"I know, boy - your mother's darkened mind."

Jim nodded.

"When I see that queer glitter in her eyes it goes through me like a knife. Will she ever get over it?"

"We can't tell yet. It takes time. I believe she will."

"You'll do the best you can for her, Doc?" he pleaded pathetically. "You won't forget her a single day? If you can't cure her, nobody can."

"I'll do my level best, boy."

Jim pressed his hand again.

"Gee, but you've been a friend to me! I didn't know that there were such men in the world as you!"

For six months the Doctor watched the transplanted child of the slums grow into a sturdy manhood in his new environment. He snapped at every suggestion his friend gave and with quick wit improved on it. He not only discovered and developed a mica mine on his mother's farm, he invented new machinery for its working that doubled the market output. Within six weeks from the time he began his shipments the mine was paying a steady profit of more than five hundred dollars a month. He had made just one trip to New York and secretly returned to the police every stolen jewel and piece of plunder taken, with a full confession of the time and place of the crime. He had shipped his tools and machinery from the workshop on the east side before his sensational act and made good his departure for the South.

The tools and machinery he installed in a new workshop which he built in the yard of Nance's cabin. Here he worked day and night at his blacksmith forge making the iron hinges, and irons, shovels, tongs, fire sets and iron work complete for a log bungalow of seven rooms which he was building on the sunny slope of the mountain which overlooks the valley toward Asheville.

The Doctor had lent Jim the blue-prints of his own home and he was quietly duplicating it with loving care. His wife might refuse to see him but he could build a home for their boy. For his sake she couldn't refuse it.

With childlike obedience Nance followed him every day and watched the workmen rear the beautiful structure under Jim's keen eyes and skillful hands. The man's devotion to his mother was pathetic. Only the Doctor knew the secret of his pitiful care, and he kept his own counsel.

CHAPTER XXVII

THE BABY

The last roses of summer were bursting their topmost buds into full bloom on the lawn of the Doctor's bungalow. The martins that built each year in the little boxes he had set on poles around his garden were circling and chattering far up in the sapphire skies of a late September day. Their leaders had sensed the coming frost and were drilling for their long march across the world to their winter home. The chestnut burrs were bursting in the woods. The silent sun-wrapped Indian Summer had begun. Not a cloud flecked the skies.

A quiet joy filled the soul of the woman who smiled and heard her summons.

"You are not afraid?" the Doctor asked.

She turned her grateful eyes to his.

"The peace of God fills the world - and I owe it all to you."

"Nonsense. Your sturdy will and cultivated mind did the work. I merely made the suggestion."

"You are not going to give me an anesthetic, are you?" she said evenly.

"Why did you ask that?"

Thomas Dixon

"Because I wish to feel and know the pain and glory of it all."

"You don't wish to take it?"

"Not unless you say I should."

"What a wonderful patient you are, child! What a beautiful spirit!" He looked at her intently. "Well, I'm older and wiser in experience than you. I'm glad you added that clause 'unless you say I should.' I'm going to say it. After all my talks to you on our return to the truths and simplicity of Nature you are perhaps surprised. You needn't be. I'm going to put you into a gentle sleep. Nature will then do her physical work automatically. I do this because our daughters are the inheritors of the sins of their mothers for centuries. The over-refinement of nerves, the hothouse methods of living, and the maiming of their bodies with the inventions of fashion have made the pains of this supreme hour beyond endurance. This should not be. It will not be so when our race has come into its own. But it will take many generations and perhaps many centuries before we reach the ideal. No physician who has a soul could permit a woman of your physique, your culture and refinement to walk barefoot and blindfolded into such a hell of physical torture. I will not permit it."

He walked quietly into his laboratory, prepared the sleeping powders and gave them to her.

Six hours later she opened her eyes with eager wonder. Aunt Abbie was busy over a bundle of fluffy clothes. The Doctor was standing with his arms folded behind his back, his fine, clean-shaven face in profile looking thoughtfully over the sun-lit valley. There was just one moment of agonized fear. If they had failed! If her child were hideous - or deformed! Her lips moved in silent prayer.

"Doctor?" she whispered.

In a moment he was bending over her, a look of exaltation in his brown eyes.

"Tell me quick!"

"A wonderful boy, little mother! The most beautiful babe I have ever seen. He didn't even cry - just opened his big, wide eyes and grunted contentedly."

"Give him to me."

Aunt Abbie laid the warm bundle in her arms and she pressed it gently until the sweet, red flesh touched her own. She lay still for a moment, a smile on her lips.

"Lift him and let me look!"

"What a funny little pug nose," she laughed.

"Yes - exactly like his mother's!" the Doctor replied.

She gazed with breathless reverence.

"He is beautiful, isn't he?" she sighed.

"And you have observed the chin and mouth?"

"Exactly like yours. It's wonderful!"

CHAPTER XXVIII

WHAT IS LOVE?

Eighteen months swiftly passed with the little mother and her boy still in Dr. Mulford's sanitarium. She had allowed herself to be persuaded that he had the right to be her guide and helper in the first year's training of the child.

The boy had steadily grown in strength and beauty of body and mind. The Doctor persuaded her to spend one more winter basking in his sun-parlor and finishing the final chapters of his book. Her mind was singularly clever and helpful in the interpretation of the experiences and emotions of motherhood.

She had stubbornly resisted every suggestion to see her husband or allow him to see the child. The Doctor had managed twice to give Jim an hour with the baby while she had gone to Asheville on shopping trips. He was rewarded for his trouble in the devotion with which the young father worshiped his son. The Doctor watched the slumbering fires kindle in the man's deep blue eyes with increasing wonder at the strength and tenderness of his newfound soul.

Jim had completed the furnishing of the bungalow with the advice and guidance of his friend, and every room stood ready and waiting for its mistress. He had insisted on making every piece of furniture for Mary's room and the nursery adjoining. The Doctor was amazed at the mechanical genius he displayed in its construction. He had taken a month's instruction at a cabinet maker's in Asheville and the bed, bureau, tables and chairs which he had turned out were astonishingly beautiful. Their lines were copied from old models and each piece was a work of art. The iron work was even more tastefully and beautifully wrought. He had toiled day and night with an enthusiasm and patience that gave the physician a new revelation in the possibility of the development of human character.

His friend came at last with a cheering message. He began smilingly:

"I'm going to make the big fight today, boy, to get her to see you."

"You think she will?"

"There's a good chance. Her savings have all been used up from her bank account in New York. She is determined to go to her father in Kentucky. I'll have a talk with her, bring her over to the bungalow, show her through it on the pretext of its model construction and then you can tell her that you built it with your own hands for her and the baby. You might be loafing around the place about that time."

Jim's hand was suddenly lifted.

"I got ye, Doc, I got ye! I'll be there - all day."

"Don't let her see you until I give the signal."

"Caution's my name."

"We'll see what happens."

Jim pressed close.

"Say, Doc, if you know how to pray, I wish you'd send up a

little word for me while you're talkin' to her. Could ye now?"

"I'll do my best for you, boy - and I think you've got a chance. She's been watching the blue eyes of that baby lately with a rather curious look of unrest."

"They're just like mine, ain't they?" Jim broke in with pride.

"Time has softened the old hurt," the Doctor went on. "The boy may win for you -"

The square jaw came together with a smash.

"Gee - I hope so. I'll wait there all day for you and I'm goin' to try my own hand at a little prayer or two on the side while I'm waiting. Maybe God'll think He's hit me hard enough by this time to give me another trial."

With a friendly wave of his hand the Doctor hurried home.

He found Mary seated under the rose trellis beside the drive, watching for his coming. The day was still and warm for the end of April. Birds were singing and chattering in every branch and tree. A quail on the top fence-rail of the wheat field called loudly to his mate.

The boy was screaming his joy over a new wagon to which Aunt Abbie had hitched his goat. He drove by in style, lifted his chubby hand to his mother and shouted:

"Dood-by, Doc-ter!"

The Doctor waved a smiling answer, and lapsed into a long silence.

He waked at last from his absorption to notice that Mary was day-dreaming. The fair brow was drawn into deep lines of brooding.

"Why shadows in your eyes a day like this, little mother?" he asked softly.

"Just thinking -"

"About a past that you should forget?"

"Yes and no," she answered thoughtfully. "I was just thinking in this flood of spring sunlight of the mystery of my love for such a man as the one I married. How could it have been possible to really love him?"

"You are sure that you loved him?"

"Sure."

"How did you know?"

"By all the signs. I trembled at his footstep. The touch of his hand, the sound of his voice thrilled me. I was drawn by a power that was resistless. I was mad with happiness those wonderful days that preceded our marriage. I was madder still during our honeymoon - until the shadows began to fall that fatal Christmas Eve." She paused and her lips trembled. "Oh, Doctor, what is love?"

The drooping shoulders of the man bent lower. He picked up a pebble from the ground and flicked it carelessly across the drive, lifted his head at last and asked earnestly:

"Shall I tell you the truth?"

"Yes - your own particular brand, please - the truth, the whole truth and nothing but the truth."

"I'll try," he began soberly. "If I were a poet, naturally I would use different language. As I'm only a prosaic doctor and physiologist I may shock your ideals a little."

"No matter," she interrupted. "They couldn't well get a harder jolt than they have had already."

He nodded and went on:

"There are two elemental human forces that maintain life - hunger and love. They are both utterly simple, otherwise they could not be universal. Hunger compels the race to live. Love compels it to reproduce itself. There has never been anything mysterious about either of these forces and there never will be - except in the imagination of sentimentalists.

"Nature begins with hunger. For about thirteen years she first applies this force to the development of the body before she begins to lay the foundation of the second. Until this second development is complete the passion known as love cannot be experienced.

"What is this second development? Very simple again. At the base of the brain of every child there is a vacant space during the first twelve or fifteen years. During the age of twelve to fourteen in girls, thirteen to fifteen in boys, this vacant space is slowly filled by a new lobe of the brain and with its growth comes the consciousness of sex and the development of sex powers.

"This new nerve center becomes on maturity a powerful physical magnet. The moment this magnet comes into contact with an organization which answers its needs, as certain kinds of food answer the needs of hunger, violent desire is excited. If both these magnets should be equally powerful, the disturbance to both will be great. The longer the personal association is continued the more violent becomes this disturbance, until in highly sensitive natures it develops into an obsession which obscures reason and crushes the will.

"The meaning of this impulse is again very simple - the unconscious desire of the male to be a father, of the female to become a mother."

"And there is but one man on earth who could thus affect me?" Mary asked excitedly.

"Rubbish! There are thousands."

"Thousands?"

"Literally thousands. The reason you never happen to meet them is purely an accident of our poor social organization. Every woman has thousands of true physical mates if she could only meet them. Every man has thousands of true physical mates if he could only meet them. And in every such meeting, if mind and body are in normal condition, the same violent disturbance would result - whether married or single, free or bound.

"Marriage therefore is not based merely on the passion of love. It is a crime for any man or woman to marry without love. It is the sheerest insanity to believe that this passion within itself is sufficient to justify marriage. All who marry should love. Many love who should not marry.

"The institution of marriage is the great SOCIAL ordinance of the race. Its sanctity and perpetuity are not based on the violence of the passion of love, but something else."

He paused and listened to the call of the quail again from the field.

"You hear that bob white calling his mate?"

"Yes - and she's answering him now very softly. I can hear them both."

"They have mated this spring to build a home and rear a brood of young. Within six months their babies will all be full grown and next spring a new alignment of lovers will be made. Their marriage lasts during the period of infancy of their offspring. This is Nature's law.

"It happens in the case of man that the period of infancy of a human being is about twenty-four years. This is the most wonderful fact in nature. It means that the capacity of man for the improvement of his breed is practically limitless. A quail has a few months in which to rear her young. God gives to woman a quarter of a century in which to mold her immortal offspring. Because the period of infancy of one child covers the entire period of motherhood capacity, marriage binds for life, and the sanctity of marriage rests squarely on this law of Nature."

He paused again and looked over the sunlit valley.

"I wish our boys and girls could all know these simple truths of their being. It would save much unhappiness and many tragic blunders.

"You were swept completely off your feet by the rush of the first emotion caused by meeting a man who was your physical mate. You imagined this emotion to be a mysterious revelation which can come but once. Your imagination in its excited condition, of course, gave to your first-found mate all sorts of divine attributes which he did not possess. You were 'in love' with a puppet of your own creation, and hypnotized yourself into the delusion that James Anthony was your one and only mate, your knight, your hero.

"In a very important sense this was true. Your intuitions could not make a mistake on so vital an issue. But you immediately rushed into marriage and your union has been perfected by the birth of a child. Whether you are happy or unhappy in marriage does not depend on the reality of love. Happiness in marriage is based on something else."

"On what?"

"The joy and peace that comes from oneness of spirit, tastes, culture and character. I know this from the deepest experiences of life and the widest observation."

"You have loved?" she asked softly.

"Twice -"

A silence fell between them.

"Shall I tell you, little mother?" he finally asked quietly.

"Please."

He seated himself and looked into the skies beyond the peaks across the valley.

"Ten years ago I met my first mate. The meeting was fortunate for both. She was a woman of gentle birth, of beautiful spirit. Our courtship was ideal. We thought alike, we felt alike, she loved my profession even - an unusual trait in a woman. She thought it so noble in its aims that the petty jealousy that sometimes wrecks a doctor's life was to her an unthinkable crime. The first year was the nearest to heaven that I had ever gotten down here.

"And then, little mother, by one of those inexplicable mysteries of nature she died when our baby was born. For a while the light of the world went out. I quit New York, gave up my profession and came here just to lie in the sun on this mountainside and try to pull myself together. I didn't think life could ever be worth living again. But it was. I found about me so much of human need - so much ignorance and helplessness - so much to pity and love, I forgot the ache in my own heart in bringing joy to others.

"I had money enough. I gave up the ambitions of greed and strife and set my soul to higher tasks. For nine years I've devoted my leisure hours to the study of Motherhood as the hope of a nobler humanity. But for the great personal sorrow that came to me in the death of my wife and baby I should never have realized the truths I now see so clearly.

"And then the other woman suddenly came into my life. I never expected to love again - not because I thought it impossible, but because I thought it improbable in my little world here that I could ever again meet a woman I would ask to be my wife. But she dropped one day out of the sky."

He paused and took a deep breath.

"I recognized her instantly as my mate, gentle and pure and capable of infinite joy or infinite pain. She did not realize the secret of my interest in her. I didn't expect it. I knew that under the conditions she could not. But I waited."

He paused and searched for Mary's eyes.

"And you married her?" she asked in even tones.

"I have never allowed her to know that I love her."

"Why?"

"She was married."

Mary threw him a startled look and he went on evenly:

"I could have used my power over mind and body to separate her from her husband. I confess that I was tempted. But there was a child. Their union had been sealed with the strongest tie that can bind two human beings. I have never allowed her to realize that she might love me. Had I chosen to break the silence between us I could have revealed this to her, taken her and torn her from the man to whom she had borne a babe. I had no right to commit that crime, no matter how deep the love that cried for its own. Marriage is based on the period of infancy of the child which spans the maternal life of woman. God had joined these two people together and no man had the right to put them asunder!"

"And you gave her up?"

"I had to, little mother. On the recognition of this eternal law the whole structure of our civilization rests."

Mary bent her gaze steadily on his face for a moment in silence.

"And you are telling me that I should be reconciled to the man who choked me into insensibility?"

"I am telling you that he is the father of your son - that he has rights which you cannot deny; that when you gave yourself to him in the first impulse of love a deed was done which Almighty God can never undo. Your tragic blunder was the rush into marriage with a man about whose character you knew so little. It's the timid, shrinking, home-loving girl that makes this mistake. You must face it now. You are responsible as deeply and truly as the man who married you. That he happened at that moment to be a brute and a criminal is no more his fault than yours. It was YOUR business to KNOW before you made him the father of your child."

"I tried to appeal to his better nature that awful night," Mary interrupted, "but he only laughed at me!"

"You owe him another trial, little mother - you owe it to his boy, too."

Mary shook her head bitterly.

"I can't - I just can't!"

"You won't see him once?"

She sprang to her feet trembling.

"No - no!"

"I don't think it's fair."

"I'm afraid of him! You can't understand his power over my will."

"Come, come, this is sheer cowardice - give the devil his dues. Face him and fight it out. Tell him you're done forever with him and his life, if you will - but don't hedge and trim and run away like this. I'm ashamed of you."

"I won't see him - I've made up my mind."

The Doctor threw up both hands.

"All right. If you won't, you won't. We'll let it go at that."

He paused and changed his tones to friendly personal interest.

"And you're determined to leave me and take my kid away tomorrow?"

"We must go. I've no money to pay my board. I can't impose on you -"

"It's going to be awfully lonely."

He looked at her with a strange, deep gaze, lifted his stooping shoulders with sudden resolution and changed his manner to light banter.

"I suppose I couldn't persuade you to give me that boy?"

She smiled tenderly.

"You know his father did leave his mark on him after all! The eyes are all his. Of course, I will admit that those drooping lids have often been the mark of genius - perhaps a genius for evil in this case. If you don't want to take the risk - now's your chance. I will -"

Mary shook her head in reproachful protest.

"Don't tease me, dear doctor man. I've just this one day more with you. I'm counting each precious hour."

"Forgive me!" he cried gayly. "I won't tease you any more. Come, we'll run over now and see our neighbor's new bungalow before you go. You admire this one and threaten to duplicate it. He has built a better one."

"I don't believe it."

"You'll go?"

"If you wish it -"

"Good. We'll take the boy, too. He can drive his new wagon the whole way. It's only half a mile.

CHAPTER XXIX

THE NEW MAN

The door of the bungalow stood wide open. Mary paused in rapture over the rich beds of wood violets that carpeted the spaces between the drive and the log walls.

"Aren't they beautiful!" she cried. "A perfect carpet of dazzling green and purple!"

"Come right in," the Doctor urged from the steps. "My neighbor's a patient of mine. He hasn't moved in yet but he told me always to make myself at home."

Mary lifted the boy from his wagon, tied the goat and led the child into the house. The Doctor showed her through without comment. None was needed. The woman's keen eye saw at a glance the perfection of care with which the master builder had wrought the slightest detail of every room. The floors were immaculate native hard-wood - its grain brought out through shining mirrors of clean varnish. There was not one shoddy piece of work from the kitchen sink to the big open fireplace in the spacious hall and living-room.

"It's exquisite!" she exclaimed at last. "It seems all hand-made - doesn't it?"

"It is, too. The owner literally built it with his own hands - a work of love."

"For himself?" Mary asked with a smile.

"For the woman he loves, of course! My neighbor's a sort of crank and insisted on expressing himself in this way. Come, I want you to see two rooms upstairs."

He led her into the room Jim had built for his wife.

"Observe this furniture, if you please."

"Don't tell me that he built that too?" she laughed.

"That's exactly what I'm going to tell you."

"Impossible!" she protested. "Why, the line and finish would do credit to the finest artisan in America."

"So I say. Look at the perfect polish of that table! It's like the finish of a rosewood piano." He touched the smooth surface.

"Of course you're joking?" Mary answered. "No amateur could have done such work."

"So I'd have said if I had not seen him do it."

"What on earth possessed him to undertake such a task?"

"The love of a beautiful woman - what else?"

"He learned a trade - just to furnish this room with his own hand?"

"Yes."

"His love must be the real thing," she mused.

"That's what I've said. Look at this iron work, too - the stately andirons in that big fireplace, the shovel, the tongs, and the massive strop-hinges on the doors."

"He did that, too?" she asked in amazement.

"Every piece of iron on the place he beat out with his own hand at his forge."

"And all for the love of a woman? The age of romance hasn't passed after all, has it?"

"No."

Mary paused before the window looking south.

"What a glorious view!" she cried. "It's even grander than yours, Doctor."

"Yes. I claim some of the credit, though, for that. I helped him lay out the grounds."

"Who is this remarkable man?" she asked at last.

"A friend of mine. I'll introduce him directly. He should be here at any moment now."

"We're intruding," Mary whispered. "We must go. I mustn't look any more. I'll be coveting my neighbor's house."

The doctor turned to the window and signaled to someone on the lawn, as Mary hurried down the stairs.

She fairly ran into Jim, who was being pulled into the house by the boy.

"'Ook, Mamma! 'Ook! I found a Daddy! He says he be my Daddy if you let him. Please let him. I want a Daddy, an' I like him. Please!"

Jim blushed and trembled and lifted his eyes appealingly, while Mary stood white and still watching him in a sort of helpless terror.

The child moved on to his wagon.

"Say, little girl," Jim began in low tones, "it's been a thousand years since I saw you. Don't drive me away - just give me one chance for God's sake and this baby's that He sent us! I've gone straight. I've sent back every dishonest dollar. I'm earning a clean living down here and a good one. I've practiced for two years cutting out the slang, too."

He paused for breath and she turned her head away.

"Just listen a minute! I know I was a beast that night. I'm not the same now. I've been through the fires of hell and I've come out a cleaner man. Let me show you how much I love you! Life's too short, but just give me a chance. If I could undo that awful hour when I hurt you so, I'd crawl 'round the world on my hands and knees - and I'll show you that I mean it! I built this house for you and the baby."

Mary turned suddenly with wide dilated eyes.

"You - YOU built this house?" she gasped.

"I've worked on it every hour, day and night, the past two years when I wasn't earning a living in the mine. I made every stick of that furniture in the rooms up there - for you and my boy. The house is yours - whether you let me stay or not."

"I - I can't take it, Jim," she faltered.

"You've got to, girlie. You can't throw a gift like this back in a fellow's face - it cost too much! Your money's all gone. You've got to bring up that kid. He's mine, too. I'm man enough to support my wife and baby and I'm going to do it. I don't care what you say. You've got to let me. I'm going to work for you, live for you and die for you - whether you stay with me or not. I've got the right to do that, you know."

She lifted her head and faced him squarely for the first time, amazed at the new dignity and strength of his quiet bearing.

"You HAVE changed, Jim -"

Her eyes sought the depths of his soul in a moment's silence, and she slowly extended her hand:

"We'll try again!"

He bent and kissed the tips of her fingers reverently.

They stood for a moment hand in hand and looked over the sunlit valley of the Swannanoa shimmering in peace and beauty between its sheltering walls of blue mountains. The bees were humming spring music among the flowers at their feet and the faint odor of fruit trees in blossom came from the orchard Jim had planted two years before.

"I'll show you, little girl - I'll show you!" he whispered tensely.

Choose from Thousands of 1stWorldLibrary Classics By

A. M. Barnard	Charles Dudley Warner	Enilor Macartney Lane
Ada Leverson	Charles Farrar Browne	Erasmus W. Jones
Adolphus William Ward	Charles Ives	Ernie Howard Pie
Aesop	Charles Kingsley	Ethel Turner
Agatha Christie	Charles Klein	Ethel Watts Mumford
Alexander Aaronsohn	Charles Amory Beach	Eugenie Foa
Alexander Kielland	Charles Hanson Towne	Eugene Wood
Alexandre Dumas	Charles Lathrop Pack	Eustace Hale Ball
Alfred Gatty	Charles Whibley	Evelyn Everett-green
Alfred Ollivant	Charles Willing Beale	Everard Cotes
Alice Duer Miller	Charlotte M. Braeme	F. H. Cheley
Alice Turner Curtis	Charlotte M. Yonge	F. J. Cross
Alice Dunbar	Charlotte Perkins Stetson	Federick Austin Ogg
Ambrose Bierce	Clair W. Hayes	Ferdinand Ossendowski
Amelia E. Barr	Clarence Day Jr.	Francis Bacon
Amory H. Bradford	Clarence E. Mulford	Francis Darwin
Andrew Lang	Clemence Housman	Frances Hodgson Burnett
Andrew McFarland Davis	Confucius	Frances Parkinson Keyes
Andy Adams	Cornelis DeWitt Wilcox	Frank Gee Patchin
Anna Sewell	Cyril Burleigh	Frank Harris
Annie Besant	D. H. Lawrence	Frank Jewett Mather
Annie Hamilton Donnell	Daniel Defoe	Frank L. Packard
Annie Payson Call	David Garnett	Frank V. Webster
Annonaymous	Dinah Craik	Frederic Stewart Isham
Anton Chekhov	Don Carlos Janes	Frederick Trevor Hill
Arnold Bennett	Donald Keyhoe	Frederick Winslow Taylor
Arthur Conan Doyle	Dorothy Kilner	Friedrich Kerst
Arthur M. Winfield	Dougan Clark	Friedrich Nietzsche
Arthur Ransome	Douglas Fairbanks	Fyodor Dostoyevsky
Atticus	E. Nesbit	G.A. Henty
B.H. Baden-Powell	E.P.Roe	G.K. Chesterton
B. M. Bower	E. Phillips Oppenheim	Gabrielle E. Jackson
Baroness Emmuska Orczy	Earl Barnes	Garrett P. Serviss
Baroness Orczy	Edgar Rice Burroughs	Gaston Leroux
Basil King	Edith Van Dyne	George A. Warren
Bayard Taylor	Edith Wharton	George Ade
Ben Macomber	Edward J. O'Biren	Geroge Bernard Shaw
Bertha Muzzy Bower	Edward S. Ellis	George Durston
Bjornstjerne Bjornson	Edwin L. Arnold	George Ebers
Booth Tarkington	Eleanor Atkins	George Eliot
Boyd Cable	Eliot Gregory	George Gissing
Bram Stoker	Elizabeth Gaskell	George MacDonald
C. Collodi	Elizabeth McCracken	George Meredith
C. E. Orr	Elizabeth Von Arnim	George Orwell
C. M. Ingleby	Ellem Key	George Sylvester Viereck
Carolyn Wells	Emerson Hough	George Tucker
Catherine Parr Traill	Emilie F. Carlen	George W. Cable
Charles A. Eastman	Emily Dickinson	George Wharton James
Charles Dickens	Enid Bagnold	Gertrude Atherton

Grace E. King
Grace Gallatin
Grant Allen
Guillermo A. Sherwell
Gulielma Zollinger
Gustav Flaubert
H. A. Cody
H. B. Irving
H.C. Bailey
H. G. Wells
H. H. Munro
H. Irving Hancock
II. Rider Haggard
H. W. C. Davis
Hamilton Wright Mabie
Hans Christian Andersen
Harold Avery
Harold McGrath
Harriet Beecher Stowe
Harry Houidini
Helent Hunt Jackson
Helen Nicolay
Hendrik Conscience
Hendy David Thoreau
Henri Barbusse
Henrik Ibsen
Henry Adams
Henry Ford
Henry Frost
Henry James
Henry Jones Ford
Henry Seton Merriman
Henry W Longfellow
Herbert A. Giles
Herbert N. Casson
Herman Hesse
Homer
Honore De Balzac
Horace Walpole
Horatio Alger Jr.
Howard Pyle
Howard R. Garis
Hugh Lofting
Hugh Walpole
Humphry Ward
Ian Maclaren
Inez Haynes Gillmore
Irving Bacheller
Israel Abrahams
Ivan Turgenev
J.G.Austin

J. Henri Fabre
J. M. Barrie
J. Macdonald Oxley
J. S. Fletcher
J. S. Knowles
J. Storer Clouston
Jack London
Jacob Abbott
James Allen
James Andrews
James Baldwin
James DeMille
James Joyce
James Lane Allen
James Lane Allen
James Oliver Curwood
James Oppenheim
James Otis
James R. Driscoll
Jane Austen
Janet Aldridge
Jens Peter Jacobsen
Jerome K. Jerome
John Burroughs
John Cournos
John F. Kennedy
John Gay
John Glasworthy
John Habberton
John Joy Bell
John Kendrick Bangs
John Milton
John Philip Sousa
Jonas Lauritz Idemil Lie
Jonathan Swift
Joseph A. Altsheler
Joseph Carey
Joseph Conrad
Joseph E. Badger Jr
Joseph Hergesheimer
Joseph Jacobs
Jules Vernes
Julian Hawthrone
Julie A Lippmann
Justin Huntly McCarthy
Kakuzo Okakura
Kenneth Grahame
Kenneth McGaffey
Kate Langley Bosher
Kate Langley Bosher
Katherine Cecil Thurston

Katherine Stokes
L. A. Abbot
L. T. Meade
L. Frank Baum
Latta Griswold
Laura Lee Hope
Laurence Housman
Lawrence Beasley
Leo Tolstoy
Leonid Andreyev
Lewis Carroll
Lewis Sperry Chafer
Lilian Bell
Lloyd Osbourne
Louis Hughes
Louis Tracy
Louisa May Alcott
Lucy Fitch Perkins
Lucy Maud Montgomery
Lydia Miller Middleton
Lyndon Orr
M. Corvus
M. H. Adams
Margaret E. Sangster
Margaret Vandercook
Margret Penrose
Maria Edgeworth
Maria Thompson Daviess
Mariano Azuela
Marion Polk Angellotti
Mark Overton
Mark Twain
Mary Austin
Mary Catherine Crowley
Mary Cole
Mary Hastings Bradley
Mary Roberts Rinehart
Mary Rowlandson
M. Wollstonecraft Shelley
Maud Lindsay
Max Beerbohm
Myra Kelly
Nathaniel Hawthrone
Nicolo Machiavelli
O. F. Walton
Oscar Wilde
Owen Johnson
P.G. Wodehouse
Paul and Mabel Thorne
Paul G. Tomlinson
Paul Severing

Percy Brebner
Peter B. Kyne
Plato
R. Derby Holmes
R. L. Stevenson
R. S. Ball
Rabindranath Tagore
Rahul Alvares
Ralph Bonehill
Ralph Henry Barbour
Ralph Victor
Ralph Waldo Emmerson
Rene Descartes
Rex Beach
Rex E. Beach
Richard Harding Davis
Richard Jefferies
Richard Le Gallienne
Robert Barr
Robert Frost
Robert Gordon Anderson
Robert L. Drake
Robert Lansing
Robert Lynd
Robert Michael Ballantyne
Robert W. Chambers
Rosa Nouchette Carey
Rudyard Kipling
Samuel B. Allison

Samuel Hopkins Adams
Sarah Bernhardt
Sarah C. Hallowell
Selma Lagerlof
Sherwood Anderson
Sigmund Freud
Standish O'Grady
Stanley Weyman
Stella Benson
Stephen Crane
Stewart Edward White
Stijn Streuvels
Swami Abhedananda
Swami Parmananda
T. S. Ackland
T. S. Arthur
The Princess Der Ling
Thomas A. Janvier
Thomas A Kempis
Thomas Anderton
Thomas Bailey Aldrich
Thomas Bulfinch
Thomas De Quincey
Thomas H. Huxley
Thomas Hardy
Thomas More
Thornton W. Burgess
U. S. Grant
Valentine Williams

Various Authors
Vaughan Kester
Victor Appleton
Virginia Woolf
Walter Camp
Walter Scott
Washington Irving
Wilbur Lawton
Wilkie Collins
Willa Cather
Willard F. Baker
William Dean Howells
William le Queux
W. Makepeace Thackeray
William W. Walter
Winston Churchill
Yei Theodora Ozaki
Yogi Ramacharaka
Young E. Allison
Zane Grey